JAMESON FOX

NINA LEVINE

Published by Nina Levine

authorninalevine@gmail.com

www.ninalevinebooks.com

ISBN: 9780994585844

Cover Design by Letitia at Romantic Book Affair Designs

Proofreading provided by Read by Rose

This one's dedicated to my OG who taught me all I know about bossy alphas. I never did tell you that you helped me write my alphas. I was always just too busy arguing with you.

PROLOGUE

Adeline

"Here's to Mr. and Mrs. Fox." Hudson raises his glass and smiles at me. "I wish Adeline all the best surviving my brother. I hope you know what you've gotten yourself into, gorgeous."

My husband's arm tightens around my waist right before his lips brush my cheek. "She knows."

I do.

I know very well what the future holds for me.

Turning to Jameson, I cup his face. "Maybe he's the one who needs the best wishes. Maybe *he'll* have to survive me."

Those dark eyes of Jameson's flash with a warning only I can see as laughter erupts among our guests.

"Oh, he'll survive you," Owen, one of Jameson's

closest friends, calls out. "How could he not? A man would be a fool if he didn't."

I look at Owen in time to catch the wink he shoots me. It helps ease the nerves still racing through me. Thank God for him. This isn't the first time he's helped me and I'm sure it won't be the last.

"Eyes on me, Adeline," Jameson commands in a hushed tone for my ears only. His rough huskiness scatters desire over my skin. Desire I don't want anything to do with.

I meet his gaze again. What I see there sucks the breath from my lungs. Desire that matches my own. Jameson hasn't made any secret of the fact he wants to fuck me, but this, what I'm seeing now, is on a whole new level.

He tightens his hold on me, pulling my body hard against his. Far too close for my liking.

Everything about him invades me.

His arm around me that is made of the kind of muscle most men never know in their lifetime.

His breath against my skin.

His spicy, woody, way-too-fucking-masculine scent that I've come to hate over the last three months because it drives me to distraction in a way I don't want to be driven to distraction.

Bending his face to mine, he kisses me. It's not our first kiss; that was after we exchanged vows. But this is the first time he's forced me to give him more of myself than I want to give.

I wasn't ready for this.

Certainly not in front of our 200 guests.

But fuck, the man can kiss. And I like it. I like it more

than I should. I like it a whole lot more than I want to. Even with that goddamn beard of his.

Keeping one hand on my waist, he brings his other hand up to my face and threads his fingers through my hair while deepening the kiss. His tongue slides over mine, as dominant as he is, and I have to use every ounce of control not to moan.

I've kissed a lot of men in my life, but none as skilled as Jameson. He kisses like he lives: intensely, demanding, taking what he wants.

It sweeps me away.

Shuts my brain down.

Turns me into the kind of woman I swore I'd never be again.

The kind that gives a man too much power.

I press my hands to his chest and push, attempting to disentangle my lips from his. I don't push hard, only enough for him to feel it, not for anyone to see it.

He feels it, all right, and he ignores it, holding me in place, keeping our lips locked.

I push again.

A little harder this time.

Again, he ignores me, his lips demanding my submission. But I'm done. He might think he has all the power here, but he doesn't. Not by a long shot.

Taking charge, I pull my mouth from his. Our eyes meet and it gives me great satisfaction to see his displeasure. That's something I've started to strive for over the last three months, and every time I achieve my goal, it helps ease some of the pain he inflicted on me five years ago.

Our guests, who can't see our power struggle, cheer

us on. They only see the love we take great care to project to the world. They want more of our whirlwind romance.

Ignoring them, Jameson leans in close and growls, "Don't ever do that again."

"Since when did the definition of husband change to dictator?"

He works his jaw, his eyes flashing with more displeasure. "You'll do well to remember what you're getting out of this marriage."

"And *you'll* do well to remember that I am not, and never will be, the kind of woman you can control. I went over every line of our marriage contract, every single word, and not once did it mention that I have to allow you to force yourself on me."

He keeps his hands on me, unwilling to yield. In the end, it's his phone that causes him to let go. A call comes in and he pulls the phone from his pocket.

Glancing back up at me after checking the caller ID, he says, "This conversation isn't finished, Adeline." Then, stabbing at the phone, he barks, "This better be important, Ashton. I'm at my wedding."

Ashton says something to him that causes him to walk away and exit the room. I watch him leave, my hate for him roaring to life.

How dare he think he can tell me what I can and can't do?

We survived our engagement, just, and I thought I'd made it clear I won't be controlled. It seems I haven't been clear enough. Going forward, I will be. I'll make it crystal fucking clear that I have no intention of bowing down to his demands. We might be husband and wife now, and we might have to get through a year together, but that doesn't mean I have to ask "how fucking high" whenever he says "jump."

Jameson Fox might reign over everything in his kingdom, but he'll never reign over me.

1

Jameson

Removing my jacket, I drop it on the armchair in the corner of my bedroom before undoing the buttons on my vest. My eyes are firmly on my wife as she walks into her walk-in closet. Hell, I can't take my eyes off her. This displeases me as much as her behavior has today. But Adeline is not a woman any man can take his eyes off.

It's not her beauty that commands my attention, but rather the way she holds herself. The way she owns a room without an ounce of effort. And as much as it fucking pains me, it's also the way she doesn't back down from me.

"I'm going to need more space," she says, rejoining me in the bedroom.

I lift my brows. "One thousand square feet isn't enough for you?"

"No."

The challenge in her tone hits my dick.

Christ.

It's been three months since I've fucked anyone. It's also been three months of living and breathing Adeline. To say my dick is on edge is a fucking understatement.

I remove my vest and undo the top button of my shirt. "It'll have to do."

"No, Jameson, it won't do. If I have to live here for a year, I'll be bringing more stuff with me than will fit in there." She eyes my closet on the other side of the bed. "It's an easy fix. Remodel yours so it's smaller and give me the extra space."

This is the first time Adeline's been in my bedroom. After I proposed my marriage deal to her three months ago, she's barely been to my penthouse. Any time we've spent together has been out. For show.

I work my way down my buttons. "It's one year, Adeline. I'm not remodeling." Everything in this penthouse was custom designed. I'm not changing it for this.

Pulling my shirt off, I walk into my bathroom and drop it in the laundry basket, wondering why the fuck I didn't anticipate this. Foreseeing future problems is a strength of mine, but I clearly didn't put enough thought into my marriage and the issues it would throw up.

After showering, during which I try to solve the hotel development challenges Ashton detailed for me earlier when he called during the wedding reception, I wrap my towel around my waist and enter the bedroom again. Adeline is nowhere to be seen, so I pull on some sweatpants and go in search of her. Failing to locate her in the kitchen, library, or great room, I check the other end of the penthouse and find her in one of my five spare bedrooms.

She's changed out of the dress she wore for the reception, the one that hugged her curves in ways I know I'll struggle to remove from my memory, and now wears a pair of white satin pajamas. The shorts cover her ass, but show off her long, tanned legs. I appreciate all parts of a woman's body, but legs are my downfall. Legs and breasts, and Adeline has been built for my destruction in these areas.

"Why are you in here?" I ask.

Glancing up from the bed where she sits, she says, "I've decided to sleep in here."

"That's not what we agreed upon."

"Well, I also didn't agree upon other things that happened today or that I've now been presented with here, so I guess we've both got to learn to be adaptable."

"So, because you didn't get your way with an outlandish request for a closet the size of some people's homes, you're going to sulk in here?"

"I'm not sulking. I simply don't want to sleep in the same bed as you, and I don't see why I have to. We're not really husband and wife, so—"

"You know why you have to sleep in there with me. Don't be childish. It doesn't become you."

She moves off the bed and comes to me, her features schooled as if she's unruffled by this conversation. I know different, though. After three months of being around her, I've come to know what pushes her buttons, and if there's one thing Adeline doesn't like, it's being told how to behave.

"Bill isn't going to drop by unannounced at night to check if we're sleeping together. It's absurd to think that. We only saw him five times during our engagement. He's not checking up on you."

Adeline doesn't know Bill Johnson like I do. The man is ruthless when it comes to his business and fierce when it comes to family. The fact both are involved in this means I can't leave anything to chance.

"Bill has eyes everywhere. I'm not taking the risk. Get your ass back in my room."

Her glare is glacial. "Does this kind of approach work on women? Or is it your money that keeps them coming back for more?"

"It doesn't matter what works on other women. You and I have a contract, and the terms are more than clear. I can print you a copy if you need the refresher."

"Yes, the terms are more than clear. They state we'll live as husband and wife for one year. And do you know what husbands and wives do, Jameson? They fight and they sleep in separate rooms. If Bill drops by, we had a fight. And if you need it to feel real, I can make that happen."

Her tone makes it clear she's not even close to moving that ass back to my bed.

I rest my shoulder against the doorjamb and cross my arms, settling in for the conversation she appears to want to have. "This is because I kissed you at the reception." She was less than happy about that kiss and didn't fail to let me know. She spent every minute after I kissed her making sure I was aware of her feelings over it.

"No, this is because I need some space. We've barely been apart for three months, and we've been together all day today. Trust me when I tell you that tomorrow morning will go a lot more smoothly if we sleep apart tonight."

I press my lips together, unimpressed with her. "You told me you had a year in you. This doesn't give me faith you do."

"Oh, for fuck's sake, Jameson. Do you always have to be an overbearing asshole?"

I run my eyes over those long legs of hers again before pushing off from the doorjamb. "This isn't me being an asshole, Adeline, but that can be arranged. I expect to see you in my bed in the next twenty minutes."

Without another word, I exit the bedroom and head to my office. I need to finalize a few things before I call it a night, one of them being a tour we're taking on our honeymoon in Italy, which we leave for tomorrow. My assistant, Shantel, emailed me an hour ago to let me know some issues with it cropped up.

I reach my office and pull out my phone as a text comes through from my brother.

Hudson: Is your dick still attached?

Me: Firmly.

Hudson: Impressive. I thought for sure she would have hacked it off by now.

I'm not a fan of texting when a conversation can be had, so I call him.

He answers the call. "You know what's not impressive?"

"What?"

"The fact you haven't slept with her yet. You're losing your touch."

"You're forgetting the fact I married her so I could inherit a company. The minute I fuck her is the minute I lose that company."

"How the hell do you figure that? I would have thought sex in your marriage would only help convince Bill it's a real marriage."

"Sex complicates relationships, and Adeline is far too fiery and impulsive to risk complicating this relationship. She wouldn't last the year. Her emotions would get in the way."

"I don't agree. Have you seen how driven that woman is in business? I think she'd be able to stick out five years with you if it meant she'd get her company back. Even if you were fucking her and complicating the shit out of the marriage."

He's right that she's driven, but I'm not convinced he's right about the rest. After all, I was the recipient of her violent emotions when I took her company from her five years ago. I've seen her in action. Adeline is not the kind of woman who easily controls herself when she's worked up about something. She's wild and hot-headed. The only reason I entered into this marriage with her is the legal contract she's bound by. And the fact I know she'd do anything to regain control of the company she started, that I now own.

My attention is drawn from our conversation when I hear the elevator opening out in the foyer.

Stepping out of my office, I close the distance between it and the foyer. When my gaze lands on the man I think of like a father, I say to Hudson, "I have to go."

As we end the call, Bill turns to face me. His eyes narrow as he takes me in. Bill is a shrewd man and I have no doubt he's running through multiple scenarios in his mind right now. He's been skeptical of my marriage to Adeline from the moment I announced our engagement. The past three months have been ninety days of non-stop effort to convince him otherwise. I'm far from surprised to see him here.

He looks down the hallway before his eyes meet mine again. "Adeline's asleep already?"

My lips quirk, amused by the dance he's insisting on doing with me over this. "It was a long day for her."

His brows arch in his signature way that indicates his disbelief. "It's her wedding night, son. I'm surprised to find you here alone."

I open my mouth to reply when Adeline's voice floats down the hall. "Bill, what a lovely surprise."

My eyes are glued to her as she makes her way into the great room.

Gone are the white pajamas.

In their place is a scrap of sexy red material that barely covers anything it should.

Her long brunette hair hangs in loose curls that draw my eyes to her breasts and then down the curves of her body to those legs that are permanently etched into my memory. Hell, I've looked at them often enough over the last few months that I have muscle memory when it comes to running my eyes over them.

When she reaches me, she slides her arm around my

waist and leans into me, curling her other hand around my neck.

Pulling my mouth down to hers, she kisses me.

It's not a deep kiss or a particularly long one, but it's sexy as hell with the way she's positioned her body next to mine and with the way she's got her hands on me.

Fuck if it doesn't get me hard, but then a kiss like this after three months of no sex will get any man hard.

I slide my hand down over her ass, letting it settle there as she ends the kiss.

Looking at Bill, she says, "As much as I always love seeing you, I hope you're not staying long." Her hand comes to my chest. "I've got plans for Jameson and they involve him not leaving our bed for the rest of the night."

Bill's eyes narrow on me again before shifting to Adeline. "I was under the impression you were asleep."

She traces her fingers over my chest as if she's doing it absentmindedly. Smiling up at me, she says, "I kind of was. My husband wore me out." Then, glancing back at Bill, she says, "Between you and me, he's got skills that ruin me in all the good ways."

Adeline's a smart woman and I make a note never to underestimate her. She's studied Bill and knows him well enough to know he doesn't believe a couple's sex life should be discussed with others. She knows he won't spend long here now because of what she just said.

"Right," Bill says, "I just wanted to stop by and congratulate you both again." He gives Adeline one of his rare smiles. "You've made an old man very happy today. I've watched Jameson lose himself to his work over the last decade and I don't want him to make the same mistakes I did. I want him to grow old with you instead of with his work."

Adeline presses herself harder against me. "I want that too, Bill," she says softly, and so fucking convincingly that even I'd believe it if I didn't know better.

Bill smiles again and nods once. "Safe travels tomorrow. I'll see you when you return home."

As he turns to leave, I say, "I'll get Shantel to plan dinner for when we get home. We need to go over the Brown deal."

He looks back at me. "We do, but first we'll catch up and you can tell me about your honeymoon." He eyes Adeline. "I look forward to hearing all about it, Adeline."

I nod and watch him leave.

Once we hear the elevator close, Adeline removes herself from me and says, "He just told me he wants me at that dinner, didn't he?"

"Yes."

"And I'm guessing the Brown deal isn't one you'd want anyone but your actual wife knowing the details of."

"Correct. He's testing me."

She tries to hide her smile but isn't successful. "This year might be fun after all." She pauses before adding, "I'm going to bed now. In my bedroom."

"Your bedroom?"

Her defiance is bright in her eyes. Unmistakable as she says, "Yes, *my* bedroom. And when you ask Shantel to book that dinner, also have her find someone to remodel our closets."

I reach for her as she turns to leave. "We have a contract that very clearly states you'll live with me for twelve months as my wife. As far as I'm concerned, wives sleep in the same bed as their husband, regardless of whether they've fought or not." I pause, my eyes boring into hers. "If you want your company returned to you at the end of our contract, you'll sleep next to me for the next 365 nights. And I'm not remodeling. You'll make it work."

Without waiting for her response, I let her go and stride back into my office.

I won't be going to bed for some time. I need space from her attitude, her body, her. All of it is fucking with me in ways I don't need to be dealing with. The only thing standing between me inheriting the company I learned the ropes at is my ability to withstand Adeline and I'll be damned if I don't succeed at this.

2

Adeline

My husband is the best-looking man I've ever laid eyes on and that pisses me the hell off.

The worst thing about it is that he doesn't even have the look I'm usually attracted to, and yet I find it hard to drag my attention from him.

He wears his dark hair in a man bun.

I fucking hate man buns.

Just cut your damn hair, for God's sake.

Almost half his face is covered by a beard I'd rather not let anywhere near my skin.

Don't men know this is why razors exist?

And don't even get me started on the ink ruining that tanned skin of his.

Jameson's tattoos run the length of his left arm, down to his hand.

I have no idea what they're of.

I haven't bothered to take a good look. Possibly because I can't remove my damn eyes from the rest of him.

The list of what I do like is far longer than what I don't.

Arm and leg muscles that annihilate my ability to think straight.

Hands that distract me at every turn.

I mean, what is it about men's hands?

I can't even begin to understand my attraction to them.

And don't get me started on his lips, his cheek bones, his eyes.

Oh God, those eyes.

Who knew brown could look so hot?

The kicker, though, was when he walked into my bedroom last night without a shirt on.

It was the first time I've seen him shirtless.

I almost died.

Breath actually stopped making its way into my lungs.

Someone needs to stop him working out for the next year and start feeding him a lot of fucking sugar and fat.

Jameson has abs of sin.

Or maybe it's abs made for sin.

Either way, he has abs—*holy hell, does he have abs*—and they make me think of very sinful things.

I didn't even chance letting my eyes drift down to the V I know for sure he has. No man has the kind of abs he does without having that V, and it would be my absolute downfall if I even glanced at it. That, I am more than certain of.

Jameson is six foot four of trouble.

The kind of trouble that could pull me under if I allow it to.

It's because of all this, and that kiss he caught me by surprise with yesterday, that I'm in the hateful mood I'm in today. Also, the fact he forced me to sleep in the same bed as him last night.

I'm convinced the only reason I actually got any sleep last night was because I crashed after the three-month build up to yesterday. I'm unsure how I made it through those months pretending to love a man I despise. Last night, my mind was so exhausted by the effort that it finally allowed me to sleep for a solid five hours. If not for that, I doubt I would have slept at all. Not with Jameson lying so damn close to me.

I told him this morning would go a lot more smoothly if we slept apart. He didn't listen to me. As predicted, I woke highly annoyed. And since he's been his usual bossy, demanding self from the minute he spotted me in the kitchen this morning, I haven't been able to let go of that annoyance.

"We leave in fifteen minutes," he says overbearingly, striding into my dressing room where I'm packing my suitcase.

I straighten, glaring at him and his arrogance. I know we leave in fifteen minutes. There's no need for him to come in here and tell me this like I require the reminder. Also, I don't appreciate him intruding on my privacy. The small amount I now have. "You do know this is *my* dressing room now, right?"

He doesn't respond straight away. He just stands there in all his suit glory—goddamn, the man can wear a suit

—and gives me that bored look of his that I hate almost as much as I hate him. Finally, he says, "I'll be waiting in the foyer. Don't take your time."

"Jameson," I say as he exits the dressing room.

He looks back at me, waiting for whatever I have to say.

"Don't come in here again."

"Don't make it so I need to." With that, he turns and leaves before I have a chance to process the assholeness of what he just said.

Usually, I'm fast with my processing and never miss the chance to get my thoughts across to people, but Jameson has a way of catching me unawares and a way of screwing with my thoughts.

The last three months have been filled with these kinds of interactions. From the minute he proposed this fake marriage to me, he's been messing with my ability to respond to bullshit. I don't know what it is or how he does it, but I seriously need to work on my game.

Determined to do that, I finish with my suitcase and head out to the foyer in plenty of time to meet his deadline. My best friend texts me as I deposit my suitcase near the elevator for his driver to collect, and since Jameson isn't here yet, I reply to her message.

Natalie: What time are you leaving today?

Me: MA's schedule says in six minutes.

Natalie: Oh Jesus, MA and his schedules. 364 more nights, babe. You've got this.

Me: I really fucking do, but MA's balls may not survive all of those 364 nights if he continues on with his assholey ways.

Natalie: I mean, does your contract say anything about them surviving?

Me: Not a thing. I think I'm still good if he suddenly loses them.

Natalie: Well, if you need a hand to bury them, I'm your girl.

Me: This is why I love you and am going to miss you next week.

Natalie: Remind me again why you two even need a honeymoon. Jameson is a known workaholic. It wouldn't have been suspicious if he didn't take one.

Me: God, do not remind me of the argument he and I had over this damn honeymoon. I do not need to ever relive that day.

When Jameson sprung the honeymoon on me three weeks ago, I told him that over my dead body was I going away with him for a week. He told me to kiss my company goodbye if I refused. The company he's giving back to me when our marriage contract is fulfilled. We then engaged in six hours of warfare over it. In the end, he won, and I drowned my sorrows at a bar I thought he'd never find me in. That was the night I learned that Jameson Fox has super-fucking-powers when it comes to keeping an eye on a person. It was also the night I learned he'd had one of his men watching me 24/7 since the day I agreed to marry him.

Natalie: I've gotta go. I just wanted to check in and make sure you're doing okay and to remind you I'm here if you need to yell or scream or plan mass ball extraction.

Adeline: I love you. See you in a week.

Natalie: Oh, and if Mr. Asshole doesn't take care of

you, I'm coming for him. And trust me, losing his balls will be the least of his worries if I'm unleashed on him. Love you, too xx

She's not joking.

My best friend is hardcore when it comes to men and the amount of bullshit from them that she won't put up with.

I log into my emails on my phone and am scrolling through them when Jameson joins me.

"You're ready?"

I meet his gaze. "I'm not standing here waiting for you for the fun of it, Jameson."

He works his jaw but doesn't respond to what I said. Instead, he presses the button for the elevator and waits silently.

I go back to checking my emails.

When the elevator arrives, he motions for me to enter first and then follows me in.

We ride down to his waiting Mercedes in silence. Five minutes later, I'm sitting next to him in the back of the car. As the driver pulls out into traffic, Jameson and I both scroll our phones, continuing the routine we've developed while together over the last few months.

Bill Johnson wants Jameson to grow old knowing the love of a woman. He has prostate cancer and changed his will six months ago to stipulate that unless Jameson was married for at least a year, he would not inherit Bill's company. I don't know the intricacies of their relationship, but my research enlightened me to the fact that Jameson began working for Bill at the age of twenty. Bill taught him everything he knew about business, and at twenty-five, Jameson spread his wings and started his own property development company. Since then, he's spent nine years branching out and building an empire of luxury brands. Hotels, retail, and real estate, including my fashion company that he stole from me.

Well, stole might be a slight exaggeration, but he swooped in during a difficult time in my life and launched a hostile takeover when I was least expecting it, so in my opinion, stole is the right word for what he did.

The only reason I agreed to this marriage was to get that company back. I might not need it anymore, thanks to the new company I built after he took Chatoyer, but I can be a sentimental bitch at times, and I want my first baby back.

If Jameson and I stay married for a year, he gets Bill's company and I get mine.

And so long as we continue this routine we've got of barely conversing while together, we'll make that year.

"Fuck," he mutters beside me, drawing my attention from my phone.

Glancing around at the traffic before looking at him, I frown. "What?"

His phone is to his ear and whoever he's called has answered before he can reply to me. "We need to go over this report," he barks into the phone, leaving no doubt that he's displeased with the report.

As he listens to the reply, his eyes meet mine.

"Tonight," he says, still with the bite to his tone. "I arrive in Rome at six p.m. our time. I'll call you when I'm at the hotel. Make sure you've got all the information for me. We don't have time to fuck around on this."

His eyes drop to my throat as he listens to the person for another few moments before ending the call.

His eyes linger on my body.

It's enough to spark a sensation I don't want sparked.

"I hope your late-night work won't interfere with our tour tomorrow. I'm not a fan of tired Jameson," I say. The time difference between New York and Rome means he'll be making that call after midnight Rome time. God knows how late he'll stay up working. In my experience with him these past months, he tends to exhibit even greater asshole ways when he's tired. And since we're spending the entire day tomorrow touring Rome, a city I've visited numerous times for work but have barely explored, I could do without asshole Jameson by my side.

He finally brings his gaze back to mine. "So you're aware, our trip to Amalfi has been postponed to Friday."

"I love how you just ignore half the things I say to you. It's not rude at all."

"There was nothing to respond to in what you said."

I could actually smash my phone into his face.

Like, the images rolling through my mind right now involve me going through the motions of lifting my hand with my phone in it and making him hurt.

"I honestly have no clue how you get people to like you," I say.

"I'll forward you this email with the updated details of our Amalfi tour."

"Yeah, you do that," I mutter with a shake of my head before giving my attention back to my phone.

He taps away on his phone for a few moments before saying, "Is this how our entire week is going to go?"

My head snaps up. "That depends on whether you continue ignoring my questions."

"You didn't ask me a question, Adeline. You made a statement regarding your feelings."

"Good God, are you like this with all the women you date?"

"We're not dating."

"And thank fuck for that."

His eyes bore into mine like he's assessing me. "Is this conversation going anywhere?"

I squeeze my phone, willing myself to ignore his condescending tone.

One year.

That's all I have to last.

I can do one fucking year of this for my company.

"No, actually, it's not."

He watches me silently for another moment before going back to his phone.

I follow suit while practicing the visualization techniques I've utilized over the last three months to make it through to this point.

Me running my company again.

Me divorced.

Me cutting Jameson's balls off.

I think it's that last one that really gets me through.

Jameson Fox may be the best-looking man I've ever laid eyes on, but he's also the biggest asshole I've ever had the displeasure of knowing.

His balls need to go.

Since that's against the law, I intend to find as many other ways as possible to cause him pain over the next year.

It may be the only thing that'll get me through.

3

Jameson

I scrapped my way to wealth.

Bill found me at an underground fight late one night when I was twenty. I worked as a mechanic during the day and fought at night, and I saved every last cent I could after giving my mother whatever money she needed to keep a roof over our family's head and food on the table.

Bill ended up hiring me on his security team, but I kept fighting at night for another couple of years while slowly working my way up the ranks in his company.

I told myself I kept fighting for the cash.

The truth is it was in my veins.

I craved the adrenaline rush.

The violence.

The blood.

But most of all, I craved the victory.

The pure annihilation of my opponent.

I haven't fought in over ten years, but I get what I still crave when I crush a rival in business.

When assholes come after me and throw down a challenge that requires me to show no mercy to win, it feeds my hunger.

Right now, my need is being fed in ways it never has with my business.

My biggest rival in the hotel industry is currently trying to tear me apart limb from fucking limb, so to speak.

Profits are taking a hit.

They have been for months.

And as much as I try to fix it, the problem persists.

The challenge remains.

Josiah, my executive in charge of this, calls again as I watch Adeline buckle herself in across from me on my private jet. He called on the way here, advising me that profits are down for a second month in a row. Another call so soon can't be good news.

"Yes?" I answer the call, directing my attention away from Adeline. She's wearing the tightest jeans I've ever come across on a woman, a tiny white T-shirt that clings to her breasts, and gold heels. She's also wearing that perfume she loves that reaches straight for my dick. Between all that and her attitude, it's an assault on my senses. If I had the time this morning, I'd invest in another jet and fly her to Rome on it while I take this one.

"Carlene just quit," Josiah says, sounding like he'd

rather be having a conversation with a lion than with me. I can't blame him. I'm tense at the moment thanks to not only my business but also my marriage, and I've been taking it out on him.

"Fuck." I exhale a long breath.

Carlene is the woman I hired two months ago to advise us on our hotel brand and how to fix our problems after our previous consultant caused me no end of headaches. I knew Carlene and I were butting heads, but I didn't realize she was getting ready to walk.

"I'm going over the list of suitable replacements," Josiah says. "I'll have it to you by the time you land in Rome."

"No, I'll cancel Rome and head into the office instead. Meet me there in an hour."

Josiah doesn't hesitate to agree. It doesn't matter that it's a Sunday; work always comes first.

"I'll call Hudson in too," I say. "I want a new plan in motion by tonight."

We end the call and I get up to speak with the flight attendant so she can let the pilot know of the change to our flight. I then text Max, my driver, to bring the car back, and Hudson who agrees to meet Josiah and me at the office. As I slip my phone back into my pocket, Adeline catches my eye.

"I take it our honeymoon is canceled." She appears anything but disappointed.

"Yes. Something's come up at work. Once I've got it under control, I'll look into a weekend away to replace the honeymoon." Bill's eyes will be on us, and I know he'll be looking to see us take some time away alone.

She undoes her seat belt. "My weekends are busy, Jameson. That may not work."

"It'll have to work."

With a purse of her lips, she gives me one last annoyed look before gathering her belongings and standing.

Adeline has been particularly argumentative today, from the minute she told me not to enter her dressing room this morning, to the minute she engaged in a pointless conversation with me on the way here. Although she's barely said a word to me after that conversation, I felt every word she didn't say.

She keeps it to herself, but I sense every ounce of tension vibrating off her. The time I've spent with her the past few months has taught me to spot it.

Proposing our marriage contract to Adeline wasn't something I did without a great deal of consideration. After shortlisting five women for the marriage, I believed her to be the best option. I've since discovered the issue with marrying a woman you don't know intimately: you can't foresee the problems that will arise from who they are underneath the mask they wear in public.

Adeline's mask is perfect.

She embodies everything I'm attracted to in a woman.

Strength, determination, grit, confidence.

Not to mention beauty and an easy way of getting on with people.

That ability, however, does not extend to me.

She can barely stand us being in the same room.

This wasn't news to me.

The fact I haven't been able to change that *has* been news to me.

I didn't predict that outcome correctly.

I assumed three months of working together to convince everyone that we were in love would end with her coming around to me. At least enough for us to live together for a year with some semblance of friendliness and civility.

It escapes me why she won't let go of her issues and just get on with the job at hand, but she seems intent on carrying on with her hostility and making both our lives difficult.

Adeline's mask is firmly off when she's around me these days, and hell if it wasn't hiding a whole storm of problems that could ruin my chance of inheriting Bill's company if I don't manage the fuck out of them.

I exhale a long breath and rake my fingers through my hair as my phone rings.

Pulling it out, I see it's my mother calling.

I answer the call, putting the phone to my ear while I follow Adeline off the jet. "Hi."

"Oh good," she says, "I wasn't sure I'd catch you two before you leave for Rome."

"We've had a change of plans. Rome has been canceled. I have to head into the office instead."

"Oh, Jameson. Why? Surely your work can wait. This is your honeymoon. Adeline must be so disappointed."

"My work can't wait," I say. Then, changing the subject, I ask, "How are you?" She was tired last night after a long day at the wedding and reception.

"I didn't call to talk about me, darling. I called to see how you and Adeline are. It's not every day my son, who swore he'd never get married, gets married. I'm dying to know everything."

I've done a good job of containing my mother's excitement over my marriage throughout the last three months, but now Adeline and I are married I haven't got a hope in hell of containing it any longer.

She isn't aware the marriage is fake.

I'm not proud of myself for this.

Lying to my mother isn't something I've ever done.

Until now.

The only people who know the truth are Hudson and Adeline's best friend, Natalie. We agreed to keep it to just these two because the less who know, the better.

"Adeline is good," I say as I watch my wife slide into the back seat of the car, my eyes glued to her legs.

"Pfft, Jameson, that tells me nothing about how she is. I really should have done a better job of teaching you how to get in touch with your feelings. I want to know how happy she is to finally be alone with you and how excited she is for your honeymoon." She stops abruptly. "You *are* still going to take a honeymoon, aren't you?"

"We'll go away for a weekend."

"A weekend? That's barely more than a day by the time you factor in travel time."

"It's all I can manage at the moment." A text comes through from Hudson, distracting me. "Mom, I have to go."

"Don't think this conversation is finished. We'll pick it up on Tuesday night. I assume since you're not going away, you'll both be able to make it for Taco Tuesday."

My mother is easygoing, except when it comes to Taco Tuesday. My brother and I are expected at her home every Tuesday night for dinner. Adeline has attended three Taco Tuesdays. I've been pleasantly surprised at how well she and my mother get along. She also gets along well with Hudson, choosing not to extend her dislike of me to my family. However, while Mom has been a little reserved with Adeline during our engagement, I'm more than aware she won't be reserved going forward. As far as she's concerned, Adeline is now part of our family. I fully expect she'll treat her like a daughter. Our next Taco Tuesday will be vastly different to the three Adeline has experienced.

"We'll be there," I say as I take the seat next to Adeline in my Mercedes. "I have to go."

"I love you, Jameson. Tell Adeline I'll call her later. I want to check in on her to make sure she's okay while you're busy working, not to mention find out how happy she is and get all her thoughts on your wedding."

"I'll let her know."

"See you on Tuesday."

We end the call and I reply to Hudson's text. Another work issue.

"How is your mother?" Adeline asks, drawing my attention.

I look at her. She only initiates conversation with me when necessary, but always asks after my mother. "How do you know it was her?"

"All traces of asshole disappear from your voice when you speak with her. No one else gets that special treatment."

I ignore her attitude. I'm going to have to if I'm to survive this day because she seems intent on keeping hold of it. "She's concerned your happiness has been interfered with by the cancellation of our honeymoon. You should expect a call from her today."

"I'll find it in me to project disappointment," she says drily. She then glances out the window at the passing traffic for a long moment before looking back at me. "I've asked Max to drop me at my office. I take it you'll be busy all day."

"Yes, I imagine so."

"And just to confirm, our honeymoon is canceled, which means I can schedule work commitments in now?"

"Yes. If I can manage it, we'll go away next weekend."

"And if *I* can't manage it?"

"The only thing you had on your schedule for next weekend was our honeymoon, Adeline. You can manage it."

The glare she gives me could light a fire. "Make sure Shantel checks my calendar before scheduling anything in. I'm as busy as you are, and our marriage contract doesn't have a clause that says my needs come last."

With that, she directs her attention to her phone, making it clear she's finished with this conversation. Since I have no desire to continue it either, I engross myself in emails, pushing thoughts of Adeline to the side. It's a good thing my assistant is tasked with coordinating my calendar with Adeline's; it would drive me insane to deal with her unpredictable nature and inclination to fight with me over every fucking thing.

~

I SPEND the day going over the state of my hotel business with Hudson and Josiah. By the time I leave the office just after 8:00 p.m., we've formulated a new plan and scheduled an appointment for tomorrow morning with Paulina

Rossi, an expert in hotel branding and strategy. She's known as a ballbuster within the industry, an agitator, and I've hesitated to work with her due to this reputation. I support agitation when it's required, but I don't always believe it is required. However, she recently impressed me at a conference we both attended, so I'm interested to hear more from her to see if we may be a good fit now.

A text comes through from my mother as I step off the elevator into my penthouse.

Mom: I'm working on our Christmas plans. We have to get the tree soon. Tell Adeline I know the best place for a tree this year.

I stare at my phone. It's like reading a foreign language. I knew Christmas was coming up in three weeks, but I hadn't thought through what this season now means to my mother.

Jameson: She's not big on Christmas.

Mom: Everyone's big on Christmas, Jameson. You've obviously misunderstood her.

Jameson: I can assure you I haven't. She'll attend Christmas dinner, but she won't want to be involved in the tree or decorating it.

Mom: Please talk with her about this. Christmas is important to our family. I think she'll want to be involved for you. I also want us to discuss a date to all go ice skating.

Jesus.

Christmas *is* important to my mother. She goes all out with decorations, baking, gifts, and over-the-top traditions. Hudson and I go along with it all because we know what it means to her. When my father was alive, our family didn't touch Christmas. He didn't allow it, and besides, we didn't have much to be happy about with him around. Since his death when I was eighteen, Mom has made it her mission to embrace everything she can about the season.

I have no idea if Adeline likes Christmas, but I've never met a woman who doesn't. I make a mental note to bring it up with her before Tuesday so we can get on the same page about it. I'll require her to involve herself in some of Mom's traditions, but we don't have to go overboard. The last thing either of us need is to spend excessive time together this season. And as for her family, I doubt they celebrate much of Christmas together, but we'll have to plan to see them too.

I walk through the great room toward my bedroom when Jeff, my butler, comes my way. "A minute, Sir?"

Jeff has worked for me for eight years. In that time, I've tried to remove the 'Sir' from his vocabulary. My preference is for all staff to use my name, but I've never managed to convert Jeff.

I nod at him. "Yes."

I change course to my office and a minute later, we go over some maintenance issues he's noted need taking care of.

Once he's finished his update, he says, "I've also spoken with Mrs. Fox tonight, as you requested, about having her belongings brought here."

"When is that taking place?"

A slight frown creases his forehead, understandably so. It would be confusing for him that I'm unaware of my own wife's activities. I asked him to oversee Adeline moving in, not simply because he's my butler, but because neither she nor I want my involvement in that. I have no doubt she'd attempt to physically harm me if her belongings don't fit in the space I've allocated her.

Still frowning, he says, "I was under the impression she's waiting for her closet to be remodeled before she brings most of her things here. I have it on my list to contact—"

"No," I interrupt him. "There's no need to contact anyone about that. We're not remodeling. I'll speak with Adeline about this. Is there anything else?"

His frown disappears but I see the lingering effect in his eyes. "No, Sir, that is all."

After he exits my office, I take a minute alone before going in search of Adeline. It's been a long day and the last thing I want to do is engage in another argument with her over this damn remodel she wants. However, it's not happening, so another conversation is required. I'm about to leave the office to do this when I hear the elevator arrive with a guest. Adeline's heels sound a moment later as she walks down the hallway.

I meet her outside my office, taking in the flimsy black material she's wearing that constitutes a dress. It strangles her hips, drops low between her breasts, and doesn't come close to reaching her knees.

Her green eyes meet mine. "I didn't realize you were home." The ice in her voice lets me know she's still in a mood with me. I've never known a woman who can hold a mood for as long as Adeline can.

"You're intending on going out?"

"No, I'm not *intending*, Jameson. I *am* going out."

"Where?"

"A friend is opening a club tonight. He asked me to attend." Her gaze cuts to Jeff who has joined us.

"Miss Murphy is here," he says, letting Adeline know her assistant is waiting. He hands her a large envelope. "She asked me to give you this, but she also has a matter to discuss with you. She advised it will only take five minutes."

"Thank you, Jeff," Adeline says, giving him a smile. "Please let her know I won't be long."

"You're not going out," I say after Jeff leaves us.

Her head snaps back to face me and I don't miss the fire that's now in her eyes. "I'll go out whenever I damn well want."

"Not on the first night of what is supposed to be our honeymoon, you won't. Not when the whole world is watching this marriage."

Thanks to Adeline's celebrity status, Bill isn't the only one watching us. Adeline was a fashion model before starting her own fashion company. After losing control of it to me, she started another company, Adeline, a brand that she's built bigger than her first. Fashion, beauty, fragrance, and jewelry. Not to mention the celebrity endorsements that bring in millions. She perfectly leveraged her celebrity status to build a cult following around the world. Hundreds of millions of social media followers later, and she feeds that fan base to the point where I wonder how the hell she maintains her sanity.

"This is my work," she says. "Surely that's something you understand."

"I understand needing to work, but right now, I'm focused on the success of this marriage. You showing your face in public without me on the second night of our marriage won't help us convince Bill that we're in love."

She stares at me in silence for a good ten seconds before snapping, "Well, you'll have to come with me then because I've made a commitment to attend, and I don't break my commitments."

Not giving me a chance to counter, she moves past me to go to her assistant. It's my turn to stare now and not just because she has the best damn ass I've had the pleasure of looking at, but because I know I have to go out with her.

My preference in life is to always manage the situations I find myself in. It's not so much that I want control, it's that I don't ever want to be ambushed. I don't ever want to chance losing everything I've worked hard for. So, I take charge at all times to ensure that never happens.

Managing this marriage is my current top priority because the stakes are so high. Up until now, I've framed the marriage as a job in my mind. Simply another situation to be managed. I thought I could establish rules and guidelines to be followed by both of us. I thought that so long as we had a blueprint and followed it, we'd make it through the twelve months. It was a no-brainer for me, but I see now it's not that for Adeline. I see how vastly different our approach to life is.

There's a push and pull between us I haven't allowed for in my plan.

I'm used to being the one who pushes in any given situation, and whenever I encounter pushback, I always find a way to achieve what I want. That way rarely involves me backing down or compromising.

Adeline is more like me than I gave her credit for and

I'm fast understanding that she's going to push against me just as much as I push against her. And unless I want a fucking headache for the next 364 days straight, I need to learn the art of compromise.

Tonight, that's going to involve me going out with her.

4

Jameson

Nights out at clubs aren't something I enjoy. Changing my plans at the last minute is also something I don't enjoy. Since this night out with Adeline involves both, as well as her bad mood, it was never going to be anything less than a shitshow. And it's been that right from the minute we shared the drive here.

I've endured two hours of it now and I'm almost certain Adeline is intentionally trying to push my buttons. She knows I have little patience for her celebrity status. I understand it's part of her business strategy, but I don't tolerate the social-media-worthy moments well, or the constant attention when we're out. Pausing a moment in my life to take a fucking photo to post to social media is not how I want to live. I was introduced to some of her world during our engagement period, but tonight has been on another level altogether and she's worked it all to frustrate the hell out of me.

She's drawn attention with public displays of affection.

She's encouraged photos with people.

She's snapped a million fucking photos and videos of us and shared them online.

I've had enough.

Of the photos, of the people, of the goddamn music in this club.

"No more photos," I say as we take a seat in one of the VIP rooms on the top level of the club. I've never been more fucking grateful for a private room.

"It's the first day after our marriage, Jameson. I think photos are called for. And this club is the perfect place for some great photos." The challenge in her voice is unmistakable, proving my assumption correct that her behavior tonight has been an attempt to push me.

"You've taken enough for tonight."

"I'll be the judge of that."

"If I leave it up to you to be the judge of that, you'll be snapping fucking photos in your sleep."

She presses her lips together. "And you'll be thanking me for helping convince Bill this marriage isn't a sham."

"This isn't up for discussion." I reach for my whiskey as I signal to our security head that his team can take a break while we're in here. "We're not taking any more photos tonight, and we're done with all the displays of affection."

"Right, so because you say so, it is?"

"On this, yes. I indulged you, but I'm done now."

She holds my gaze, unflinching. "No."

"No?"

She stands. "No, we're not done. I take a lot of photos and share them to social media. People expect that from me. If I stop that, and if I don't share you in them, it'll give Bill reason to doubt us." She pauses before adding, "I'm going to the bathroom. Please order me champagne while I'm gone and figure out how you're going to get on board with all of this. I refuse to give Bill any reason to question this marriage."

With that, she walks away from me, making sure to swing that ass of hers from side to side exactly how I fucking like.

Jesus Christ.

The hostess comes and I order a bottle of champagne.

Ten minutes pass in which I check my emails.

Adeline doesn't return to the room.

Another five minutes pass and I go in search of her. It pisses me off to have to leave the quiet hush of the private room to go back out into the club.

I find Adeline talking with a woman. Her eyes meet mine when I draw close, and her mouth spreads out in a dazzling smile as she slides her arm around my waist.

"Jameson," she says, her voice full of affection I know she doesn't feel. "Lucia was just telling me about this amazing little restaurant we should check out." Her body turns toward mine and she brings a hand to my stomach as she gazes up at me. "She said their salmon is to die for."

Adeline's hands on me are the last thing I need because even though I'm annoyed with her, my body never fails to respond to hers. Something she's more than aware of because I've never bothered to hide it.

Keeping up our marriage charade, I put my arm around her and smile at the woman she's been talking with. "Thank you for the recommendation."

Adeline presses herself against me, allowing her hand to travel down my stomach. "I told her how much you love salmon, darling."

I place my hand over hers, halting her progress down my body, and gripping it hard enough to warn her against this course of action.

"I do." I shift my gaze from Lucia to Adeline and am about to let her know we're done with this conversation when a voice comes from behind me.

"Jameson. I didn't think clubs were your scene."

I turn to find an old business acquaintance of mine running his eyes appreciatively over Adeline.

"Ian." I introduce him to Adeline, my attention firmly on the fact he's leering at her.

Lucia leaves us and Adeline smiles at Ian. "It's lovely to meet you. How do you know Brax?"

Brax is the owner of the club, and since tonight is invite only, everyone has a connection to him. My research into Adeline months ago let me know Brax is a man she had a short relationship with after her marriage ended five years ago. It was obvious when I met him earlier that he still wants her. My research also let me know Brax is a man with a reputation for sleeping with married women. To Adeline's credit, she made it clear she's not interested. If I was actually in love with her, I wouldn't hesitate to find my own way to make it clear to him that a married woman is off limits. I've made a mental note to have Gabriel, my fixer, keep an eye on this asshole.

Ian keeps his eyes glued to Adeline. Desire blazes from him but that's not something new for her. Most men she's met while in my presence have had the same experience. "I met Brax through an old girlfriend," he says. "We barely know each other. How about you?" His gaze drops to her breasts. "I imagine you know him much better than me."

My arm tightens around Adeline as a surge of unexpected possessiveness hits me.

Her eyes meet mine and she arches a brow. Fleetingly, just for me, before glancing back at Ian. "I dated Brax years ago. Only for a short time. We've stayed friends since." The easy friendliness has disappeared from her tone, but I doubt Ian would notice. I only note it because I've had the time to learn the nuances of her voice, expressions, and body language.

Glancing at me briefly before looking back at Adeline, he says, "He must be disappointed you're married now. Although, from what I've heard about Brax, he doesn't let a husband get in the way of his time with a friend." He says this suggestively while eye-fucking her.

I fist my hand by my side, doing my best to let Adeline handle this because the one thing I know for sure about her is that she'll want my balls if I dare attempt to assume control of this situation. If she were my real wife, we wouldn't still be standing here. There's no way Ian would have made it past his first leer.

Stiffening in my hold, she's perfectly arctic when she says, "A friend is just that to me, Ian. A friend. Nothing more." The tone she takes with him is one I know well.

It's the one that tells whoever's on the receiving end of it to back the hell off.

There were numerous stories written about Adeline when her first marriage ended. Stories that insinuated she cheated with a friend of theirs. I've never discussed it with her. Mostly because it's none of my business, but also because I don't believe it for a second.

Ian pays no attention to her caution, continuing to eye-fuck her while drawling, "Well, if I was Jameson, I'd keep a close eye on Brax. With a woman like you, with your history, he'll probably think he's got a shot."

Unwilling and unable to tolerate another second of this bullshit, I step in. "That's enough." I only utter two words, but they fall between the three of us with furious weight. Ian's a lucky man tonight; if there weren't hundreds of eyes on me and Adeline, he'd be lying at my feet now.

Adeline is angrier than I am. Moving forward, out of my hold and closer to Ian, she says, "It's men like you who remind me that there are some real assholes out there. I used to be married to one of them and I vowed never to put up with his kind of shit again. I'm only going to say this once, Ian. Don't ever look at me again. Don't ever come near me again. And don't ever fucking talk to me again."

Ian's cheeks redden and he looks at Adeline with distaste. "That was a mistake. A big fucking one. But bitches like you don't—"

My fury blazes, filling my chest with scorching, caustic anger, the likes of which I haven't felt in a long time. "Get the fuck out of my sight. And if you ever come near my wife again, I'll make you regret that decision."

He looks at me, directing his dislike my way now. "Now *you're* making a mistake, my friend."

"We were never friends, and we never will be. And the only mistake I'm making is the one in which I'm allowing you to continue to stand in front of Adeline without my fist in your face."

He glares at me for another couple of moments before finally stalking away from us.

Adeline turns her body to face me, her eyes filled with fierce fire. "I don't need you to fight my battles."

I watch Ian until I can no longer see him. He's angered me to the point where I may need to take it to my gym when we get home.

"Jameson," Adeline snaps, her outrage flaring brighter. "Did you hear what I said?"

I look at her. "You may not need me to, but you're mine to protect now, so I won't hesitate to fight your battles."

Her eyes widen. "I am not yours and never will be."

"You *are* mine, for twelve months, and you need to get used to that."

Determination bleeds from her as she says, "The only one of us who needs to get used to anything is *you*. Don't go to battle for me again."

She turns and walks away from me, into the restroom.

Unable to let this go, I stride after her, finding her standing at the sink when I enter the bathroom.

Her gaze meets mine in the mirror when I move behind her.

She doesn't say a word; she simply issues a challenge with those beautiful eyes of hers.

I bend my mouth to her ear. "I am your husband now,

Adeline, and I will act accordingly. Any man who comes near you will have my eye on him. And any man who treats you the way Ian did will be made to understand never to do it again." I snake my arm around her waist and pull her hard against me. "You can tell me not to fight your battles, but you don't have a hope in hell of me listening to you." My voice drops low as I add, "In time, you will learn I am not a man who can be told what to do."

She shoots daggers at me in the mirror. "Take your hands off me."

I glide my hand across her stomach, splaying my fingers against the smooth material of her dress. I move slowly, deliberately. Adeline needs to understand I will never be a man who acts on demand.

Her breathing slows as her anger intensifies.

Desire too.

It's written all over her.

White hot anger and desire all mixed together, raging between us, meeting my own anger and desire.

We do the dance we're becoming adept at.

The push and pull.

The refusal to give an inch.

Neither of us speak another word.

We simply wait each other out.

In the end, she grabs my hands and forcibly removes them from her body before stalking out of the bathroom with one last glare at me.

As I promised, she will learn.

I'll allow her to win some of our battles, but only when it suits me.

5

Adeline

Natalie: I saw your Insta stories tonight. Why must MA look so good in a suit?

I stretch my legs out in front of me on the bed I now share with Jameson and reply to her text. It's just after 1:00 a.m. which is a time we often catch up after the events of the day. We both struggle with sleep, so this nightly debrief sometimes helps with that.

Adeline: He doesn't. He doesn't look good in anything.

Natalie: I see we've moved back to the first stage of grief.

Adeline: I'm in all the stages of grief at fucking once right now. Oh wait, no, I'm not in the last stage. I'll never accept any of this. Seriously, the man is unbear-

able. I have no idea how he has that long line of women he's dated behind him.

Natalie: Not to mention the long line still waiting. I accidentally tapped his Insta hashtag tonight. I can't wrap my head around how many women post about him.

Adeline: Accidentally?

Natalie: Okay, so that was a lie. I was curious.

Adeline: Ugh, please talk to me about anything other than my husband. I had to survive hours of him tonight and let's just say he's lucky to still be breathing.

Natalie: I thought you were going to Brax's club by yourself?

Adeline: I was, but Jameson didn't want me to go. I stood my ground and ended up with him along for the ride.

A text comes through from Vanessa, my assistant. We've been going back and forth all night with work stuff. Vanessa works almost as many hours as I do.

Vanessa: I just realized your meeting with Jenna has been scheduled for Tuesday, not tomorrow.

Jenna Pearce and I are in the early stages of putting together our plans for the fashion company we're building together. I asked Vanessa to schedule a meeting for tomorrow and confirmed with her earlier when she came over that it was going ahead. She assured me it was.

Adeline: Why is it scheduled for Tuesday?

Perhaps Jenna can't make it tomorrow.

I try to give Vanessa the benefit of the doubt, but she's been making a lot of mistakes recently, so I'm finding this hard.

Vanessa: I apologize. This was my error. I can call

her first thing in the morning and see if she can change it.

I quickly check my calendar, noting that I don't have even a spare five-minute slot during my day. There's no other time I can meet with Jenna. I had her down for a 9:00 a.m. meeting; I highly doubt she'll be able to rearrange her own day to make that happen at such late notice.

Adeline: No, leave it as it is.

Vanessa: I'm sorry, Adeline. This won't happen again.

Adeline: Is everything okay, Ness?

Vanessa: Yes. I really am sorry I messed this up.

Vanessa has worked with me for four years and has never made the kinds of mistakes she's currently making. I've been convinced for a couple of weeks something is going on that she's not telling me about. Vanessa is the member of my team who usually starts her day with a recap of everything that happened to her since we saw her the day before. She loves to talk, but lately she's been closed off.

I go back to my messages with Natalie.

Natalie: In other news, I'm seeing that mechanic again tomorrow night.

I sit up straight at the mention of this guy.

Adeline: Wait. Tank?

Seriously, Natalie meets the worst men. On her last date, the guy took her to a sports bar and proceeded to watch football with five of his friends who were also there to watch the game. He turned out to be a waste of her time, but she got on well with one of his friends instead. The mechanic who I nicknamed Tank because she couldn't remember his name. They got drunk together on bad beer and stories about their worst first dates. They both have a history of bad dates in common.

Natalie: Yes. I found out his name is Ryan. He promised there will be no football in sight.

Jameson strides into the bedroom as I read Natalie's message, his suit jacket in his hand, the top few buttons of his shirt undone. He ignores me completely and goes into his bathroom, leaving a trail of his cologne in his wake.

The scent causes memories of his body against mine earlier.

His mouth to my ear.

His hand on my stomach.

His arrogance as he told me I'm his for the next year.

You are mine, for twelve months, and you need to get used to that.

Anger burns through my veins again as the memory settles in.

Desire sparks right alongside that anger because I can't think of Jameson's body, or his hands on me, or his breath against my skin without those memories affecting me this way.

This only makes me more furious with him.

Adeline: Sorry to change the subject for a minute, but you'll visit me in prison, right?

Natalie: After you harm MA? Of course. I'll also bring all your favorite food. I've got you covered.

Adeline: Good. Now, back to Tank. Please have sex with him. I need to live vicariously through you for the next year.

Natalie: I can't even fathom that you're going to give

up sex for that long. I mean, do you really think Jameson will go that long? Because I doubt it, and if he doesn't, you shouldn't have to either.

Adeline: IDK. I'm keeping a close eye on this situation.

Natalie: Speaking of keeping a close eye on situations, you might wanna keep an eye on Ian Swift. I saw Donna Hartford's Insta story tonight and she was hooking up with him. He said something about you fucking Brax while married to Jameson. It was drunken ramble, but still, it could be damaging.

Jameson exits his bathroom as Natalie's last text comes through. He sits on his side of the bed with his back to me and scrolls his phone reading something. Probably an email. From what I've seen, Jameson rarely looks at anything else on his phone and he certainly doesn't have any social media accounts.

Adeline: Thanks for that. Gotta go. MA is here. Talk tomorrow xx

I pull up Instagram and search for Donna's stories.

"Christ, do we need that right now?" Jameson says as I watch the videos she's posted. I do my best to ignore all those muscles of his I can see thanks to the fact he's now shirtless. I also do my best to ignore the way he just spoke to me.

"Ian's spreading lies about me sleeping with Brax. I'm watching this to hear exactly what he said."

He turns to look at me. "Ian's a piece of shit who you don't need to worry about."

I stare at him, processing the way he minimizes so many things I mention, and once again I want to smash my phone into his face. Instead of doing that, I move off the bed and stalk into my bathroom without even bothering to respond to him.

Men who dismiss me and trivialize things that are important to me are men I don't want a thing to do with. I was married for three years to a man who slowly chipped away at my confidence by repeatedly dismissing me, talking down to me, and treating me like I was less than him. He did it so insidiously most of the time that I didn't even recognize it for what it was. I made a vow to myself that I'd never allow another man the same privilege.

I've been labeled a bitch in the years since my divorce. By both men and women. Apparently, insisting on strong boundaries and refusing to be treated badly means a woman is a bitch. I've learned not to listen. I've also learned to stand the fuck up for myself, and Jameson has a long year ahead of him if he thinks that I'll just lie down and accept his dismissal of the things I have to say.

I spend fifteen minutes in the bathroom, moisturizing my body and gathering the strength to go on without doing harm to the man I have to share a bed with. When I walk back into the bedroom, I find him showered and sitting on the bed reading a paperback.

Trying to distract myself from him, I sit on the bed and gaze out the window at Manhattan while taking some breaths. Jameson's master suite is sumptuous with its luxury finishes and furnishings, and is easily the largest bedroom I've ever seen. It includes a sitting room, dual walk-through closets that take you to separate bathrooms, each complete with spectacular views. The space is open and light with a smattering of darker gray accents.

Without glancing at me, he asks, "Have you calmed down?"

I peel the bed covers back and slip under them while keeping my emotions in check as best I can. I've never met a man who provokes me like Jameson does. "I've calmed down as much as you've stopped being an asshole."

Still not giving me even a sideways glance, he says, "Are you anticipating this will last long?"

"Yes. My best projection is twelve months."

That catches his attention.

Closing his book and placing it down, he finally looks at me. "This is all because I told you that Ian isn't someone you need to worry about? Or because I stepped in and told him to fuck off tonight?"

"I see now why you're an unmarried man. You really are clueless about women."

He eyes me with his bored look. The one I want to do serious damage to. "Which one is it, Adeline? I don't intend on spending the entire night getting to the bottom of this."

"You know what? It's not my job to educate you on how to be a better person. And quite honestly, I doubt you'd even listen to me if I enlightened you. My projection still stands. You're looking at a year of this if you can't figure out your own shit." With that, I switch my light off, pull the covers over me, and lie on my side. I face away from him and ensure I'm as far from him as possible. Thank God this is an Alaskan King bed. I'd have to insist on replacing it if it was anything smaller.

Jameson uses his brain for the first time tonight and doesn't speak to me again. He goes back to reading and allows me the space to go to sleep.

I'm just as tired tonight as I was last night, however

sleep eludes me. I'm still awake when Jameson turns his light out. And I'm still awake hours later at 4:00 a.m. when he leaves the bedroom. I fall asleep soon after that, grateful to have the bed to myself. How I'm going to make it through a year of sleeping next to this man, I have no idea.

~

WAKING up to find photos of your mother half-naked while supposedly getting drunk and high with random men isn't a great way to wake up. It's also not a great way to begin a week. Or a marriage, especially one in which you're spending almost all your energy to make it look real. When you have little energy because you only got two hours of sleep, you don't have much available for any of this bullshit.

This is how my Monday begins.

It's not a good sign that the day is going to go well.

I spend my first half hour messaging with my team about it, which is something I don't like to do. I work a lot, but I try to keep the time just after I wake free. It angers me that I have to skip my morning workout for this.

It's lies. All of it. Well, not the bits about Mom sleeping with a lot of different men, but everything else is a lie.

My mother doesn't take drugs or drink alcohol. Her parents were alcoholics who beat her often as a child. She's completely against all substances.

Sex, though, *is* her drug of choice. I have no doubt the photos published across social media and in the tabloids are all real. It's only the words printed with them that are manufactured.

It's not a good way to start any damn day.

After I finish messaging with my team, I shower and dress, spritz some of my favorite perfume on, and leave the safety of the bedroom to report to my husband.

Yes, report, because that's what it feels like.

Jameson is in the kitchen, pouring himself a coffee. He glances up at me and I work hard to keep my eyes on his rather than letting them drop to his body while he says, "Would you like coffee?" Not for the first time, I wonder why I had to fake marry a man with this body. It's a cruel joke the Universe is playing on me.

He's dressed in a black suit, his broad shoulders drawing my eyes to them and then to the rest of him. I try to fight it but it's a pointless endeavor. There's simply no way I'll ever not be attracted to him.

"Yes, please," I say to his offer of coffee as I slide onto one of the breakfast bar stools.

Jameson's kitchen is as opulent as the rest of his penthouse. Ninety-six floors above Manhattan, the penthouse takes up the entire top floor and has stunning views of the city. With fifteen-foot ceilings, top-of-the-line finishes throughout, and twenty-four 10x10 foot windows enclosing the penthouse, his home is the most luxurious home I've ever been in. And that's saying something because my condo is plush.

The kitchen has marble floors, countertops, and backsplashes. It's all white and natural oak, which surprised me. I imagined Jameson's home to be filled with grays and darker, masculine colors rather than the light and airy feel of white. His bedroom and office have some darker tones, but mostly the penthouse is made up of a lot of white. And while I love the feel he's created, I'd personally add a whole lot more color if this was my penthouse. That's the beauty of white; splashes of color can add so much more personality than what Jameson's home has.

Sitting at the breakfast bar that overlooks Central Park, I say, "Have you seen the news this morning?"

"I've seen it." He brings my coffee over before going back to the island.

I look at him while taking a sip of my drink. "And?" Surely he's not as calm about this as he appears. Neither of us need the attention the story about my mother will bring.

His phone sounds with a text and he glances down to read it. He then proceeds to reply to it before looking back up at me and saying, "I doubt this story will last even one news cycle, Adeline. I wouldn't give it any of your attention." He then goes back to his phone, doing what he does best, dismissing me.

I calmly take another long sip of coffee before placing my mug down and moving off the stool. Walking to the island, I stand across from Jameson. "I've changed my mind about educating you on how to be a better person. This thing you do where you dismiss me needs to stop. If it doesn't, I can't be held accountable for my actions."

That fucking bored look of his makes an appearance. "I'm not dismissing you. I listened to what you said and then gave you my best assessment of the situation."

My eyes widen. "Did you just? Well, let me tell you what *my* best assessment of the situation is: I'm the one out of the two of us with more social media and tabloid lies experience, so I think I'm the one who knows more about how this situation may go. I don't think it'll blow over in one news cycle."

"Even if it doesn't, it's trash talk that isn't worthy of your focus."

"Honestly, you have no idea." *This conversation* isn't worthy of my damn focus. I'm saved from it when Lara, my social media manager, texts me.

Lara: I'm at the office. How long until you'll be in?

Lara is one of the most hardworking members of my team. She's worked with me for two years, and in that time her work has done more for my brand growth than many of the things I've tried. I'm convinced she wakes up with her phone in her hand and her brain already kicked into high gear after formulating new strategies in her sleep.

Adeline: I'll leave now. See you soon.

I glance up at Jameson. "I'm heading into the office now to strategize with my social media manager. She'll likely want to book a shoot with us to get a range of images to use in her campaigns, and she'll likely want that to happen today or tomorrow. I hope you have some free time or are able to make some. We'll need about an hour." I look at my phone as a couple more texts come in from Lara before meeting Jameson's gaze again. "I think she'll probably want photos taken here." Another round of texts hit my phone, causing me to mutter, "Shit, I have to go" before striding out of the kitchen to gather my laptop and purse from the bedroom.

I'm applying lipstick in the bedroom when Jameson joins me. "We're not doing a photo shoot," he says, using the tone that conveys he won't be entering into a discussion over this.

I use the tone that conveys I will be. "We are. You get to choose whether it will happen today or tomorrow." God knows where I'll find time today, but if he chooses today, I'll make it happen.

"Married couples don't fucking do photo shoots for social media, Adeline."

I finish with my lips and look at him. "And this is why your take on anything to do with social media is incorrect. You don't know how the machine works. I do, and this is exactly what married couples in the spotlight do. More to the point, it's what *I* do, and since you are now involved with me, it's also what *you* do."

"Perhaps it's time for you to alter what you do." His phone buzzes with a text and after checking it, he says, "Max has the car ready."

When he sweeps his arm to the side for me to exit the bedroom ahead of him, like he's coming with me, I frown. "What are you doing?"

"What does it look like I'm doing?" He utters this question like mine was the dumbest question ever asked.

I refrain from locating a knife to stab him with. Instead, I say, "We don't need to drive to work together."

"No, but we are."

"Jameson," I start, but his phone rings and he takes the call, striding out of the bedroom.

I stare after him, willing myself not to follow him and tell him what I think of the way he engages with me or what I think of the fact he expects us to share the drive to work.

During our engagement period, we negotiated how to

handle certain aspects of our marriage. Jameson insisted I give up my driver and use his. He told me Bill would expect that. This was just one thing we negotiated, but it was one thing that took months for me to compromise on.

In the end, I agreed to begin the marriage this way, but I made it clear I reserved the right to change my mind if it didn't work for me. What I did not make clear enough was that I intended on traveling to work each day by myself. Jameson and I will have to spend enough time together at night and on weekends; we certainly don't need to spend any unnecessary time together.

I grab my laptop and purse and make my way out to the elevator. Jameson is nowhere in sight when I step into it, but a few minutes later, I find him in the car, still on the phone.

His eyes come to mine as I slide into my seat. "I'll see you soon," he says into the phone before ending the call. Then, to me, he says, "You're ready to go?"

I nod without saying any of the things I want to say to him. Instead, I simply say, "Yes."

We settle into a tense silence while Max pulls out into traffic. Well, it's tense for me. I have no idea if Jameson ever feels anything. I try to concentrate on my emails but it's a hopeless endeavor. I'm still stuck in the conversation we didn't finish about the photo shoot we're going to have to do.

Jameson may think we don't need it, but experience tells me we do. I won't bring it up with him again because he was an asshole about it. I'll get Vanessa to contact Shantel to schedule it in. However, the irritation I feel with him over the way he ignored what I had to say about it sits in my chest and I know it'll sit there for many hours.

A text comes through from Natalie five minutes into the trip, providing me with a good distraction from all this.

Natalie: I saw the stuff about your mom. Are you okay?

Adeline: You know how it goes. This isn't anything new. I'm good.

Natalie: Yeah, I know, babe, but this is your mom. They've never really gone there before.

She's right; my mother and sister haven't made it into the news too much over the years. Not the real story, anyway. Mostly, the lies printed about me focus on my sex life. Natalie is the only person who knows I'd rather those kinds of lies any day over the truth about my family.

Adeline: I've got my team on it. If anyone can spin this away from Mom, it's Lara. And Simon won't hesitate to sink his teeth into anything he can, too.

My lawyer is savage. Most don't win against him.

Natalie: True. Okay, let me know if you need me. I'm busy this morning with patients, but I'm free this afternoon.

Adeline: Love you. Thank you.

Natalie: If you really loved me, you'd convince Simon to give up dick and come to the dark side for me.

Max brakes suddenly, jerking me forward and sending my phone flying out of my hand across the car toward Jameson.

He retrieves it and passes it back to me. "Are you okay?"

I blink.

This may be the first time he's ever checked on my wellbeing. It throws me off enough that I stumble with my reply. I don't answer him straight away, but finally, I say, "I'm fine." They're only two words, but even I can admit they come out a little coldly. Not that it matters. I doubt Jameson even notices how I say things. He certainly doesn't notice anything else about me, so why would he pay attention to this?

He gives me a brusque nod before going back to his phone.

I return to my messages, trying to ignore the way his cologne has started to affect me. Well, *started* isn't quite accurate. I've been keenly aware of it from the second I joined him in the kitchen this morning. Being as close as we are now, for this length of time, is only intensifying my response.

I hate him even more for affecting me in this way.

Adeline: If you really loved me, you'd find a way to get my company back that doesn't involve me staying married for a year.

Natalie: I see MA is still being an asshole.

Adeline: We don't seriously think he'll ever stop being an asshole, do we?

Natalie: I live in hope.

Adeline: I don't bother. Well, I do hope I don't end up in jail for murder at some point in the next twelve months.

Natalie: I have to go. I hope you have a good day.

And you've only got 363 more nights to go. You've got this x

I go back to my emails. I've worked through two of them when Max stops the car. I frown as I glance outside. We're not at my office which is on the way to Jameson's. We're parked outside a coffee shop.

"What would you like for breakfast?" Jameson asks.

I look at him. "Sorry?" I could swear he just asked me what I'd like for breakfast, but surely that's not what he asked.

"You didn't eat. What do you feel like?"

I glance at the coffee shop again before looking back at him. "I'm not hungry."

He inhales a breath like I'm testing him, which, let the record show, I'm not. I wish I was, because it's fast becoming my favorite thing to do, but right now, I'm just confused. "I'll get you a bagel and coffee," he says before exiting the car.

It takes a few moments for my brain to catch up with what's happening. Once it does catch up, I'm out of the car, following him into the shop.

By the time I join him, Jameson's talking with the woman behind the counter. They're smiling at each other like they're old friends, and if I'm not mistaken, she's teasing him about something. When she lays eyes on me, her smile grows bigger, and she claps her hands together. "You must be Adeline! We've been dying to meet you." She gives Jameson a chastising look. "This one has been keeping you hidden away from us."

If I thought I was confused before, I'm really confused now.

One: I'm not sure I've ever seen Jameson smile.

Two: I don't think I've ever seen him inspire a smile in someone else.

And three: The man is actually engaging in banter with another human. Who knew he had it in him?

I smile at her. "He certainly has been."

Jameson's eyes find mine. That dark brown of his flashes with something I've not seen yet: warmth. It baffles me, slowing all my thoughts down and tying them all together in a big fat mess.

"Well," the woman says, "I'm glad to finally meet you. I'm Brenda. My husband is Vinnie." She gestures at nothing in particular in her shop. "He's around here somewhere. You'll meet him soon enough, but for now, what can I get you?"

"She'll have a bagel with cream cheese and—" Jameson starts, but I cut him off.

"No, I'll have one of those please," I say, pointing at the Nutella rolls I just spotted. How anyone can go past Nutella is beyond me.

"For breakfast?" Jameson murmurs. His tone suggests he's judging my choice.

I look up at him. "You seem intent on me eating. This is what I want to eat. Do you have a problem with that?"

"Suit yourself." Gone is the warmth but the judgment remains. I'm sure of it.

"Seriously," I say softly enough for only him to hear, "don't bring me to a coffee shop that serves Nutella rolls or anything with Nutella and expect me not to buy it. And put your judgment away or I'll make you regret bringing it out."

With one last "as you wish, suit yourself" look, he

glances back at Brenda. "We'll take a salted caramel latte too."

Brenda gets to work on the coffee while I stand silently next to Jameson processing the fact he's memorized my coffee preference. The time we've spent together during the last three months has mostly been at night. We've probably only drunk coffee together three times. I'm impressed (frustratingly so) that he's remembered I drink salted caramel lattes. I'm also impressed he remembers I like bagels. I mean, I can't even put it down to his assistant remembering for him. Shantel isn't here prompting him.

While I try to decide what trick he uses to remember information like this, Brenda says, "Jameson, is it okay if Mark calls you this week for some advice? He's been talking his father's ear off about scaling his business, and quite honestly, between the three of us, Vinnie isn't the person to go to for that advice. And if you repeat that"—she gives us a stern look—"I will deny it."

She says all of this with such expressiveness that a laugh falls from my lips. God how I adore mothers like Brenda. Mothers so unlike the one I was raised by.

When she looks at me, I say, "My lips are sealed. Your secret is safe with me."

She grins. "I knew I was gonna like you." She then gives her attention to Jameson and says, "Why'd you take so long to find Adeline?"

I eye him, amused, and say, "Yes, darling, why did you take so long?"

He looks at me, nowhere near as amused as I am.

Brenda's husband saves him from answering my question when he calls out from the kitchen, "Bren, hurry your ass along, woman. We just got an order through for twenty coffees and a whole lotta food."

Brenda rolls her eyes. "I've been married for twenty-four years, Adeline, and honest to God, there are some days I wonder how I've managed not to kill him."

I smile. "I've been married for two days, Brenda, and I've already wondered the same thing about my husband."

She barks out a laugh and nods conspiratorially. "These men take some managing. Marriage ain't easy, that's for damn sure."

She switches her attention to my order and five minutes later, after he agrees for her son to call him, Jameson and I leave the shop. The chill of the morning greets me with a blast of cold air as I step outside and pass Jameson's security guys who have left the car they followed us in to wait on the sidewalk. I pull my coat in tighter and hurry to the car.

Jameson uses his dictator voice on me when he opens my door and says, "Bill is a daily customer here, so tone it down. Every word you utter to Brenda will be repeated."

"Oh, for God's sake, Jameson, she thought I was joking."

"Just keep in mind what I've said."

I only just manage to keep all my thoughts to myself over this. If it wasn't so cold, I'd stand on the sidewalk and argue with him, but since it is, I slide into the car and push my annoyance away.

He closes my door. A few moments later, he's sitting beside me, and Max is pulling back out into traffic.

I take a sip of my latte and realize why Jameson and Bill frequent Brenda's shop. Before I can stop myself from starting a conversation with him, I say, "Brenda knows her coffee."

He nods. "She's the best in the city."

"How long have you been going there?"

"Ever since Bill took me there fourteen years ago. Vinnie's father owned the shop then. Bill was a customer of his for years."

"Is he still around?"

"No. He passed away four years ago. Brenda and Vinnie took over then."

I sip some more coffee before taking a bite of the Nutella roll. I was going to wait until I got to work, but I have to know if Brenda's coffee-making skills extend to food.

They do.

"Oh my God," I mumble as I shove more of the roll into my mouth. "This is amazing. Seriously, I need to know her recipe."

"You bake?"

"Don't sound so surprised. I know how to do many things."

"I don't doubt it," he says before glancing down at his phone.

I watch him while finishing the Nutella roll. I try hard to keep my eyes on his face, but I fail. That suit he's wearing today is doing things to me. Things I'd rather it not be doing.

And then there are his hands.

I skim my gaze down his body to them. I'm not sure how he manages to get work done on his phone. Not with the size of those hands.

Jesus.

And now I'm thinking about what said hands *would* be good at.

Abort, abort, abort.

I quickly shift my attention to *my* hands and focus very intently on watching my Nutella roll disappear. Much safer than watching Jameson work his phone.

I spend the next little while guzzling coffee faster than I've ever drunk coffee. When Max pulls the car up outside my office, I can't exit fast enough.

I need to put space between me and that suit and those hands and all the thoughts those things are inspiring.

I gather my belongings and juggle them with my coffee cup. I'm in the middle of trying not to spill what's left of my drink when Jameson opens my door. He managed to exit the car and come around to my side with me barely noticing. That's because all I could think about was escaping him. And now he's standing outside the car, watching and waiting.

"I'm capable of opening my own door," I say after thanking Max and getting out of the car. If Jameson was my real husband, I'd be all for this, but he's not, and I don't want him doing things for me. Yes, when Bill is around, but there's no need for this right now.

"I'm aware." His tone is terse. "Perhaps you could just let me do the things a husband should do without making a fuss every damn time."

"Perhaps we need to exchange a list of what we deem are husband jobs. The top item on my list would be ensuring his wife has room for all her belongings in her bedroom."

His lips press together but he doesn't bite. Instead, he

says, "Let Max know when you're ready to go home. I'll likely be working late tonight."

I don't really care to know his plans. Actually, no, that's not true. I do care to know what time I need to prepare myself for him tonight, so this is good news. I refrain from telling him the later the better.

I simply nod and turn to walk into my building.

"You forgot something, Adeline," he says as I take my first step.

I glance back with a frown. "What?"

He comes to me, and before I know what's happening, he's got his arm around my waist, he's got my body against his, and he's got his lips on mine.

Holy hell.

All my senses go into overdrive.

His scent.

His touch.

His taste.

Why, God?

Why must Jameson smell, and feel, and taste so fucking good?

I want to force him away.

I can't because my hands are full of too many things.

But, also, I actually can't.

To the world, I'm his wife, and unfortunately, the world is watching.

And for once, Jameson is giving them a good show.

He knows cameras are out, so he's taking his time with this kiss. He's giving it his all, including his tongue. And Jesus if it doesn't feel like he's enjoying it.

I would be too if I wasn't hating every second of it.

The problem is that the way I'm kissing him back doesn't signal that hate.

My body is leaning into his a little too desperately.

I'm giving him just as much tongue as he's giving me.

And shamefully, I think I just moaned.

Jameson pretty much confirms that when he ends the kiss and looks down at me with a knowing look. The asshole then murmurs, "I'll take that response as confirmation this should stay on my husband list."

"You shouldn't ever assume anything when it comes to me."

His eyes flash with something that looks a lot like amusement, but since I've never known him to be amused by anything, I know I'm mistaken. He's probably got gas that's making him grimace. "The only thing I assume with you is that I shouldn't assume anything."

Jesus, that's not confusing. I mean, maybe it isn't, but it is to me right now. I can't form a straight thought even if I try. Not after that kiss. Trying to make sense of anything he says is just as hard, so I don't even attempt it.

"I'll see you late tonight. In fact, if you come home late enough, I'll be asleep." I give him a long, pointed look before walking away from him.

Thankfully, this time, he doesn't stop me and demand anything else from me.

I think I'd just pretend I didn't hear if he did.

This morning has been far too much already; I need at least a year to recover from it all.

"RIGHT," Lara says, a few hours after Jameson drops me at work. "I've got posts going out on all our accounts and have altered our monthly campaigns to help shift attention from where we don't want it. I don't expect this to go away fast, but I think with some work, we can bury it." She glances down at her phone for a moment before meeting my gaze again. "Simon asked me to send him everything that pops up, so I'll keep on top of that too." She pauses. "Now, about this photo shoot. I know you said Jameson is super busy and that he's not keen on doing it, but we need him to, Addy. Surely he can find time for you?"

Rule number one if you're going to fake marry a man should be: only marry him if you like him and he likes you. Everything is too hard if you hate each other.

I nod. "I know we need him to. I'll work on him. Also, please keep an eye on Ian Swift and anything he has to say about me sleeping with Brax."

"I'm all over it." Lara knows the last thing we need are lies about me cheating on Jameson. What she doesn't know is it's the last thing Jameson and I need. I'm determined to stop anything that threatens my chance at getting my company back.

"Adeline," Vanessa says, popping her head into my office, "Jenna just confirmed that she can move your meeting to tomorrow morning."

"Great. Thanks, Ness."

She pops back out as Lara says, "Let me know ASAP about the photo shoot. We'll do it at your place. People are dying to see inside Jameson's penthouse."

God, I'm aware of this. I'm also aware the interest in his penthouse and his life don't impress him. He's one of the most private people I know; he's made it more than clear the last thing he wants is the world knowing his private business. He goes along with me snapping photos of us outside of his home, but I know he's not keen on photos taken inside it.

I sigh.

"I'll message you as soon as he gives it the green light."

"Good. Okay, I'll leave you to it unless there's anything else you want to go over?"

"No, I think we've covered everything," I say as my phone rings.

It's Jameson's mother.

She called me yesterday to see how I was after my wedding day and to make sure I wasn't too disappointed about the honeymoon cancellation. I did as I promised Jameson; I faked disappointment.

Reese Fox is a beautiful woman, inside and out. How she managed to raise an asshole like Jameson is something I haven't worked out yet. I've chosen not to let it interfere with my relationship with her. I figure she did a good job with her other son, so Jameson's character can't be attributed to her mothering.

"Reese," I greet her with a smile. I do enjoy conversations with her even though I have to pretend to be in love with her son. "How are you?"

Her smile is apparent in her voice. At least the twelve months ahead will hold some sunshine; we get on well. "Hello my darling, I'm good. You?"

"Well, I'm not sure if you've seen anything about it yet, but some lies have been published about my mother this morning. It wasn't a good way to start the day, but things are looking up. I'm well, apart from that."

"Oh, I'm glad to hear it. That was why I was calling. I wanted to make sure you were okay."

"Thank you, I appreciate the call." I really do. Her son blew off my concerns, so it's nice to know she understands this is upsetting.

"Do you have an update on when your honeymoon will take place? That would surely cheer you up."

Oh, if only she knew just how much that would not cheer me up.

"No, we haven't made any plans yet. We've both got a lot going on with work now. It may be a while until we can get away, but honestly, we're both okay with this."

"It's not right, Adeline. Jameson should not have put his work before your marriage. I'll have another word with him."

I want to tell her to absolutely have another word with him. I'd love to see him make it through that conversation. But I don't. I continue faking my love for him instead. "You really don't need to, Reese. I know he's upset about this already, and that he'd go away in a heartbeat if he could. And quite honestly, I can't really get away now either. I think it's best if we just leave it how it is."

I practically hear her lips pressing together in her tone when she says, "Well, if you think so, darling, but you let me know if you want me to say something. Sometimes men need to hear it from their mother."

Another call is coming through and when I check to see who it is, I say, "Actually, Jameson is calling me now. I'd better take his call. Thank you for checking in on me."

"I hope your day continues improving. Tell Jameson to call me when he gets a chance. I need a quick conversation with him about tomorrow night."

I have no idea what she's referring to, but since I don't need to know, I simply say, "Will do."

We end the call and I answer Jameson's as I lean back in my seat. "This must be urgent for you to pick your own phone up and call." Usually, he has conversations with me through our assistants.

He doesn't respond to that, but his voice communicates his impatience with me. "We're going to a dinner party tonight. It's last minute and not on your schedule, so I didn't want you to make alternative plans before being made aware of it."

"And what if I already have plans?" God, the arrogance of this man never fails to astound me. To call and tell me rather than ask just pisses me off.

"You don't."

"How do you know I don't?"

I hear the breath he exhales. That pisses me off too. Like I'm the cause of his problems rather than taking any ownership of them himself. "Your calendar for tonight is empty." He pauses. "Must we go through this, or can you just get on board with what we're both trying to achieve here?"

"Yes, we must go through this. Why do you think it's okay to order me around? Why can't you *ask* me if I want to go to this dinner party?"

"Because want doesn't come into it, Adeline. You married me for a reason, and for both of us to be successful with this, we have to show up to things together like a fucking married couple would."

I grind my teeth, willing myself not to tell him what I think of his asshole ways. Taking a deep breath, I say, "Fine, I'll go to this dinner party with you, but for future reference, do not call me and *tell* me I have to do something. I won't agree to the next thing you order me to do."

With that, I jab my phone to end the call.

Jameson will regret his approach today.

Of that, I will make sure.

6

Jameson

After a long day at work meeting with Paulina Rossi, hiring her and strategizing our next moves, and dealing with a million other headaches that came up, Adeline and I arrive at the dinner party she wants nothing to do with just after 7:30 p.m.

She's been in a mood from the minute I stepped foot inside my penthouse an hour ago. I'd anticipated it, but perhaps not the full extent of it. How we'll make it through tonight without the dinner party guests picking up on the fact there's not one ounce of love between us, I have no idea.

"Do not kiss me tonight," she hisses under her breath as we enter the home of one of my business acquaintances.

"I've no intention of it," I assure her. The kiss this morning was purely for show. And while I did enjoy it, kissing her is something I'll only do when absolutely necessary.

"And take your eyes off my legs."

She's looking for a fight. Thanks to her winter coat, I haven't laid eyes on her damn legs once tonight. However, I do now that she's put the idea in my head. And fuck if I wish I didn't, because on the way down to those legs, I run my eyes over her ass, causing my gut to tighten.

Adeline's wearing a gold dress that covers most of her legs, except for the long slit in the front that reveals her left thigh. It's figure-hugging, pulling in tight at her waist, and curving over her ass like it's been painted on. Thin straps hold it up, with more of that painted-on fabric covering her breasts.

It's the kind of dress that will drive me to fucking distraction all night.

"Jameson!" Lionel Wrest's greeting is heartier than I expected. The last time we spoke, we both left the conversation a little warier of the other. I quietly threatened to kill a property development he was involved in if he continued fucking with one of mine.

Receiving this dinner invitation this morning came as a surprise. I was intent on declining, but Hudson pointed out the potential benefits of me attending. Lionel owns land Hudson has identified as being valuable to us and has suggested a relationship with him may help us win it if Lionel ever sells. Lionel is known for preferencing acquaintances when he sells off assets.

"Lionel," I greet him as I put my arm around Adeline's

waist and pull her close. "I'd like you to meet my wife, Adeline."

He smiles warmly at her. "It's lovely to meet you, Adeline. My wife is around here somewhere. She'll be by soon, no doubt. She's a big fan of yours."

The reason for the dinner invitation clicks into place. This was for Adeline, not me. Still, now that Hudson has opened my eyes, I'll make the most of it.

Adeline's body is stiff in my hold but she's doing a good job of appearing happy to be by my side. "I look forward to meeting her," she says.

Lionel glances at a woman motioning for his attention. He excuses himself to go and talk with her, at which point Adeline attempts to step away from me.

I tighten my hold, not allowing her to move. "You *are* aware people are watching, aren't you?"

"Jameson, in case you need the reminder, I've lived my entire adult life in the public eye. I'm aware people are always watching."

Fuck, she's testy tonight.

"So perhaps you could also remember you're my wife now, and as such, there's an expectation that two days after our wedding, you'd want to fucking stand next to me."

"Of course, I remember I'm your wife," she snaps. "I wish I could forget, but there you are, always in my head."

Just like she's always in my damn head.

Even when I tried to push thoughts of her from my mind today, I struggled.

I thought about sleeping next to her the last two nights, something that's been harder than I imagined. I have a large bed and yet it's still not large enough for me to avoid her.

I thought about all the social media and tabloid lies published about her. I mentioned them to Gabriel and asked him to look into them. Adeline is convinced she needs to do photo shoots and concoct a new social media strategy to fix the problem. I wouldn't bother. I'd simply have someone fix the problem for me.

I also thought about the honeymoon we need to have.

On top of all that, her scent clung to me for hours after I dropped her at work this morning, so even when I managed to move past thoughts of her, that scent ensured they circled right back around.

A blonde woman who looks to be about fifty comes over to us, her eyes blazing with excitement. "Oh my gosh, Adeline! I'm so glad you and Jameson could make it tonight! I'm Sarah, Lionel's wife."

Adeline flashes her a smile. "It's so lovely to meet you, Sarah. Thank you for inviting us." She leans into me, snaking one arm around my waist while bringing her other hand to my stomach. Settling it lower than I'd prefer, she continues, "Jameson was just saying how much he loves your art. You'll have to take him on a tour later and share with him how you came across each piece."

Christ.

Adeline knows I have little patience for shit like this. I can appreciate art, but I'm not interested in knowing anything about it. We had an argument about this topic weeks ago. She has a deep interest in art and couldn't believe I have zero interest. She didn't hesitate to tell me what she thinks of my unrefined ways. I didn't hesitate to tell her what I think of her snobbery.

Sarah beams at me. "Oh, I would love that, Jameson. We'll find some time after dinner for me to do that. It's not often I find friends of Lionel's who want to know about my art."

I return her smile. "Thank you. I look forward to it."

Adeline gazes up at me like she loves everything about me before looking back at Lionel's wife. "I need to use your powder room, Sarah. Would you mind telling me where it is?"

Sarah gives Adeline instructions before leaving us to welcome another couple.

Adeline keeps her hand on my stomach as she looks up at me again. "I won't be long, darling," she purrs. "Be a good husband and get me a drink while I'm gone."

"You can cut the bullshit," I mutter. "No one can hear you."

Her hand drifts lower. "No, but I know you're very concerned about people watching us, so I'm just playing the part you want me to."

I place my hand over hers, gripping it. "Enough." It's a growl that falls between us in a way that anyone other than Adeline would pay attention to. She, however, never pays attention in the way I'd like.

"How long are you intending for us to stay tonight?"

"However long it takes me to do what I need to do."

"Well, that's enlightening and super useful information." She drops her hand. "Perhaps you could get to work while I'm gone so we don't have to stay hours after dinner."

She walks away from me in the direction Sarah gave her, and I take the steadying breath I need.

It's going to be a long fucking night.

"How romantic," Sarah says as we finish dessert. "I wish I had a story like that for how Lionel proposed to me, but I don't." She looks at her husband. "He doesn't have a romantic bone in his body."

Adeline has just recounted to the group of ten here tonight the story she weaved together months ago that we now use when asked how I proposed to her. It involves a spontaneous flight in my jet to Paris, a romantic weekend there, a famous restaurant I had closed to just the two of us for the proposal, the rock she's wearing on her finger now, and many intricate details of the things we did in Paris that weekend. The parts about the jet and the restaurant are true; the rest is bullshit. People love to hear it, though, and Adeline is a talented storyteller, so they hang off every word she says. When I'm asked for the story, they're lucky to get even a quarter of it.

Adeline rests her hand on my thigh and leans in close to me. "Jameson has his moments. I'm a very lucky woman." She takes the opportunity to run that hand up and down my thigh, moving far closer to my dick than I appreciate. This is something she's been doing throughout dinner; something we'll be having words about later.

"That, you are," says the woman sitting on my other side. She's been eyeing me all night. Every time Adeline notices, she makes sure to touch me in some way. I've no fucking idea why. I just know we'll also be having words about that.

We need to make people think we're in love; we don't need to go fucking overboard with it.

"So, Adeline," a woman sitting across from us says, "how do you maintain your sanity with all the things posted about you on social media that I'm assuming aren't true? I don't think I'd survive it if it were me going through what you've had to deal with today."

Adeline reaches for her glass of wine. I've noticed tonight that whenever someone mentions anything to do with her family, she reaches for that wine. I know the basics of her family and their history, the information my team researched for me. And I've had conversations and spent a little time with her mother and sister, but I'm fast forming the opinion there's a lot I don't know.

What I do know is that Adeline and her sister, Sabrina, grew up without their father after he took off when Sabrina was born. Adeline was three. Their mother struggled to hold a job, either waitressing or cleaning to earn money.

Adeline isn't close with her mother but would like to be. She's also not close with Sabrina. She does, however, tend to pay most of their bills from what I can work out.

Her family is a touchy subject and whenever I've broached it, she's shut the conversation down fast. I haven't been interested enough to dig more. My only requirement when we negotiated our marriage contract was to know the basics so that if Bill asks me anything, I can provide him with an answer.

Adeline sips her drink before answering the woman.

"You get used to it over time. It's my job, and I've been doing it for fourteen years, so it's second nature now."

"Yes," the woman says, "but even though it's your job, this must be hard. Dragging your family into it makes everything so much more personal. I don't know how you do it."

Adeline smiles, but it's a tight, controlled smile. The one I know she uses when she's feeling anything but happy about whatever she has to discuss. "It's hard, yes, but I'm blessed to have a great team around me who help me get through it." She looks up at me. "And now I also have Jameson. He's my rock."

"Well, you were right when you said you're a lucky woman," the woman says. "Whenever I have work problems that turn a little personal, my husband has no idea what I really need from him. He's practical and solution oriented, whereas I'm looking for some emotional support, you know? Honestly, I just want him to listen to me, and nod, and give me some form of 'everything will be okay', but he just wants to tell me what he thinks I should do to fix it. I have no idea how we've made it through fifteen years of marriage without him figuring out I don't find this helpful."

That starts a chorus of agreement from the women around the table.

I reach for my drink and throw some whiskey down my throat while taking hold of Adeline's hand that's still resting on my thigh and placing it back in her lap.

Her eyes find mine as I do this, and they flash with what looks like satisfaction.

While the conversation around us is noisy, I take the

opportunity to lean toward her and warn in a hushed tone, "You're playing a dangerous game here."

"And for once, I'm enjoying every minute of it." Her eyes are fixed on mine as she takes a sip of her wine. Placing her glass down, she adds, "It's almost time for your art tour. How fun for you."

I work my jaw. "This is a conversation we'll be continuing when we get home."

"I have no doubt. You do like to play dictator with me, after all, so I imagine you've got a lot of new orders for me to follow."

My phone sounds with a text, saving her from hearing my thoughts on that. Adeline thinks I'm dictatorial; she has no idea how little she's observed of my dictatorial capabilities. If she insists on pushing me, though, she'll learn fast just how wrong she was.

Shantel: Paulina wants to see you tomorrow. I'm shifting your first meeting to 1pm so you can fit her in.

Jameson: Make sure that time works for Hudson too. I want him sitting in on every meeting I have with her.

Shantel: You do realize that after working for you for five years, I've reached the point where I can read your mind, right? I've already scheduled him in too.

Jameson: Good.

Shantel: As you were.

"I like it when Shantel messages you," Adeline says.

I glance at her, my brows pulling in. I'm unsure of where she's going with this.

She gives me an amused look. "I can tell when it's her by the expressions you pull. It's like you're simultaneously pleased with her and perplexed by her. I like it when people perplex you. It gives me great joy."

"Is this conversation necessary?"

She reaches for her wine. "I believe so."

"I don't see a need for it at all."

"And that's the difference between us, Jameson. You only see the need for conversations and activities that are practical and useful to your agenda, while I look for so much more."

The conversation around us begins to quiet down, so I don't respond to what she says. I don't want anyone to overhear our true feelings about each other.

"Jameson," Lionel says, pushing his chair back and standing. "I'd like a word with you."

I nod and follow him to his office.

Lionel and Sarah's condo is a few blocks from mine and reveals their taste for gaudy art and ostentatious furniture. None of it is my preference, but then, there's not much about Lionel that I connect with. I'm only here for business.

His office is just as garish as the rest of his home. I endure fifteen minutes with him while he talks with me about a development he's looking into. Nothing he mentions is of interest to me, but I remain attentive while keeping my eye on the bigger picture here.

After those fifteen minutes, I endure twenty minutes with his wife while she shows me her art collection. Adeline is nowhere in sight, and when I finish with Sarah, I find her sipping wine alone on the terrace.

She turns when she hears my approach. "You're finished your tour?" I don't miss her delight.

Not bothering with an answer to her question, I say, "We're leaving."

"Your mother just texted me. It reminded me that she asked me to get you to call her earlier. I'm sorry I forgot."

Adeline's apology catches me by surprise. That, and the genuineness in it. I can't recall an apology from her to date. She does like my mother, though, so I assume that's where this is coming from. And that's something I appreciate. "I spoke with her a few hours ago."

She finishes her wine. "Good." She glances past me into the condo. "Okay, let's go. I'm tired and I still have work to do."

I usher her out after we say our goodbyes. My eyes are on her ass while I follow her. I hope to God she never wears this dress again, or one like it. I also need to locate her bottles of perfume and throw them all out. Between the dress and her scent, I'm finding it difficult to concentrate. And right now, with all the work issues I'm dealing with, I need to fucking concentrate.

This marriage has already distracted me enough over the last few months. I'm convinced that's why my hotels are in the state they're in.

We drive home in silence and when we arrive, Adeline rides up in the elevator alone while I take a call in the car that comes in from Hudson. Fifteen minutes later, I'm greeted by Jeff when I step off the elevator. He details a few issues that cropped up today before saying, "As for Mrs. Fox's belongings, she's assured me you'll help her with them."

I frown. "Help her how?"

"I phoned her when they arrived earlier and asked her for guidance on where to put everything. I followed that guidance, but as you'll see, there's just not the room for everything. She advised you'll take care of it for her."

Christ.

"Thank you, Jeff. I will."

I stride down the hallway to the bedroom in search of my wife and all her belongings.

When I reach the bedroom, I come to a dead stop as I take in the boxes piled everywhere in there.

She will be the fucking death of me.

"Adeline," I bellow, unable to stop myself as I push past boxes. There are so many of the fucking things I can barely move. I also can't see the bed because they're stacked three high in some places.

When she doesn't respond, I assume she's in her bathroom, so I make my way to it. Not an easy feat.

The bathroom door is closed, and I can hear the shower running.

"Adeline," I call out as I knock on the door. When she still doesn't respond, I bang harder and raise my voice. "Adeline!"

"What?"

"Get your ass out here. We need to speak."

"I'm not finished showering."

"Well, finish. And do it fast. I'll have Jeff take care of these boxes while you're in there if you don't."

I pull at the buttons on my shirt, undoing them as I stalk back through the maze of boxes and go into my bathroom. My anger increases when I realize three of her fucking boxes are stored in there also.

Like I told her earlier, she's playing a dangerous game here, and she won't enjoy the consequences if she keeps it up.

I've just stripped out of my shirt when her voice floats through the air behind me. "How may I be of service to you, master?"

I turn to face her, fury sitting deep in my chest. "For a start, you can cut this fucking bullshit. I don't appreciate your attitude. And then you can tell me why the hell I'm surrounded by boxes?"

Jesus, she's wrapped that body of hers in the tiniest towel known to mankind. It must be one of hers because I sure as hell don't have towels made for children in my home. It only just fits around her, and only just covers what it should. I'm staring at far too much skin right along with all that attitude she's throwing my way.

"These are my belongings, darling. When a wife moves in with her husband, it's generally accepted that she'll bring all her things with her. I think I may need you to help me find room for them."

Before she sees me coming, I close the distance between us, push her up against the tiled bathroom wall, grip both her wrists, and press our hands to the wall either side of her head so she can't move. Leaning my face close to hers, I growl, "Now is not the time to test me, Adeline. Not after subjecting me to you all night."

Hostility blazes from every pore of her. "I do believe you're the one who subjected me to *you*. I didn't want to go to that dinner party, but you forced me to, so you only have yourself to blame for that. And as far as my belongings go, I told you that what I own won't fit in the space you've allocated me. This should not be a surprise to you. And take your fucking hands off me or everyone in your penthouse will hear the screams of a wife being terrorized by her husband."

I keep my hands right where they are. "I don't tolerate women playing games with me. I didn't take you to be the kind to engage in them."

"Oh, I'm not playing games, Jameson. I want my belongings here and you will have to find a way to make that happen. And when I tell you I'll scream for all to hear, I mean it."

Right now, the only staff members in my home are Jeff and two of my security team. I'm not concerned about them hearing Adeline scream, but I don't doubt she'd put the effort in to scream loud enough for the entire building to hear. I'm not convinced, though, that her threat is real. She has too much riding on this marriage for that.

I tighten my grip on her wrists, doing my best to ignore that fucking perfume of hers. I'm furious with her, and yet, my dick hasn't gotten the memo. Between her scent, her closeness, and the tension that's always crackling between us, I want to throttle her as much as I want to tear that damn towel off right now. "If you want your company back, you won't make a sound."

"Is that going to be your standard response for the next year whenever you refuse to compromise?"

"There's nothing to compromise on. You'll only be living with me for twelve months. You don't need to bring every belonging you own with you for that short a time."

"God, you are so fucking arrogant thinking that you know best for other people. You have no idea what items I'll need for a year."

"I know you don't need a million boxes of clothes to get through a year. I'm presuming that's what's in those boxes."

"And there you go, showing your ignorance. I have other things in those boxes too." She presses her lips together while her beautiful green eyes flash with the kind of fire I'm drawn to. "Now, fucking let me go or I promise you, I will scream, and I will do it very loudly."

This time, I believe her, so I let her go. When she tries to push me out of the way, I say, "This conversation is not over."

She stares defiantly at me. "This conversation is absolutely over. The only thing not over for you is dealing with my boxes."

With that, she exits my bathroom, leaving me wondering how the fuck I'm in this mess, and how the hell she's managed to get me here.

I rake my fingers through my hair and exhale a long, frustrated breath.

If Adeline wants her belongings here, she can have them, but I'm not fucking remodeling.

7

Adeline

Waking to your ex-husband making comments on the lies being spread about you and your family is worse than waking up to the original lies.

There are two reasons for this.

One: Thomas's comments are lies in themselves, but that's what he does best. He will say and do anything if he thinks it'll increase his profile and benefit him in some way, regardless of who he hurts on the way up.

And two: Thomas is one of the most popular actors in the world right now, so anything he has to say spreads fast and is eaten up.

I hate that I loved him at one point and decided to marry him. I've made many bad decisions in my life, but Thomas Miller was the worst.

I've finished dressing for the day and am about to go in search of coffee and food when a text comes through.

Lara: I hope to God that you've convinced Jameson to do this photo shoot. With this bullshit that Thomas has said overnight, we need something to shift attention.

Adeline: I'm still working on him.

Lara: Jesus, Addy, hurry up. This is urgent.

If only she knew how fucking difficult dealing with my husband is.

Vanessa got nowhere with trying to schedule the shoot through Shantel yesterday, so I'm going to have to bring it up with him again.

I survey the bedroom after spritzing some perfume on. Jameson had the boxes cleared into one of his spare bedrooms last night after I made it clear I had no intention of living without my belongings. He's still refusing to remodel. Instead, he'll turn the spare bedroom into a closet for me.

It wasn't what I wanted, but I know when I've reached the end of the road on something, and I am more than sure Jameson won't budge on this. And as much as I want to push him some more, because God does he infuriate me with that arrogance and dismissiveness of his, he was right about me not being a woman who plays games.

I'm not.

In fact, I detest them as much as he does.

I barely recognized myself at dinner last night when I insisted on testing him and then when I told Jeff to put all my boxes in the bedroom. But that's what Jameson does to me. I find myself saying and doing things I'd not normally do.

I'm letting the remodel idea go and moving on. Goodness knows, I've got enough other problems to focus on right now.

"Mrs. Fox," Jeff says when I meet him halfway to the kitchen. "I should have your belongings stored by the time you arrive home tonight."

I smile. Jameson might be an asshole, but he's surrounded by good people. In fact, there's not one person I've met through him that I don't like. "Thank you, Jeff. I appreciate it."

He nods and continues down the hallway while I finish making my way to the kitchen.

I was hoping not to run into Jameson in here, but he's sitting at the table drinking coffee while scrolling his phone. I don't acknowledge him; I simply head straight for the coffee machine and breakfast food Jeff has prepared for us.

While I'm filling my plate, Jameson says, "It's Taco Tuesday at Mom's tonight. We need to leave here around seven."

I stare at him. "You didn't think to put this on my calendar or tell me about it earlier than now?"

"I'm telling you now. Besides, you know she does it every Tuesday."

I continue staring at him. "You've taken me three times, Jameson. Weeks ago. And I'm not sure if you made it that clear it's a weekly thing."

He takes a deep breath before standing and bringing his coffee mug over. After he places it on the island, he says, "It's a weekly thing. We're going tonight. Don't be late."

He doesn't wait for my response before striding out of the kitchen.

It's my turn to take a deep breath. If I don't, I may go after him and attempt to inflict damage.

I'm almost certain Lara is going to want to inflict her own damage when I break the news to her that I can't get him to agree to a photo shoot. Because I doubt very much Jameson has any intention of doing one.

I eat my breakfast and drink my coffee in the ten minutes I'm alone before he returns. He looks at me expectantly. "Are you ready to leave?"

"Yes."

He nods. "Good." With that, he exits the kitchen and heads for the elevator.

We don't speak on the drive to work. I don't have it in me to, and Jameson is busy on his phone. I'd usually spend the time going through emails, but I'm tired this morning after not much sleep again last night. Instead, I stare out the window and contemplate how much staying married to Jameson means to me.

I knew it wouldn't be easy, but I made some assumptions about how we'd navigate daily life that I shouldn't have made.

I didn't expect to have to share a bedroom with him.

I didn't expect to have to travel to work with him every day.

And I didn't expect he'd insist on keeping up the pretense of being in love when Bill isn't around.

That kiss we shared yesterday has played over and over in my mind. I'm attracted to Jameson whether I want to be or not, and it's proving difficult to be around him so much. Especially at night.

Separate bedrooms would give us space to recharge alone after our busy days. To withdraw from the other and regroup, because goodness knows I need to regroup. Jameson has me on high alert at all times and I'm finding it difficult without that downtime by myself at night.

I resolve to find the right time to bring this up with him and revisit his decision for us to sleep together. Now is not the right time. Not after last night. I'll see how tonight goes and then perhaps talk with him when we get home. And I'll use today to build my case to present to him.

We arrive at my office and have a replay of yesterday morning.

Jameson comes around to my side of the car and helps me out. He then closes my door and says, "Adeline," in his deep voice as I take a few steps away from him.

I stop and meet his gaze. "I'm not in the mood this morning, Jameson."

His eyes flash with that never-ending supply of impatience he seems to have for me. "Find the mood," he says, his voice rumbly and extremely dictatorial.

Without giving me time to even begin trying to do that, he closes the distance between us and invades me.

With his arm around my waist, he pulls my body close and bends his face to mine. His kiss this morning starts out slow. He doesn't put much effort into it. This lulls me into a false sense of security that we're not going all out today in our show for the world.

He ends the kiss much faster than he did yesterday, however something stops him as he pulls away.

His eyes find mine, searching them, and his hand tightens its hold on my waist.

I have no idea what he's thinking, but I feel him.

God, do I feel him.

It begins low in my stomach.

A spark that quickly spreads throughout my body.

My skin feels warm.

My head feels light.

My heart makes itself known more than it ever has.

It beats fast and hard, and I-don't-even-know-what's-occurring-right-now.

We stand on the sidewalk like this for what feels like forever.

I flounder under the assault of my senses.

I wish I understood my responses to this man, but I understand nothing.

Not one thing I've done since he proposed this marriage makes any sense to me.

"Fuck," he growls, and for the first time, I know exactly what he's thinking because I'm thinking it too.

I want to get closer to him. Have his hands all over me. His mouth on mine. Our limbs tangled.

And as much as I really don't want any of that, I'm helpless but to stop myself from moving into him at the exact moment he moves into me.

I grip his suit jacket while he slides his hand into my hair.

Our lips crash together, and the spark that started low in my stomach flares to life in a way no spark has before.

I kiss Jameson with everything in me.

It's a heated frenzy of lust and anger and so many emotions I can't even begin to label.

I'm not thinking.

I can't.

This is my body taking control of my brain. Taking what it needs. And what that is, is Jameson.

His fingers dig into my hair as his tongue finds mine.

He kisses me deeply, thoroughly, demanding I do the same. Not that there's any risk I won't. I'm all in on this kiss. I want everything he has to give me.

When he growls into the kiss, I swear my ovaries explode.

I lose every last sense of control I've been trying to cling to.

Jameson could demand anything from me now and I would give it to him.

Of that, I am sure.

I have no idea how long we stand here kissing.

It could be a few minutes; it could be hours.

He's ruining me and I am allowing it.

And then, he's pulling his mouth from mine, growling and swearing all at once, and putting his phone to his ear while barking, "What?" into it.

I blink a few times and draw breath in.

What is happening right now?

Jameson's body is still against mine, so I take a step back, trying to put distance between us, that kiss, and all the confusion rushing through me.

He lets me go but his eyes don't. They stay firmly on mine.

I suck more air in.

I blink another couple times.

I gather my thoughts.

When Jameson finishes his phone call and slips his phone back into his pocket, I say, "Don't ever do that again."

His brows arch. "That wasn't all on me."

"It absolutely was." I know that's not true, but I refuse to take any credit for that kiss.

He receives a text, and after quickly checking it, he says, "I have to go. Don't be late tonight."

"I swear I will stab you if you continue treating me like this," I snap, unable to keep my thoughts to myself.

His lips twitch like he's amused. "Like what?"

"Like a fucking child. You don't have to remind me of things after you've told me once."

Another call comes through on his phone. He glances at it. "I'll see you tonight." He then puts the phone to his ear, turns, and walks around to his side of the car.

I stare after him for longer than I wish. My body refuses to let go of thoughts about our kiss. She demands I dedicate time to his suit, his body, his hair. It's at that point, when I'm checking out his hair, that I know I've completely lost all good sense.

I don't even like his fucking hair.

"Jesus," I mutter to my body as I turn to go into my building. "You need to get a grip. I don't like that man and I would kindly appreciate it if you could remember that the next time he assaults you."

"Are you talking to yourself?"

I jump at the sound of my best friend's voice next to me. I was so engrossed in my thoughts about Jameson, I didn't see her coming.

"Yes." I look at her while also eyeing the security detail Jameson insists I have at all times. Thank God they're discreet about what they see and hear. "I'm giving myself a good talking to."

She grins. "Over that kiss I just witnessed?"

"Yes."

"You actually looked like you were into it. Have you been taking acting lessons?"

I stop walking and turn to face her, all my confused thoughts and feelings spilling out of me. "I don't know what's happening, Nat. The man threw himself at me and I just went along with it. Like, willingly went along with it, as in I wanted him to kiss me. And I didn't want him to stop. You need to tell me how to fix myself, because I can't let him do that again."

She laughs. "Oh, babe, come here." She opens her arms and pulls me in for a hug, which I accept without hesitation. When she lets me go, she gently says, "You've got a lot going on, Addy, with the marriage and now with all this new gossip about your family." Her voice softens more when she adds, "Thomas coming out and getting involved too is bound to stir up a lot of things for you. And because your divorce is tied in your mind with Jameson taking over your company, it's all a tangled mess."

Natalie is a therapist. She's not mine, but she often helps me make sense of myself. She always knows when I'll be triggered by something, and she always knows what I need to hear.

"None of that should make me want to kiss Jameson, though."

"No, you did that simply because you're attracted to him."

"I honestly don't know who I am at the moment. I am not this woman. I mean, I can't stop myself from arguing with him over every little thing. You know that's not me."

She nods. "I know. I think a lot of this might be

coming from how Jameson made you feel five years ago when you lost your company to him. I imagine that's all been stirred up thanks to him being in your life now. You're likely overcompensating by challenging him over everything and trying to prove to yourself that the past won't be repeated."

Jameson was able to take my company because my eye was off the ball thanks to my divorce. I went through a long period of self-doubt after that. Both to do with the divorce and with the loss of my company. I vowed never to doubt myself again. I think Natalie is correct to link all this together.

I inhale a breath. "This is why I love you. You just get me. Even when I don't get me." I pause. "How am I going to make it through a year of this? We're only three days into this marriage and I can't decide if I want to kill him or tear his clothes off."

"Firstly, don't kill him. I will miss you too much while you're in prison. And second, you need to tell him his no-sex rule must go. Along with his rule you sleep in the same bed."

I sigh. "I know all this, but you should try having a conversation with that man. I don't know how he does it, but half the time I forget what I want to discuss with him and simply end up arguing with him instead."

"Have you been diffusing your lavender oil?"

"No."

"Do it tonight before you see him."

She's right. Lavender oil does help calm me. It also helps me sleep, something I desperately need.

"Thank you for being you. I sometimes forget the things that help me, but you never do. Now, we're going to get coffee and you're going to tell me all about your date last night. Since I didn't hear from you, I'm guessing you spent the night with Ryan."

"Let's just say that the crappy date I went on with his friend was so worth it to meet Ryan."

She shares as many of the details from her date as possible in the fifteen minutes we can both spare. I don't want to let her go when she looks at her watch and tells me our time is up, but I also have to leave. Jenna will be here soon for our meeting, and I need a little time with Vanessa and Lara before that.

We promise to connect late tonight for a full catch up before going our separate ways.

I'm stepping off the elevator onto my floor when my sister calls.

My chest tightens as I read her name on the screen. Sabrina only ever calls for one thing, and today I just don't want to deal with her. But I do, because she won't stop calling until I answer.

I put my phone to my ear. "Hi."

"So, Thomas is a dick."

Sabrina never changes. I have no idea how I ended up with a sister who is so different from me. "Yes."

"I can't believe the shit he's saying about Mom and me. What an asshole."

When asked for a comment on the story about Mom, Thomas said he'd witnessed her getting high with men many times and sleeping with a lot of them. He also mentioned that he'd witnessed Sabrina doing the same. That part about Sabrina was the only thing he didn't lie about.

I don't comment on what she says because I don't

want to get into an argument with her this morning. And we *would* end up in an argument, because that's where we always end up. "What do you need, Sabrina?"

"Why do you think I need something? Maybe I just called to talk to you about Thomas." Her defensiveness tells me otherwise.

"Did you?" I rub at my temple, feeling a headache forming.

"Well, no, but if it wasn't for Mom needing help, I would have just called for that."

We both know that's a lie, but I don't touch it. "What does Mom need help with?"

"Her plumbing."

Right, I should have known. "How much?"

"I don't know. A few grand maybe."

I highly doubt she needs that much, and if it was any other day, I'd likely point that out. But since it's today, and I don't have it in me to get into this with her, I say, "I'll take care of it."

"I'll let her know. And maybe get your lawyer onto shutting Thomas the hell up."

The call disconnects and I take a minute to center myself before walking into my office.

If I thought I needed a year to recover from yesterday morning, I need longer today.

~

I SURVIVE THE DAY.

Actually, my day goes well.

Jenna and I make good headway on our business plans and set a few new things in motion that we've been talking about for weeks. It feels good to get the ball rolling on these plans.

Lara only brings up the photo shoot with Jameson twice. I make it clear to her that it won't happen and that I don't want to hear about it again.

I get through a lot of work throughout the day and arrive home feeling like I achieved a lot. I then shower and get dressed for dinner with Jameson's family. I take Natalie's advice and diffuse lavender oil while getting ready, hoping it will help me remain calm during dinner.

Jameson strides into the bedroom at 6:45 p.m. He glances at me on his way through but doesn't speak. He takes a shower and emerges looking like he was styled by a professional. I find it highly annoying that he can do this, and that he can do it in less than ten minutes. It takes me far longer to achieve that level of styling.

He's changed into jeans, and a high neck black-and-white cashmere sweater. I may hate his hair, beard, and ink, but I like his style. Jameson has this way of making even the most casual outfit sexy. I'm convinced the man could wear anything and I'd like it.

"I'll wait in the car for you," he says, grabbing his black wool overcoat and exiting the bedroom without waiting for my reply.

I swipe some lipstick on, run my fingers through my hair one last time, and join him in the car.

I spent time today going over what I want to talk with him about later tonight. I also spent time trying to rid my mind of the kiss we shared this morning. I thought I'd done a good job of moving past it, but being in his presence, for even this short amount of time, shows me I didn't do a good job at all.

Max hasn't even exited the garage before my skin heats and my thoughts start jumbling. I swear I feel the air around us stir with a new energy.

How is this possible?

I don't want to feel any of this with this man.

"Shantel has gone over my calendar trying to find a weekend for our honeymoon," he says. "It looks like December is out. We'll have to wait until January."

I meet his gaze. "Have her check in with Vanessa. I may not have any spare weekends in January."

He watches me silently for a long moment like he's appraising me before finally nodding.

We turn silent after that, and I work through some emails that have come in since I left work. I try to forget that Jameson is sitting next to me, but there's no hope of me doing that. Not when my body is so aware of him.

It's like I'm two people at once.

The real me who hates him, and the other me who wants to sit on his lap and do filthy things to him.

Oh, good God.

No.

No, no, no.

I squeeze my eyes closed and commence praying.

I can't recall the last time I prayed.

It seems God isn't holding that against me. Within a few moments of my prayer going up, I receive a text that takes all my attention off Jameson.

Lara: Ian Swift is an asshole and if I ever meet him, I'm going to make him eat a bag of dicks. Dirty, unclean, old dicks that will make him choke.

Adeline: What's he done?

I pull up Instagram and search his profile.

Lara: He posted a comment on Insta saying he's not surprised to read the stories about your mother and sister after meeting you, and that he also wouldn't be surprised to read similar stories about you. It's gathered a lot of other comments from people agreeing with him.

"That fucking asshole," I mutter to myself.

"What's wrong?" Jameson asks, giving me his attention again.

"Nothing." He'd just dismiss it even if I told him.

"Something is obviously bothering you and I'd rather you not take your mood to dinner. Who's the asshole tonight?"

The me who wanted to sit on his lap and do filthy things to him a moment ago no longer runs the show. "Well, besides you, Ian Swift."

"What's he done now?"

"Do you really care?"

He works his jaw. "I wouldn't ask if I didn't."

"He's made a comment on social media about me and my family. It's not flattering."

"Ignore him."

"I can't just ignore this kind of stuff, Jameson. That's not how my business works. We rely heavily on social media."

"Have you tested that?"

"Yes, as a matter of fact, I have."

"You need to find other forms of supporting your business, then. This isn't a healthy way of doing business."

My eyes go wide. "How about you stick to what you know, and I'll stick to what I know?"

"What I know is that you've always got some social media crisis to deal with. It consumes you at times. That can't be good for you."

"It's business. And may I remind you that I'm not the only one dealing with problems. Your business also has them."

"My business has problems I can fix because the issues are within my control. Your problems are out of your control."

Another text comes through. It's good timing because I need the break from listening to Jameson tell me how to run my business.

Natalie: Babe, don't go on Instagram tonight, okay?

Adeline: It's too late if this is about Ian. Lara's already told me.

Natalie: I'm sorry. Just remember these people don't know you, so anything they're saying isn't the truth.

Adeline: Thank you <3

I meet Jameson's gaze again. "Please don't talk to me about my business again. You don't know anything about it."

"That may be the case, but I know about business, Adeline. And I know that business problems can find their way into personal lives." He pauses. "Make sure that doesn't happen with this marriage."

I glare at him. "Would you say that to a man? Or are you assuming because I'm a woman, I can't keep my life under control?"

Irritation dances across his face. "This has nothing to do with you being a woman."

"I'm not sure I believe you."

"Believe what you choose, but don't fuck this up."

I don't talk to him after that.

I can't.

He's angered me so much I want nothing to do with him. Goodness knows how we're going to make it through this dinner with his family.

8

Jameson

Adeline's long legs are as distracting as her attitude is frustrating. I'm having trouble tearing my eyes from them tonight just as much as I'm having trouble with her attitude.

She's wearing black leather pants and stiletto boots with heels that can't be good for a woman's back. I do, however, find them sexy as hell. But then, I find everything about her sexy as hell, even when I don't want to.

It's only Tuesday, yet it feels like I've endured longer than just a few days of marriage to her.

"You look like you'd rather be anywhere but here," Hudson says when I join him in Mom's kitchen just after I leave Adeline in the living room with Mom.

"I'd rather be here without my wife," I mutter.

My brother chuckles and pours me a whiskey. "That bad, huh?"

I take the drink and throw some down my throat. "You've no idea."

"So, Bill is here."

I frown. "Where?"

Hudson lifts his chin in the direction of the living room. "Here. Tonight."

"Fuck." I didn't see him and I sure as hell didn't expect him. I should have, though. He knows Mom does Taco Tuesday every week. It makes sense he'd show up tonight, the first Tuesday after my wedding.

"He was taking a call on the terrace. I imagine he'll be finished with that soon, so you might want to get back out there and manage your wife."

I drink some more whiskey before nodding. "Thanks for the heads up."

"Before you go, are you still against the suggestions Paulina made this morning?"

"I haven't changed my mind."

"Why are you being stubborn about this?"

"Because I don't want to tie Adeline's name to my brand in this way. This marriage has an end date, and I don't want to have to work on this problem again when our divorce goes through. Besides, I'd have a greater chance of convincing her to jump out of a fucking plane than I would of convincing her to help me in this way."

One of Paulina's ideas to improve my hotel chain's competitive advantage was to launch a campaign featuring Adeline. I have no doubt such a campaign would work, but I have no interest in going down that path.

Hudson chuckles at the plane reference. "You may be right there, but I still think it's worth considering. We'd only have to run the campaign for six months, at which point we could launch a new one with someone else. By the time you divorce her, the brand would be tied to someone else. We maximize your involvement with her now for the short term, get as much out of that as we can, and then move on. You know her brand would deliver for the hotels. It's a no-brainer as far as I'm concerned."

"What's a no-brainer?" Bill asks, coming into the kitchen.

I turn to him. "I thought you were away this week." He mentioned something to me last week about flying to London.

"My trip was cancelled." He glances between us. "What was the no-brainer?"

I drink some more whiskey. "A suggestion Paulina Rossi made for the hotels."

Before he can ask what the suggestion was, my mother and Adeline join us.

Mom comes to me, and I lean down to kiss her. "Hello, darling. I'm happy to see you wearing that sweater I bought you."

I smile at her as Adeline moves next to me. Placing my arm around Adeline, I say to Mom, "How are you?"

Adeline slides her arm around my waist, and I try to ignore the way her touch causes my gut to tighten. As hard as I try, though, I don't succeed. Much like this morning when I couldn't rein in my desire to kiss her.

"I'm good." She looks between Adeline and me. "Very happy to see you two here tonight."

Adeline brings her hand to my stomach and gives me

a smile before looking at Mom. "We're glad to be here, Reese."

I prepare to stop Adeline's hand, which I anticipate will drift lower than I prefer, but she surprises me when she doesn't shift it as low as she usually does.

"Have you two settled on a new date for your honeymoon yet?" Bill inquires.

"We're looking at a weekend in January," I say.

His brows arch. "That far away? I thought you'd be falling over yourself to whisk your new bride away."

"He is," Adeline says. "Honestly, if Jameson had his way, he'd never let me out of his sight. But I've got so much on at work that we just can't get away this month."

Adeline surprises me again. She knows that Bill will let this go now that he thinks the lack of a honeymoon is because of her work rather than mine. I wouldn't have expected her to take one for the team like this. Not with the level of her hostility toward me.

"Right," says Mom, "enough honeymoon talk. I spoke with Adeline about it yesterday and I know you're both disappointed you have to put it on hold. Let's talk about something happier, like the news I saw about Owen last night. He must be delighted."

I nod as I shift my thoughts from the fact Adeline spoke with Mom about the honeymoon yesterday to Owen. "He is. I haven't had a chance to have a good chat with him about it yet, but I'm hoping to catch up on the weekend." My oldest friend manages a hedge fund and was nominated as a finalist in this year's Hedge Fund Industry Awards. He more than deserves it, too. He's delivered top performances in the industry for years now.

"That's great news," Adeline says, and I hear the

genuine warmth in her voice. It makes sense because she's taken a liking to Owen.

Bill frowns. "You didn't know?" He looks at me questioningly and I realize the mistake she's made.

Adeline doesn't miss a beat, though. "No, I didn't." She presses her hand harder against my stomach as she leans into me. "I was slammed at work yesterday and then Jameson and I had to attend a dinner party that didn't allow much time for us to catch up after work. And then"—she smiles sexily up at me—"well, you know how it is, Bill, when you're just married. You'd rather be doing other things than talking."

The memory of our kiss this morning crashes into me, coiling desire for Adeline through me all over again.

Christ.

It's unexpected and unwanted.

I'm attracted to her, but there's no way in hell I'm acting on that. Like I told Hudson, it's too risky to take things any further with Adeline. But fuck, it's proving harder than I thought to ignore what she does to me.

"I do remember," Bill says, his features softening. My mentor is an old romantic. Any mention of his ex-wife softens him, something Adeline knows. She played a great card there.

Bill worked too much throughout his marriage. His wife left him a few years before I met him due to his workaholic ways. He had many girlfriends after that, but he never remarried. I know he regrets choosing work over his wife because she truly was the love of his life. I also know this is why he insisted I find love in order to inherit his company.

He thinks I work too much and will end up regretting that like he does.

Bill and I aren't the same, though. I'm not interested in being married or building a family. I don't have any good memories of my parents' marriage. In fact, my mother is better off without my father.

Love fucks people up. Makes them do things that aren't good for them. I vowed years ago not to make the same mistakes my mother did.

"How about you, Hudson?" Adeline asks, turning her attention to my brother.

"How about me, what?" he says.

"Are you seeing anyone? I keep asking your brother and he keeps fobbing me off. Since we're related now, you should just expect me to come straight to you with these questions." She grins at him like she's enjoying herself.

He returns her grin. Hudson likes Adeline. "I see how we're doing things now, Addy. And if you're planning on hitting me up for details, you should plan on me hitting you up for the same."

She laughs and I feel it in her entire body as it sways against mine. "Oh, Huds, I have no secrets from you. You know this."

"Huds?" he asks. "I don't recall anyone ever calling me that."

Adeline cocks her head. "I think it's good. You don't like it?"

"I can work with it," he says. "And as for your question, I'm not seeing anyone."

"Oh, how disappointing. I was thinking we could double date," she says.

"Jesus, no," Hudson says. "I can think of nothing

worse than fucking double dating with a newly married couple."

Adeline laughs again. It's such an unusual sight that I'm captivated by it. The way her face softens and lights up at the same time. And the way her whole body laughs along with her. She's a beautiful woman; when she laughs, that beauty is magnified. "What do you think, darling?" she asks, her eyes finding mine.

I stare down at her, still thinking about how beautiful she is. Even her eyes change when she laughs. The color shifts into a different shade of green and the wariness I always see in them disappears. "I'm not willing to share you yet."

"There's the brother I know," Hudson says. "And I suspect he won't ever be willing to share you, Addy, so no double dates for us."

Adeline watches me for a few more seconds before dragging her gaze away. Looking at Mom, she says, "Is there anything I can do to help you with the tacos, Reese?"

"No, this is Jameson's and Hudson's job. You and I won't be lifting a finger tonight." She loops her arm through Adeline's and guides her back out of the kitchen while calling over her shoulder, "Adeline needs a drink, Jameson."

Hudson grins. "There's nothing quite like watching you get ordered around."

I ignore him and pour Adeline a wine. When I take it to her, I find my mother listening intently to something Adeline is saying. Slowing my pace, I watch them for a minute.

Mom is like Bill, a romantic at heart. Sadly, the man

she fell in love with at eighteen, and left her family for, turned out to be a piece of shit who didn't know what love was. She stayed with him until he died simply because she had two sons with him and thought staying was the right thing to do. I also doubt he would have let her go, but since she didn't test that theory, I'll never know.

Over the years, Mom has tried to find me love. She's invited me to lunch many times, while also inviting a woman she thought I'd like. She's dragged me to charity events under the guise of wanting me to donate money while really it was to introduce me to someone. She's also, on occasion, simply not shown up to a dinner with me, leaving me alone with a woman she also invited.

My mother wants me to fall in love.

She wants me to have a wife who will love and care for me.

And she wants grandchildren.

I hate that I'm deceiving her with my marriage. Watching her happiness now while talking with Adeline causes guilt to slice through me.

She will be devastated when I divorce Adeline, and that is something I didn't think through very well.

"Oh, there you are," Mom says when she catches sight of me.

Adeline finds my eyes and takes the glass of wine I offer her. "Thank you."

I watch her for longer than is required, slowly running my eyes down to the swell of her breasts under the black top she's wearing. The top dips between her breasts, giving me a glimpse of skin, but nowhere near enough.

"I'm sorry, Reese," Bill says, coming into the living room, "but something has just come up and I have to leave."

Mom stands and moves to him so she can hug him goodbye. "Hopefully we'll see you next week?"

He nods. "Perhaps." He then eyes me. "Have Shantel call Lisa. I want dinner in the next week."

After he says goodbye to Adeline, he leaves. I pull out my phone to ask Shantel to get in touch with his assistant about that dinner. I also make a mental note to talk with Adeline about it. She needs to be prepped. This is a test; one I won't have fucked up.

Hudson and I finish preparing the tacos, discussing Paulina's strategies while we work. I rejected the strategy involving Adeline, but she came up with a lot of other great ideas that I signed off on. I'm hopeful this month's figures will begin reflecting the changes we're going to make. If Paulina is known for anything, it's turning business around fast.

I pour drinks while everyone takes a seat at Mom's large dining table. When I take my seat, I shift it closer to Adeline's. She smiles at me as I do so, but that's not for my benefit. I see the warning in her eyes. She doesn't want me too close. However, this is for my mother and I'm not changing course. I've no doubt Bill will grill Mom about my marriage and her thoughts on it. I need her to help me convince him it's real.

Putting my arm around Adeline's shoulder, I lean in close and brush my lips over her cheek so I can murmur against her ear, "Mom needs to buy this. Make it so she does."

Her hand comes to my thigh, and she squeezes it as she says, "I love you too, darling."

Letting her go, I give her one last pointed look before turning to dinner.

"Adeline," Mom says as she fills her plate. "I was talking with your mother at the wedding, and she mentioned she's thinking of visiting this month. Has she confirmed when? I'd love to invite her to dinner while she's in town."

Adeline's mother lives in Wilmington, just over two hours from here. I haven't visited her home, and Adeline hasn't shared much with me. From what I know, she lives with Sabrina, and neither comes to New York often.

Adeline reaches for her wine and takes a sip. "She hasn't told me yet. I'll let her know you'd love to have her over for dinner. She'd like that."

I hear it in her voice that she has no intention of telling her mother about this. It doesn't surprise me. Adeline wasn't keen on inviting her mother and sister to the wedding. I had to put my foot down and insist on it.

Observing the three of them at the wedding, I noted the tension. If I read the dynamics correctly, Adeline spends her time trying to keep the peace between the three of them, while Sabrina doesn't appear to give a fuck about peace. Adeline's mother seems to live in her own world, interjecting every now and then to give her opinion on how her daughters could improve themselves.

My mother is good at reading people and by her expression, I suspect she's picked up on Adeline's hesitancy to invite her mother over. Her face softens and she says, "If you'd prefer to have her to yourself this trip, I understand. I don't want to force myself upon her or interrupt your time together."

Adeline's shoulders relax. "Thank you, Reese. I appreciate that." Her shoulders may have relaxed but her voice still holds threads of tightness.

Mom reaches out to Adeline and places her hand on her arm. "Always, my darling. I haven't seen my mother for a long time, but I remember how precious my time with her was."

I'm unsure if it's the sadness in Mom's voice that catches Adeline's attention or something else, but she looks at Mom and says, "It must have been hard to lose contact with your mother." Adeline knows the basics of my mother's history, but since they've not spent a great deal of time together, they've never discussed it.

Mom nods. "Yes, it was, but my father forbade her from seeing me after I chose to marry Jameson's father, and she never went against his wishes. I was young and too blinded by love to fully understand what I was giving up." She pats Adeline's arm. "You take all the time by yourself with your mother this trip. I'll have many more opportunities to spend time with her."

Adeline takes a breath and wraps her hand around her wine glass like she's about to lift it. She doesn't, though. She simply holds it for a moment before letting it go and saying, "Actually, Mom and I aren't that close. Not by my choice, but we just have never really found our way there." She stops speaking and swallows like she's trying to get rid of her thoughts that way.

Mom listens closely and I see her softening even further toward the woman she believes I love. "I'm sorry to hear that. Maybe she's coming to visit because she wants to change that."

"No." Adeline shakes her head. "She may have told you she's coming to visit, but I don't think she'll come. Mom is full of big plans that she never follows through on."

I sit back in my seat and take a sip of my whiskey. There's something in Adeline's voice now that I've not heard before. Vulnerability and openness.

She's always closed off with me. Watchful and ready to defend at all times. I understood why to begin with, but I hadn't expected it to continue on like it has. I thought once we signed off on the marriage contract, we'd settle into a working relationship of some sort. That has not been the case, and Adeline has refused to lower her walls around me.

"Have you spoken with her about your desire to be closer?" Mom asks.

"When I was younger, yes. I've given up now." She pauses, and when she speaks again, her voice wobbles in a very unlike-Adeline way. "My mother uses me, Reese. She was the one who pushed me into modeling when I was sixteen. She saw dollar signs and a way for her to fill her bank account. She didn't care what I had to go through to reach the top; she just pushed me until I got there. Now, she's still reaping the rewards. I've reached the point where I see her for who she truly is, and I don't think I want the kind of relationship with her that I once did."

Heartbreak fills my mother's eyes. She's one of the most empathetic people I know. "Yes," she says softly, "I imagine you don't."

Adeline shares a moment with her before finally saying, "Thank you. Not many people understand when a person says they don't want a relationship with their parent."

Mom squeezes her hand. "I know." She lets Adeline's hand go and looks at me. "Right, let's eat. And while we do that, you and Hudson can tell us girls what the plans will be for Super Bowl."

Hudson picks up his taco. "I presume they'll be what they always are."

"What's that?" Adeline asks.

"We usually gather at Jameson's for a party," Hudson says, "so prepare yourself now for the onslaught, because when I say party, I'm talking a lot of people in your place."

"I prefer to go to the game. You guys can have the penthouse to yourself," Adeline says.

Hudson whistles low. "Yeah, I don't think it works like that, Addy."

"Like what?" she says.

"We're not going to the game," I say.

"Jameson prefers to watch it at home," Hudson says.

Adeline smiles sweetly at me after eating some of her taco. "He can watch it at home."

My eyes bore into hers, holding a warning that this discussion needs to come to an end. This is the kind of conversation that will require negotiations in private. "We'll watch it at home."

"I think it would be fun to go to the game," Mom says. "Can you still get tickets?"

"I have tickets," Adeline says. "But if Jameson doesn't want to go, I have people I can give them to." She looks at me. "I don't want us to fight over this. You know I hate fighting with you."

"We'll talk about this some more," I say. I have no intention of going to the game, but I suspect Adeline has every intention of it.

"What I can tell you," Hudson says as he finishes his taco, "is that you'll enjoy the party if you don't go to the game. Jameson mightn't love crowds, but he knows how to throw one hell of a party."

Mom nods her agreement. "He's right, Adeline. It's always a good time. And while he never allows me to help him and Shantel plan it, I'm sure he'll let you."

Hudson grins. "Let's not get ahead of ourselves, Mom."

"I think I'm with Hudson on this one," Adeline says. "I love him dearly, but my husband is a control freak."

Mom shifts the conversation after that, asking Adeline about fashion week and some of the ins and outs of her business. I listen attentively to everything she says, asking questions I'm interested to know the answer to. Adeline answers them easily. It's the first conversation we've ever had that wasn't hard and I find myself enjoying it. I get the impression Adeline does too.

After we finish eating and talking, Hudson and I stand to clear the table.

Mom shoos at Adeline when she stands to help. "Sit, darling. The boys will clean up."

Adeline's lips twitch as she looks at me. "I can't say I've ever heard anyone refer to Jameson as a boy."

The last thing I hear as I carry dishes into the kitchen is Adeline asking Mom to share stories with her about me as a boy. I'm not surprised to hear her ask this. She's good at keeping up the pretense that she loves me. What I am surprised about is that she genuinely sounds interested.

Hudson and I clean up. We then spend another hour with Mom while she tells Adeline stories about our childhood. She skips the dark side of it and only shares fun stories. Adeline sits next to me on the sofa, her hand glued to my thigh, her body leaning against mine. I settle my arm across the back of the sofa behind her and concentrate on ignoring the sensations her touch is causing.

I give Mom this hour and then I tell her we have to leave. Mostly because I have work to do, but also because I don't have it in me to sit with Adeline like this for any longer.

"I like your mother," Adeline says a couple of minutes into our drive home. She's full of surprises tonight. Initiating conversation with me is something she rarely does.

"She likes you too."

"Has she had many relationships since your father died?"

This isn't a topic I ever discuss with anyone; however, I find myself answering her. "She's dated, but I suspect she's cautious after my father."

She frowns. "Why?"

I keep my private life very private. The only people who know what my father was like are my mother, Hudson, and Bill. As far as I know, they've never shared the details either. All Adeline knows is that my father died when I was eighteen, and that I didn't get along with him while he was alive.

"Dad didn't treat her well. It wasn't a very happy marriage."

She takes that in, silently processing it. "Do you think she's open to love?"

"She wants it for everyone else, so I imagine so."

"She desperately wants it for you, doesn't she? I don't get the impression she's as worried for Hudson as she is for you."

I nod. "You are correct. She's gone out of her way to find me a wife."

"I can imagine."

"I'm not sure you can."

She lifts her brows questioningly. "What has she done?"

"The most outrageous thing was to set up a dating profile for me. She responded to all the women who matched with me and then arranged dates."

Adeline's entire face lights up with a smile. It might be the most beautiful smile I've ever witnessed. "Oh my gosh. Go Reese." She shifts in her seat to face me. Every fiber in her being is invested in this conversation. "How did she get you to agree to the dates?"

"She didn't. She simply invited me to lunches and dinners with her. Then, she didn't show up and I was left to explain myself."

She laughs. "How many of these 'dates' did you actually go on? Surely you figured out what was happening pretty fast."

"One dinner the first time. One lunch the second time."

"Oh my God, she did it twice?"

"Yes. My mother is nothing if not persistent."

"I see where you get it from."

Her phone sounds with a text.

After she checks it, she says, "That was my social media manager. She told me to commend you on your kissing ability." She holds her phone out for me to read the message.

Lara: Holy woah, Addy. Jameson outdid himself today. I may let him off the hook for refusing to do the photo shoot. That kiss this morning has gone viral and from what I've heard, sales are through the roof. Most importantly, though, it's taken some of the heat off with all the other stuff being posted about you.

"So, does your directive still stand, then?" I ask.

"What directive?"

"The one in which you ordered me to never kiss you again."

If I'm not mistaken, her breathing picks up. "Yes, that directive still stands."

"You don't think it's important for people to see a husband kiss his wife goodbye for the day?"

"Well, no, that's not what I'm saying."

"What *are* you saying?"

Adeline is a confident woman who can hold her own in any situation. I've seen that firsthand many times. Right now, though, she appears slightly bewildered. Unsure of herself.

"What I'm saying, Jameson," she says, attempting to inject firmness back into her voice, "is that a goodbye kiss doesn't require that level of effort."

Adeline was just as aroused by that kiss as I was.

That much was clear to me this morning.

The difference between how we're both handling it is that while I'm not trying to downplay it, she appears determined to pretend it didn't happen.

"We're attracted to each other, Adeline. That's just biology. It doesn't mean we have to act on it. But we can use it to help us with this marriage."

"You are very good at making assumptions about other people."

"What? You're denying you're attracted to me? That you didn't enjoy that kiss?"

"I'm saying exactly what you heard me say." Her tone turns a little snappy. "You like to make assumptions."

"I run with facts based on observations. You can't tell me you didn't make the kind of sounds that a woman makes when she's enjoying a kiss. Or that you didn't give me your tongue willingly today." I pause. "Those are facts, not assumptions."

She looks anything but happy that I've brought these facts up. However, instead of running with her usual style of arguing with me, she says, "Perhaps a little less tongue tomorrow. Or no tongue. That would be acceptable."

My lips kick up at the ends. "You know, I was beginning to think you didn't have it in you."

"What?"

"The ability to compromise."

Her brows shoot for her forehead. "Are you kidding me? I'm fucking compromising all over the damn place. You're the one who doesn't have it in you. Oh, and just so you know, I'm not watching the Super Bowl on your television, so don't even think about trying to get me to change my mind."

My lips are still kicked up.

I'm enjoying this more than I should, because as much as Adeline's fire frustrates me, it turns me on more.

There's no way she's getting less tongue tomorrow.

9

Adeline

I wake early on Wednesday morning, refreshed and with the clearest mind I've had all week.

I slept last night.

Like real, deep sleep, during which I wasn't aware of who was lying next to me.

Many, many hours of it.

It's just after 5:00 a.m. when I push the bed covers back and get out of bed. Jameson has already left the room. I've no idea of his morning routine because I've not been up this early with him yet, but I imagine he's in his gym working on those muscles my eyes think they should rest in peace on.

My exercise routine has taken a hit this week and my body is feeling it, so I change into tights and a tank top, splash some water on my face, and throw my hair up into a ponytail. I then make my way to Jameson's gym to use his treadmill. I'd prefer to run outside. I'd also prefer not to work out with Jameson. But I'm not a fan of running outside in winter, so his gym it is.

It turns out I don't have to work out with him.

Jameson is exiting the gym when I arrive.

"Good morning," he says, running his eyes over my body appreciatively. No man's eyes have caused my body to respond the way Jameson's do.

The second his eyes meet my body, my core wakes up, my skin wakes up, my veins wake up.

I feel him everywhere at once.

I want him everywhere at once.

His eyes, his hands, his mouth.

Oh Jesus, I want that mouth of his in ways I should not want it.

"Morning," I say while mentally telling my body to stop thinking for itself.

She, of course, pays no attention.

Jameson is stealing all her attention with his muscles all up in her face.

Good God, are his muscles really that big?

And why am I so attracted to him while he's so damn sweaty?

I try not to stare, but that part of me that wants to sit on his lap and do filthy things to him is in full control, and she's having nothing to do with the other part of me who could stab him at the best of times.

"I'd like to leave early this morning," he says, his gravelly voice shooting another wave of lust through my body.

My thoughts crash into each other and land with a thud.

What did he just say?

Something about grinding against me?

While I sit on his lap?

And he bites my neck?

Shit, no.

That was me thinking that.

Abort, abort, abort.

"Adeline? Did you hear what I said?"

I stare at him, willing my brain to start working again.

I nod like an idiot while no words come out of my mouth.

He frowns. "I'll take that as a yes to leaving early?"

"Yes."

"Seven-thirty?"

"Yes."

"Good." With one last sweep of his eyes over my body, he moves past me.

It takes me far longer than it should to finally gather all my thoughts, and when I do, I want to slap myself for everything that just happened.

I cannot go on like this.

Not when I have a year to get through.

But I have no idea how I can change the way I react to him. I mean, short of wearing a blindfold at all times. And plugging my nose so I can't smell him. Not to mention putting earplugs in so I can't hear his voice.

Just cut your head off and be done with it.

"Oh my God," I mutter to myself as I step into the gym. "Stop it. The man is not worth your damn time. Surely you can control yourself around him. Stop thinking about sitting on his lap and start thinking about the fact he stole your damn company. Oh, and the fact he's an asshole."

"Adeline."

I spin at the sound of Jameson's voice. "What?" It comes out snappy. The man should not sneak up on me like that.

I swear his lips twitch once. I also swear his eyes do something similar. But I can't be absolutely sure because he moves straight onto what he came to say. "I need to leave at seven now."

"Fine. Yes. Seven. I've got it. I'll be ready." Jesus, can he just stop invading me like this?

This time, I know his lips twitch.

The bastard is enjoying my disheveled state.

"Jameson, it's far too early for this. I'm not good first thing in the morning. I need to run. Then I need coffee. After that, you can talk to me about whatever the hell you want."

He continues watching me like he's enjoying this.

He doesn't reply to what I said. He simply turns and leaves.

I watch him exit, and goddamn he has a fine ass.

I hate him even more for that ass.

~

I RUN on the treadmill for an hour. I need every minute of that run. I also meditate during it because I need that too. After, I shower and dress for the day, taking longer with my hair and makeup than I should considering Jameson wants to leave at seven.

I'm delaying the inevitable because I know without a shadow of a doubt that being in his presence is going to make me behave in ways I don't want to behave.

How I've gone from wanting to stab him every second of the day to wanting to sit on his lap in between stabbing him is beyond me, but here I am.

A text comes through as I'm leaving the bedroom.

Vanessa: I'm so sorry to do this to you today with all the stuff that happened overnight, but I'm not well this morning and will be late for work.

I call her. When she answers, I hear just how sick she is. "I'm sorry, Adeline. I hate doing this to you when you're super busy."

"Ness, stop. I can hear you're not well. I don't want you to come in today, okay? I don't know what stuff happened overnight but whatever it is, we'll deal with it. You just get better." I purposely didn't check social media or emails first thing today because I needed a break from it. I needed some quiet, peaceful time before the day unleashes itself on me.

"Oh my God, it's not good. No, you're going to need me today. I've taken drugs and am hoping they'll kick in fast. I'm coming in."

I don't focus on what she said about things not being good. Instead, I focus on making her understand I want her to rest. "You sound like you're at death's door with a cold. Do not come to work. I'll just send you straight home. Please rest so that you get better fast. If I need you for anything urgent, you can do it from home." I have no intention of asking her to work while she's not well, but I know she'll feel better about staying home if she thinks I'll call if needed.

She's silent for a moment before agreeing. "Okay, but definitely call me if you need me. I'm here."

"I know you are. Get better. Check in with me later to let me know you're okay."

We end the call and I pull up my social media.

I immediately wish I hadn't.

My chest tightens while I read what's been posted.

Stories about my mother being a hooker.

Stories about me being a bitch who doesn't help her family. A bitch who would rather see her mother sell her body to pay her bills.

Stories about the awful drug addiction my mother now has, thanks to having to sell her body.

If only they knew the truth of which one of us had to sell her body to pay bills. It sure as hell wasn't my mother.

And then there's the post Thomas has made about our marriage. He's lied about our sex life, saying that I pressured him into having threesomes. He's also said I cheated on him numerous times. On top of all that, he said he hopes Jameson knows just who he married and that I'll probably cheat on him too.

I never looked at or touched another man while married to Thomas. He, on the other hand, cheated on me with at least five women. I discovered this after I left him, and I suspect there were more than five women. I've left all that behind me. I've worked hard on rebuilding myself after spiraling into a dark place after my divorce. I'm in a good place now, but damn, this gossip is bad news.

It could harm my chance at getting my company back.

Taking a deep breath, I go in search of coffee and Jameson. I doubt he's going to be happy about this.

He's standing at the island when I join him in the kitchen. All suited up in a blue suit, ready for the day. Although, he's not quite fully ready because his hair isn't pulled back into that god-awful man bun yet.

My brows pull in as I look at his hair. "Did you cut your hair?" I don't recall it looking any different last night, but now that it's out, it seems shorter than when I last saw him wear it out.

He looks at me, and yes, there's something different today. "Yes."

Jameson's hair used to fall just below his shoulders. Now, it doesn't quite touch his shoulders. He has thick, wavy hair, though, so there's still a lot of it, and I'm sure he'll still wear it in a bun. But there's no denying I like it this length.

I especially like it when he runs his fingers through it to keep it off his face like he does now while watching me.

Holy hot ovary.

Thankfully, he moves along with the conversation and asks, "Would you like coffee?"

Right.

Coffee.

Food.

The matter at hand.

I hold my phone up. "Clearly you haven't seen the news this morning." At his frown, I add, "If you had, you wouldn't be offering to make me coffee." It's bad enough having to deal with the bullshit my ex is spreading about me but having to do that on Jameson's watch is going to be painful. He won't be happy with the spotlight on us in this way.

"I've seen it."

I stare at him, confused, as he reaches for a mug. "And?" He seems so unaffected by it. Not at all what I was expecting.

"And what?"

"Jesus, Jameson. My ex-husband has done a tell-all about our sex life with particular emphasis on the threesomes I supposedly used to demand from him, and the cheating I supposedly did. And here you are acting like nothing even happened. I mean, what is Bill going to make of this? Surely that's of concern to you."

He holds up the mug he just pulled out of the cupboard. "I presume you want coffee?"

Who is this man?

He looks like Jameson and moves like Jameson, but he doesn't speak Jameson's language. The asshole language, that is.

I sensed a change in him at dinner last night. We actually had a conversation in which I didn't want to take a knife to him. He listened to me when I told his family a little about my work. He asked me questions like he was interested in the answers. And then he shared that story with me about his mom trying to line up dates for him.

He was relaxed last night, something I've not witnessed before. I was relaxed too. I don't know what it is about his mother, but just being in her presence calms me. Being with her last night helped me shed the stirred-up emotions I've been feeling since the wedding.

I don't know Reese well, but I already know she's the kind of mother I always wished I had. Hell, the woman stayed married to a man who didn't make her happy for her children. While I don't necessarily think mothers should feel the need to do that, it's a lot more than my mother ever did for me. I was lucky if my mother even got out of bed to get me ready for school when I was too young to do that myself.

Last night, I decided that while my relationship with her son is fake, my relationship with her doesn't need to be. She has a beautiful energy that makes me feel good, and I want to reciprocate, so when she brought up the topic of my mother, I chose to be honest with her. I don't talk about my family with anyone but Natalie; it felt good to open up to Reese.

"Adeline?" Jameson says, his voice filled with a level of patience not common from him. "Coffee?"

"Yes, I want coffee. But please, husband dear, enlighten me as to your thoughts on this. Reading your mind is not a specialty of mine yet."

He arches his brows. "Yet?"

"Yes, yet."

He gets to work on my coffee as he says, "I look forward to the day a woman can read my mind. It'll make my life a lot fucking easier."

"I wouldn't be so sure of that. Not with this woman, anyway."

He meets my gaze. "I don't doubt that."

"Are you going to tell me what you're thinking about the shit Thomas has made up, or am I going to have to beat it out of you?"

His lips quirk, and God help him if he shows any hint of amusement. I'm not above inflicting physical pain today. It might make me feel better.

For once, Jameson plays the smart card. He reins his amusement in and says, "I don't give a fuck about the shit Thomas has made up." He narrows his eyes at me. "Do you?"

I do, but there's no way I'll ever tell him that.

"No, but I thought for sure you'd be pissed off over it."

"Why?"

I let out a frustrated breath. "Honestly, dealing with you is hard work. You're so contradictory."

"How the hell am I contradictory?"

"You're focused on us looking like we're in love and on how we appear in public, so I'm unsure why this isn't triggering concern for you."

"I only care how we appear as a couple to Bill," he says, sliding the mug of coffee across the marble countertop to me. "This kind of gossip about you won't matter. He knows your profile attracts all kinds of trash talk that's not true, so he won't bother to listen to it."

"Well, just so you know and can prepare yourself for it, this story won't go away quickly. And it'll likely grow before it fades. Thomas won't be the only one they ask to share intimate details."

He nods. "I've asked Gabriel to look into this and keep abreast of it." He pauses before adding, "For you. Not for me."

Gabriel's the guy who gets Jameson any information he asks for. God knows how he gets it. I've heard stories that Jameson will go to great lengths to get what he wants and doesn't hesitate to be ruthless when needed, so I can only imagine the lengths Gabriel goes to.

"What do you mean, 'for me?'" I'm quite capable of

looking after myself. I don't need Jameson's help, and I certainly don't want to owe him for anything.

Frustration creeps across his face. "I simply asked him to keep us updated on the situation."

"I can keep myself updated." I may not have a Gabriel, but I have a team who manage my public profile. And I can get a Gabriel if I so choose.

More of that frustration rolls on in as he says, "'Thank you, Jameson' is the appropriate thing here, Adeline."

"No, it's not. The appropriate thing here is for you to look after your own shit and to let me look after mine."

"From where I'm standing, your shit isn't getting looked after too well."

My eyes widen.

How dare he?

I'm formulating a response when he says, "Drink your coffee and eat some breakfast. We're leaving in ten minutes."

He strides out of the kitchen before I can instruct my mouth to open and tell him what he can do with that directive, let alone what I think of the other bullshit he just said to me.

I stew on this for a few minutes, preferring to focus on Jameson than on my ex-husband.

While I stew, I eat one of the pastries Jeff prepared for us and drink some coffee. I think about how Jameson is surrounded by people who know how to make great coffee. And I contemplate how I can convince Jeff to come with me when I divorce Jameson.

Fifteen minutes, later, Jameson and I are in the car on the way to work. He's on his phone with Hudson and I'm going through emails. I switch to my messages when a text comes through from Lara.

Lara: I'd just like to reiterate that I'm sending Ian Swift a bag of dicks.

Adeline: I thought you were going to make him EAT a bag of dicks?

Lara: I thank you for the reminder of my intentions. THAT is EXACTLY what I'm going to do. I'm also doing the same to Thomas. Scratch that. He's getting a truckload of dicks.

I laugh, drawing Jameson's eyes. I hold his gaze for a moment before going back to Lara.

Adeline: What's he done now?

Lara: Oh, honey, what HASN'T he done is more the question.

She calls me.

"I can't wait to see you source so many dicks," I answer with.

She doesn't laugh. Not a good sign. It means she's stressed. "We're going to need another strategy session. And a photo shoot with Jameson. And a million more of his kisses going viral. This is bad."

"Okay, tell me, so I can be the judge. We both know you're a little hardcore sometimes." I love that she goes above and beyond while trying to protect my brand. But it does mean that sometimes she worries about things that don't need worrying over.

"Addy, the next time you get married, he's going to have to go through me first, and he's going to have to sign a fucking ironclad contract that will give me superpowers over him. Thomas is screwing you royally here. If I ever come across him in person, he's going to hear exactly what I think about him."

I suspect she's blowing this out of proportion.

I know that what Thomas is doing is causing her a headache and me a PR nightmare, but it isn't something that will ruin my brand. My company is too strong foundationally for it to do that.

"I'm not getting married again," I say. She'll assume I'm saying that because I intend to spend the rest of my life with Jameson, but I truly mean it; after I divorce Jameson, I'm not ever marrying again. My marriage to Thomas was enough to cure me of wanting to commit to a man in that way again.

"Well, just know that if you do, I'm in charge of making sure you never get screwed like this again."

And there goes my sentimental side. The side I tried to put away while building my company. It's a tough gig being a woman who prefers to bring her soul to her business, and I've had enough people tell me there's no place for it here. I beg to differ, but still, I spent many years trying not to let it show. These days, I embrace it, and it hasn't let me down.

One of the reasons I adore Lara is because she brings her soul to work every day too. It's not her job to protect me in this way, but I know from experience that she means every word of what she's saying.

"Got it," I say. "You're in charge of my next marriage contract."

Jameson's brows lift as he watches me.

I've finally met a man who can multitask.

I never thought I'd see the day, but here we are. He's

carrying on a conversation of his own while eavesdropping all over the place on mine.

Lara interrupts my thoughts on his multitasking skills when she says, "I just saw a reel from Todd Boise. It was a snippet from an interview Thomas has given and it looked like it's full of more lies."

I understand why she's concerned. Todd runs the current hottest Insta gossip page with hundreds of millions of followers. However, I don't hold the same concern.

"Okay, here's what we're going to do," I say. "Nothing."

Silence greets me. And then, "I don't understand."

"We have a great strategy in place. We'll stick to it. This gossip and all the lies aren't going to stop anytime soon, and I'll be damned if we keep showing up each day trying to put out fires. So, we do nothing but stick to the plan we've already mapped out."

She's silent again before I hear her blow out a breath. "See, this is why you're the boss. I don't know how you stand strong like this. I'd collapse into a heap if my family was being smeared all over social media. Right, so we stick to the plan. Got it."

We end the call and I go back to my emails while Jameson finishes his call. When he puts his phone down, I look at him. "We need to talk about something." At his questioning look, I continue, "Actually we need to talk about two things. Your rules about sleeping in the same bed and not having sex for a year."

"My rules?"

"Well, that's what they are, aren't they?"

"They're decisions to ensure this marriage is a success."

I want to argue with him about that. Point out that they may have been decisions, but that they're decisions he made on his own and then ordered me to obey, so really, they're rules he made. But I don't. I spent time yesterday figuring out how to approach him over this, and that approach involves honey rather than vinegar. Well, as much honey as I can stomach, that is.

"Right," I say. "I understand why you think they're necessary decisions, but can we please revisit this and discuss it some more? Can you honestly see yourself not having sex for a year? That's a long time, Jameson."

His face clouds with disapproval. "Is this your way of telling me you won't last the distance?"

"And there you go making assumptions again. That's not what I said."

"No, but it doesn't give me confidence that you can."

"So, you're confident you can?"

"I wouldn't have signed up for this if I wasn't."

This man is maddening.

"Does it ever get lonely up there on your high horse?"

He ignores that. "We're not revisiting this."

I stare at him for a long moment while I process his infuriating inability to engage in give-and-take. "And you think I can't compromise."

"I can compromise when it's needed."

It's taken everything in me to get this far into the conversation without showing my real feelings. That last statement of his tips me over the edge. "You know, I don't think you can." My skin blazes with the exasperation coursing through me. "I think you think you can but trust me when I tell you that all you seem able to do is whatever works best for you."

We arrive at my office, and I gather my belongings as Jameson reaches for his door handle. "No." I look at him and shake my head. "You're not kissing me today."

Of course, he doesn't listen to me.

He meets me on the sidewalk, moving into me before I can stop him.

I try to stiffen myself against him, but my body has different ideas.

The second Jameson's hand brushes me, I flare with desire.

He slides his fingers through my hair and bends his face to mine.

Our eyes meet and I see the same level of heat in his that I'm feeling all over.

"You make this fucking difficult," he says before claiming the kiss he came for.

I want to push him away and give him my thoughts on what he just said.

I want to argue with him a whole lot more about his unreasonable rules and the way he denies me the chance to help make decisions.

But I don't.

I tell myself I don't because we're in public for the world to see, but that's not the full truth.

I don't do either of those things because I can't do them right now. Not when Jameson is consuming me the way he is.

He devours me with his kiss.

He takes ownership of me.

I lose myself willingly.

And when he demands my tongue, I don't hesitate for even a second.

He can have whatever he wants.

When his lips leave mine, I have to work hard not to beg for them back.

It's shameful how easily he turns me into this woman.

"If you need sex," he growls, keeping hold of me, his eyes burning into mine, "you come to me."

Want and need collide in my brain, in my body, all through me.

I'm instantly aware of every inch of myself in a way I wasn't already.

My legs, my fingers, my face, my nipples.

And goddamn if I'm not wet.

And angry that Jameson is the one causing all this.

"You will be the last man I will ever go to for sex."

He works his jaw. "I will be the only man you'll go to for sex this year, Adeline. Your company depends on it. Don't ever forget that."

I press my lips together. "There's no chance of that. You remind me often enough."

"Good."

With that, he lets me go and strides to the car. Without another glance, he's in the car and gone.

I never thought it was possible, but I hate Jameson Fox more now.

I hate that he's made me want to fuck him.

10

Adeline

Working in fashion is not for everyone and it's not the glamorous work many think. As Karl Lagerfeld once said, "If you are not a good bullfighter, don't enter the arena." I learned early on that if I wanted to succeed in this industry, I'd have to toughen the hell up, work long hours, and be prepared to fight for what I want.

I'm a good bullfighter.

Today, I've had to be the best goddamn bullfighter because on top of everything else I'm dealing with, I've had one of my top designers quit and I've had an argument with my creative director.

Vanessa made a monumental mistake by screwing up the date we had to get new designs to our Italian manufacturer. The due date was yesterday; she had it on my calendar for next Wednesday. Mario, my creative director was furious, and still is. It took me a good three hours to calm him down. A hell I never want to go through again. We've spent the day scrambling and begging our manufacturer to work with us to ensure the planned release date can go ahead. Thankfully, they've rearranged things on their end and will make it happen for us.

Jameson's assistant calls me just after 5:00 p.m., catching me in an exhausted moment.

"Hi, Adeline," she says when I answer. "Jameson asked me to call you to ensure you're aware of some changes he made to his schedule this week."

I sit up straight. "What changes?"

"A dinner with Bill tonight and a gala attendance on Friday night."

After the day I've had, including my conversation with Jameson this morning, I'm unable to curb the annoyance this new information flares in me. "A dinner *tonight*? It's already five. What time tonight?"

"Eight." Shantel is so talented at what she does that she doesn't stumble once with my reaction or her response. "I can alert him to the fact you may be late?"

I take a deep breath, working on my feelings over this so I don't take them out on Shantel. Making a snap decision, I say, "No, that won't be necessary, Shantel. I will take care of this myself."

"He can expect you at eight?"

I grip my phone harder. "He can expect many things, and yes, one of them is me being at dinner on time."

We end the call and I spend the next hour finishing up what I need to before I can leave. I work like a woman possessed. My only goal right now is to get to Jameson's penthouse as fast as possible so I can tell him exactly what I think of his fucking calendar.

He's not home when I walk in just after six thirty. Jeff greets me and ensures I have everything I need. I refrain from asking him to have a coffin delivered. I then make my way into the bedroom and take a shower.

I've showered, dressed, fixed my hair, and touched up my makeup by the time Jameson walks into the bedroom. I've also grown angrier with each passing minute. He has no idea what he's arrived home to.

He drops his suit jacket on the bed and has his hands to his tie before his eyes find mine. They instantly drop to my chest and then down my body as he takes in the midnight blue slip dress I'm wearing that hugs my curves in all the right places. I chose it because it makes me feel good, and I need that for the conversation Jameson and I are about to have.

I open my mouth to speak but his phone rings. He yanks it out of his pocket and stabs at it with the kind of angry energy that tells me he's in a mood too.

Stalking out of the bedroom, he barks, "I hope to fuck you've got good news for me."

He's such a wonderful human.

I can't believe how blessed I am to be married to him.

Perhaps I should have asked Jeff to source that coffin after all.

I wait for Jameson for fifteen minutes, at which point, I decide to get some work done while I wait. I head into the room that is now my home office and work through some emails that have come in since I left work.

I spend twenty minutes working, losing myself in emails until I hear footsteps outside the office. Glancing up, I see Jameson stride past. I push my chair back and go after him. Our conversation is way past due.

I stalk down the hallway, reaching him as he enters his office.

"We need to talk," I say, my chest heaving with fury.

He turns, his face a storm cloud. "I've got a call to make. Can this wait?"

I shake my head. "No. For once, you can put yourself second and give me the fucking gift of being put first."

He arches his brows, not saying a thing, but making it clear he's waiting for whatever it is I have to say.

I take a step closer to him. "Putting a dinner on my calendar at the last fucking minute can't happen again. And in future, when you add things to my calendar, I'd really appreciate it if you acknowledge that I'm just as busy as you are, and that the things I've got happening in my life are just as important as your things." I exhale a harsh breath. "I've already asked you not to order me around and told you I wouldn't do the next thing you ordered me to. I mean it this time, Jameson. This won't ever happen again. I'm done after tonight."

"Dinner was unavoidable tonight. I asked Shantel to call you as soon as I knew about it."

"That's not good enough. You should have told Bill you had to check with me first."

"Fuck." He shoves his fingers through his freshly washed hair. "I appreciate what you're saying, but since dinner was requested by Bill, and since this marriage is all for his sake, I assumed we'd both make it happen."

"You assumed. Much like you always do. Honestly, how hard is it to pick up the damn phone and call me to ask? And as for the gala that's been added to Friday night, I may not be able to make it."

"Why not?"

"Because I'm having the week from hell and I may need to keep that night free for work, that's why! And don't ever ask me a question like that again. I'm not here for it."

His brows furrow. "A question like what?"

"Like that one!" I stab my finger at him. "You made it sound like I didn't have a good reason for not being able to go to the gala."

"Christ. I asked you a simple fucking question."

"No, you didn't. There was a whole lot of subtext there."

His jaw clenches. "Do you intend on going to war with me every time you don't get your way?"

My eyes go wide, and I finally lose the last shred of control I have.

In a wild blur of energy, I'm in his face and I have my hands to his chest. "You are the most infuriating, arrogant, frustrating, presumptuous, self-important asshole I have ever met!"

He grips both my wrists with one hand and turns me in his hold so my back is to his chest. Bringing his other arm around me, he pins my body to his. "And you are the most argumentative woman *I* have ever met," he growls against my ear.

I struggle in his hold, grasping his forearm, trying to force it away from me. "Let me go!"

Tightening his hold, he rasps, "Not until we fucking work this out."

"The only one who has to work anything out is you. None of this is on me."

"How the hell is this all my fault?"

"Are you serious right now? This is why we're in this mess. You are so fucking clueless."

He spins me back around to face him, crushing our bodies together. His brown eyes meet mine and I suck in a breath at the anger and heat colliding there. When they trace their way down my face to my lips, to my throat, to my breasts, I feel every second of it deep inside.

"Fuck," he growls, bringing his gaze back to mine. "I have a mind to bend you over this desk and fuck this out of you."

When his hand glides up my stomach toward my breasts, I smack it away. "Don't you dare touch me."

Jameson Fox doesn't like being told not to do something. I see that clearly in his eyes. And, God, if I don't feel it all over me when he decides to pursue what he wants.

He grips my face and roughly pulls it to his.

Our lips crash together, and he kisses me with everything he has.

I'm helpless but to kiss him back, but I don't stop fighting him.

I press my hands to his chest and attempt to push out of his hold. He doesn't let me go. He tightens his arm around me, keeping me in place with the kind of strength I'm not match for, and continues kissing me.

I finally manage to tear my mouth from his. "Don't kiss me!"

His eyes search mine. "You want this."

"I don't fucking want this."

"You're a bad liar. You want it just as much as I do."

I slap my hands to his chest. "I hate you. Even if you were the last man alive, I wouldn't want this."

"You might hate me, but there's no denying you crave my touch."

My hands take over again, pummeling him. There's far too much energy inside me. It's savage, and intense, and unlike anything I've ever experienced. I need it out of me.

He takes it for a moment, and then in one swift move, he's got me in his arms, he's swiped everything off his desk, and he's lifted me to sit on it. Moving into me, between my legs, he takes hold of my face with both hands, and demands another kiss.

This time, my thoughts splinter into a million pieces.

His scent, his taste, his touch.

Those are the only things I'm aware of.

Not my hate for him.

Nor my desire to inflict damage on him.

And most definitely not my insistence that I don't want his mouth on mine.

Because I do want that.

I want that more than I've wanted any mouth on me.

I don't allow him to take over completely, though.

I might have lost nearly all my good sense, but I haven't forgotten that he needs to know we're equals. That he doesn't get to run this show by himself.

I tear at the buttons on his shirt. As they spill all over the floor, he growls into my mouth, deepening our kiss and sending need through every vein I have.

He lets go of my face as I rip off his shirt.

Our eyes meet.

It's a moment of white, hot need.

Fast breaths and a desperate desire for friction.

It lasts only a moment, because then I'm yanking my dress up, and his hands are on it, and he's stripping it from me. By the time it lands on the floor, his eyes are all over my body, and if I've ever felt more turned on, I don't recall it.

I reach for his face and pull it back to mine, my lips seeking his. He kisses me while cupping my breast with one hand and roughly gliding his other one down my body to my panties.

I struggle to breathe.

His touch is fucking with my ability to function.

His attention is too.

Jameson is the most intense man I've ever been with. To have all his attention on me like this is intoxicating.

When his hand slides into my panties and he finds my clit, I arch my back and shove my fingers up into his hair. Gripping him hard, I moan and grind myself against his hand.

Oh, God.

Damn him for being so skilled with a clit.

Why, God, must the man I hate know more about what he's doing right now than any other man alive?

I bring one leg up to rest a foot on his desk and hook the other one around him before placing one hand on the desk for support and rocking myself as hard into his hand as I can.

"Fuck," he rasps, looking down at my shameless need for him. He lets go of my breast and wraps his hand around my neck before kissing me again.

We're a wild torrent of lust and anger as I madly undo

his belt and then his zip. The hiss that falls from his lips when I take hold of his dick only fuels that frenzy.

He bites my bottom lip as he pushes a finger inside me.

I stroke his dick, my entire body straining for more.

He adds another finger and reaches deeper.

My body is on fire.

My nipples are needy for him.

My vagina wants him to move in.

I can't get enough of him, and I don't even care.

He finger fucks me exactly how I like it and my body finds a rhythm with him while I work his dick.

Oh, God.

Why is this the hottest thing I've ever done?

He finger fucks me faster while thrusting his dick into my hand, and suddenly, I need him inside me.

"Fuck me," I say, my words rushing out breathlessly.

I'm not even ashamed that I'm begging this man for his cock.

And for once, he does what I say.

And he doesn't waste time doing it.

Keeping a firm hold of my neck, he guides his dick to my entrance.

We both watch.

I'm practically panting for him.

He's so big.

I want him stretching me, filling me, fucking me.

His eyes find mine as the crown eases in.

I reach for the back of his neck and grip it.

He fills me some more.

It's not enough.

Goddamn, it's not enough.

My fingers dig into his skin.

I clench my vagina.

And finally, *finally*, he thrusts inside, giving me what I need, while making the kind of sound that can only be described as filthy and indecent. The kind of sound that speaks directly to my inner dirty girl.

It's disgraceful how much I like that sound.

Thank God our marriage contract insisted on a full health check, and I know it's safe to fuck him without a condom, because there's no way I'm stopping right now.

Our bodies move perfectly together, all anger and heat, frantically working the wild emotions from us.

He dips his mouth to my neck and kisses me, adding some teeth as he thrusts harder and deeper, picking up his pace, and moving me closer to what I want.

I forget myself as the pleasure Jameson delivers becomes all-consuming.

All I know is the orgasm I'm chasing and the man I'm chasing it with.

And then, it finally shatters through me, and I'm falling into it.

Jameson jerks one last time and then comes too.

He doesn't pull out straight away and I don't move fast either.

I need a minute to catch my breath and collect myself.

And then I hear Bill's voice float down the hallway.

Jameson pulls out and I reach for my clothes while wondering what the hell I've just done.

Fucking him was a bad decision. One I already regret.

He zips himself up while I finish putting my dress on.

"I'll make Bill a drink while you clean up," he says.

I nod. I'm a hot mess of dazed thoughts, unable to form any reply other than, "Okay."

He's almost out the door when he stops and looks back. "We'll sit down after dinner and go over our schedules together."

With that, he exits the office and heads toward the great room while I process everything he just did and said.

I make my way to the bedroom.

I need another shower.

I need to clean Jameson from my body.

And I need to forget this ever happened.

11

Jameson

Fucking Adeline was never in the plan, but if I'm honest with myself, I always knew it was going to happen. The attraction between us is too strong for it not to have. Watching her walk into the great room where Bill and I are sitting with a drink, I suspect she's unsure of how to deal with it, but I wouldn't know that from looking at her. She looks relaxed and confident.

She's showered and swapped the blue dress for a pink one. It's sexy but more subtle about that than the blue one was. That blue dress made me lose my goddamn mind. No, that's not true. The woman who wore the dress makes me do that without the help of anyone or anything.

"Bill," she greets him with a warm smile before coming to sit with me. She doesn't hesitate to nestle in close to me on the sofa, easily resting her hand on my thigh while I spread my arm across the back of the sofa. When she notices the wine glass sitting on the coffee table in front of us, she reaches for it and says, "Thank you, darling."

Fuck, just the thought of her is enough to get my dick's attention. Having her this close again, with her body against mine and her hand on me, causes a rush of desire and a mindfuck of thoughts.

Adeline may hate me, but I don't hate her. However, while I've now had sex with her, I wasn't lying when I told Hudson I didn't want to. Fuck knows how this will shift the dynamic between us. We were already on fragile ground. I'm unsure this marriage can sustain more fragility. Not for a year, anyway.

But hell if I don't want her again.

"How are you, Adeline?" Bill asks, taking a sip of his whiskey. "It's been a big week for you so far."

She drinks some wine. "It's been a god-awful week. I'm okay, but tired. You?"

"I've been busy, but nothing out of the ordinary," he says before eyeing me. "How's Paulina working out?"

"Better than expected." I struggle to give him more of an answer than that. I'm finding it hard to shift my focus from Adeline.

"Good," he says, happy enough with my reply. Bill was the one who convinced me to give her a go. He's a fan of her work. "I ran into her this morning. She mentioned a campaign featuring Adeline that she's hoping will go ahead." The way he says this alerts me to the fact he's aware that I said no to it, and that this has aroused his suspicions.

Paulina and I will be having words about confidentiality.

I nod. "Yes, that was one of her suggestions."

"You don't sound convinced of it," he says. Before I can reply, he glances at Adeline and asks, "What are your thoughts?"

Adeline knows nothing about this; however, she shows me why she was the woman I chose for this marriage when she says, "I think Jameson knows his business best. If he's not convinced it's the right idea, I'm not either."

"It's perfect for his business," Bill says. "Paulina knows what she's doing, Jameson. Don't waste her skill by refusing to consider this."

Adeline's phone sounds with a text, which she checks and ignores.

"The idea is still on the table," I say even though it's not.

"Good," Bill says. He drinks some more whiskey. "I have a new development you might be interested in. Lisa will send the details over tomorrow. You'll have to move fast if you're interested."

Another text comes through for Adeline. This time, she checks the message and gives me an apologetic look. Standing, she says, "I'm sorry, I have to deal with this."

I nod, but something in her expression catches my attention. Unease maybe. "Is everything okay?" She doesn't look okay.

"It's just Sabrina."

I watch her as she exits the room and find myself wondering what's going on with her sister to make Adeline look the way she just did.

Bill shares some information with me about the new development he thinks has merit while Adeline is gone. When she returns, I note that she still appears uneasy about something.

She settles in next to me again as Bill moves the conversation to the topic of babies. I'm not surprised about this. I've been waiting for it. Bill regrets not having children and has spoken with me about having a family many times.

"Have you two given much thought to having a family?" he asks.

"We've discussed it," I say. We have. Adeline knows exactly what to say here.

"I'd like three children," she says, going off script with that number. I advised her that he would believe me wanting one child, no more. "But honestly, Bill, I've got a lot more I'd like to achieve in my business before we go down that path."

"You aren't getting any younger," he says.

"That is true," she agrees. "But we still have plenty of time."

"When are you thinking?" he asks.

"In a few years," she says.

He frowns. "That may be cutting it close. Especially if you have trouble conceiving."

"There will be plenty of time," I say, steering the conversation back to where it should have gone. "Adeline may want three children, but I'd be happy with one."

She places her hand on my leg as she looks up at me. "Darling, you know I really want three. Two, at least."

My eyes search hers, trying to figure out where she's going with this and why she's not sticking to the plan.

Her eyes tell me to go with it. Against my better judgment, I do. "I know, but I've always said that may be ambitious."

She nods. "Yes, and I understand that you're worried we won't have the time to be there for three children, but I think we will. I think we'll make the time because it's so important to us to be that kind of parent."

And there it is. Where she was leading me.

Adeline is a smart woman. It makes sense that we would disagree on this topic. Based on our different personalities, that's far more believable, and Bill will buy it more than he'd buy us being on the same page. Then, bringing up that we both want to be very hands-on parents was perfect. If I did want children, that's the kind of parent I'd want to be. And Bill would know that.

I pull her close and press a kiss to her lips before eyeing Bill. "We're still figuring this out, but I want Adeline to have the time in her business that she needs before we even think about getting pregnant."

I see it in Bill's eyes that we've moved him closer to believing in our marriage with this conversation. "Just don't leave it too late. I'd hate for you to miss out on the family you want."

Jeff joins us and lets me know dinner is ready to be served.

As we stand, a text comes through for me.

Gabriel: The gossip about Adeline is all originating from Black Diamant. They want her out of business.

I glance at Adeline. "I have to make a call."

She nods and leaves the room with Bill, directing the conversation to questions about how his cancer treatment is going.

My eyes are glued to her ass while I call Hudson.

"I'm in the middle of a date," Hudson answers the call, drawing my attention back to where it should be.

"This won't take long."

"Okay, shoot."

"You were right about Black Diamant. They're feeding the gossip on Adeline. I want you to either put them out of business or take them over. I don't care which."

Hudson's main job is to identify risks to my company and execute plans to mitigate them. When I signed my marriage contract with Adeline, I asked him to learn everything there is to know about her company and advise me of potential risks for her. He put Black Diamant, one of her biggest competitors, on his list, but it was only a hunch at the time. Hudson's gut feelings usually pan out, so I asked him to keeping digging into this; however, he hasn't been able to substantiate it.

"I'm on it," he says.

We end the call and I text Gabriel back to thank him. I then head into the dining room to join Adeline and Bill.

I find them laughing over something. Adeline's eyes meet mine and I take in the flush of her cheeks. She's still got that just-fucked glow, which causes my gut to tighten as my gaze settles on it.

"Bill was just telling me the story about your mom and that time she traipsed around London with toilet paper stuck to her shoe," she says.

I sit next to her. "That's one of her favorite stories to tell." I reach for the glass of whiskey in front of me. "I'm surprised she hasn't already shared it with you. She tells anyone who will listen."

Adeline smiles. "I love that she and I have so many more stories still to tell each other."

She means every word of that. I sense it in her tone. She's really taken a liking to my mother, which was evident last night. I can't deny I like this.

"Reese is one of Gods gifts to the world," Bill says to Adeline. "Does your mother have any funny stories like this?"

Without intending to, I place my hand on her leg. She looks at me for a brief moment, her forehead creasing slightly, before looking back at Bill. "My mother isn't like Jameson's," she says softly. "If she has any funny stories like that one of Reese's, they were from before I was born, and I've never heard them."

"I'm sorry to hear that," Bill says gently.

Jeff serves dinner and we change the subject after that, keeping things light.

Adeline is the perfect partner tonight, entertaining Bill with stories about the people she met in her modeling days. Bill's an Elton John fan and is delighted to hear about the night Adeline met him, not to mention the times she met Bruce Springsteen and Chris Martin.

Over dessert, he brings up the Brown deal. The property deal that involves sensitive information about a building that will be coming up for sale in a month. Don Brown, a friend of Bill's, gave him the information a few months ago, detailing everything we need to make a successful bid. I'd prefer Adeline not be privy to this information. In the past, I've had people close to me attempt to screw me out of deals after they've discovered important details. These days, I never allow anyone to know anything. Bill is aware of this, so including her in the conversation is his way of testing me.

If the way he leaves my penthouse after dinner with a smile on his face is anything to go by, we passed tonight's tests.

Adeline finishes saying her goodbyes and looks at me. "I've got some work to do." With one last smile at Bill, she walks toward her office.

Bill meets my gaze. "Is Adeline okay? She seemed a little off tonight."

He's right; she did. However, that could be due to the fact I fucked her right before he arrived. And the fact she was furious about not being made aware of this dinner earlier.

"She's had a stressful day. She'll be okay." I have no idea if her day was stressful, but she did say she's having the week from hell, so I'm guessing it was.

"Don't let her work too late, son."

"I won't."

After he leaves, I walk down the hallway into my office. I pass Adeline's on the way. Her door is closed, and I contemplate knocking on it. I promised her we'd go over our schedules tonight, but I don't want to interrupt her work. Deciding we can do that later, I head into my office and make a start on what I have to get through tonight.

Two hours pass in a blur. I look at my watch just after 11:30 p.m. and remember my promise to Adeline. I've got probably another half hour of work to complete, but I can finish that later. I push my chair back and go in search of her.

I find her sitting in bed doing a crossword.

I've noticed she always carries a small crossword book and tends to pull it out when she's stressed or worried.

Resting my shoulder against the doorjamb, I cross my arms and watch her.

A couple of minutes pass before she says, "Are you going to stand there all night?" She does this without looking up from her crossword.

I remain where I am. "What's going on?"

This gets her attention. She studies me with a frown. "What do you mean?"

I push off from the doorjamb and walk into the bedroom. "Is Sabrina okay? You seemed off when she texted."

"It's nothing."

"Bill mentioned that he thought you weren't yourself either."

"Well, considering we'd just had sex, and considering I'd reached the end of my ability to put up with your asshole ways, I'd say I had good reason not to be myself."

I narrow my eyes at her. "That all may be the case, but you're deflecting. Can I help you with Sabrina?"

She stares at me like I've just asked her a question she has no idea how to answer. Her chest rises and falls faster than a moment ago. And her eyes flicker with confusion. Finally, she snaps her crossword book closed and says, "What you can help me with is our schedules. You promised to go over them tonight."

I nod. "I did."

"Right," she says, all business.

When she makes a move to leave the bed, I say, "Where are you going?"

"Do you want to do this in your office?"

"No. We can do it here and then you can go to sleep."

This appears to fluster her. "I'd rather do it in your office. Or mine."

I don't move. "Why?"

She stands across the bed from me, her face flushed, and shoots me a pointed look. "Because I don't want to do anything in this bed with you."

Fuck, I like her like this.

"I'm simply going through my calendar with you. Nothing more."

She gives me more of that bewildered state that's testing my resolve not to touch her again. "For the record, we are never having sex again."

I should agree with her.

Put her mind at ease.

Make it clear I'm fully on board with this.

What I shouldn't do is get into a discussion with her on this, because I know it'll just end up in an argument.

Yet, I find myself asking, "You didn't enjoy it?"

It seems I enjoy arguing with her more than I should.

Especially since I know the answer to my question.

Adeline fucking begged for my dick.

I've never wanted a woman to beg me for it as much as I wanted her to.

She doesn't bother lying to me.

Instead, she says, "Faking ignorance doesn't suit you, Jameson."

My lips quirk. "I'm learning not to make assumptions."

"Wow." She crosses her arms. "You do have a sense of humor. I'm actually stunned."

I find myself smiling. I can't recall the last time a

woman made me smile like this. It feels easy, and fuck if that doesn't surprise me. "Okay, let's get this done. I have more work still to do once we're finished."

When she hesitates after I sit on the bed, I say, "I'm not going to touch you."

She gives me a look of disbelief but finally sits back down while muttering something I can't quite make out. If I'm not mistaken, though, I think she says something about a coffin.

We spend fifteen minutes going back and forth over our next month. Adeline tells me which events are her most important and I mark them in red on my calendar. She does the same with my events on her calendar. We agree that we'll ensure we attend these functions together. The rest won't matter if we can't get to them as a couple.

It takes some negotiation because some of our events clash. I've had a couple of relationships I deemed serious at the time; however, I've never gone to this trouble for anyone because it hasn't been important to me that I show up as part of a couple to anything.

I'm not used to making space for anyone in my life. It's never been important to me to build a relationship. Not a romantic one. I don't have the time to invest in that. Or the inclination.

I realized tonight that the only way I'm going to succeed at this marriage is to make space for Adeline. If she was more like me, we'd simply exchange the information we needed through our assistants, methodically work our way through the engagements we need to show our face at, rinse and repeat.

She's not like me, though.

Adeline runs on emotion, and she requires an emotional investment.

I missed that memo during our engagement somehow. But I've received it loud and clear now. And while I'm not convinced I have the bandwidth to give her exactly what she requires, I can give her this.

"That wasn't too hard, was it?" she says as she closes her calendar on her phone. "I mean, you're still breathing, right?"

I stand. Ignoring her sarcasm, I say, "Going forward, use the red highlights when you add things that are important. And let Shantel know of any clashes."

She gives me a look of irritation, but it seems more subdued than what I'm used to from her. "One of these days, you'll stop treating me like a child. Do you think you could speed that day along?"

"I'm not treating you like a child. I'm simply ensuring we're on the same page."

"I'm not stupid, Jameson. I can put all that together for myself."

She's right. She's one of the smartest women I know. However, I've not gotten to this point in my life by assuming people won't drop the ball on me. Reiterating agreed-upon points is how I ensure shit doesn't get fucked up. I'm not about to change the way I've always done things.

I say goodnight and leave her to sleep while I go and finish the work I brought home with me.

I stay up far too late tonight, my thoughts tangled over fucking Adeline.

It was the best sex I've ever had.

That's what I keep coming back to.

I then come back to the fact I haven't had sex for three months, so any sex would have felt good.

But fuck if I can bring myself to believe that.

Adeline is fire and we burned brighter than I've burned with anyone.

I've never been good at staying away from fire.

Not even when I know it could burn me to the ground.

12

Adeline

Sabrina: Mom needs more money.

Adeline: What for?

Sabrina: Her car needs parts.

Adeline: Have her call me and let me know how much.

Sabrina: The mechanic says it could be thousands to fix.

Adeline: Yes, get her to call me.

Sabrina: She asked me to tell you.

I take a deep breath. I don't believe my sister. She wants cash and is using Mom to get it. I doubt Mom even knows what she's doing.

"Adeline," Jameson says from beside me in the car.

I look up and realize we've arrived at my office. The trip here passed by in a rush of messages back and forth with Lara, and now these texts with Sabrina. Oh, and a whole lot of me trying to ignore the man sitting next to me.

I can't stop thinking about the sex we had last night. I barely got any sleep. And not just because my brain wouldn't switch off. My body wouldn't either. I spent most of the night fighting with her every time she wanted to roll over and throw herself at him.

It's appalling how much I want to have sex with him again.

I reach for my laptop and purse while he reaches for the door handle.

My core is like Pavlov's dogs with that move of his. She knows what's coming next and she is here for all of it.

I, on the other hand, am not.

I exit the car and my eyes meet his as he rounds it. They beg him not to put me through a kiss. Not this morning.

His arm slides around my waist and he pulls me close, keeping his eyes on mine.

I'm not skilled at reading Jameson yet, but I get the impression he intends on honoring my wish.

However, the way he's bringing our bodies close tells another story, so I'm beginning to feel some of the bewilderment he causes in me. Bewilderment no other man has ever managed to cause.

His face dips to mine.

My hand moves to his chest, both to steady myself and to attempt to keep him at bay.

His lips brush my cheek before he murmurs, "I'm buying you new perfume that doesn't fuck with my dick."

With that, he lets me go and strides back around the car to his door.

I watch the car pull away from the curb, my breaths leaving my body faster than they were before he touched me.

Why must I like what he said so much?

There is something very wrong with me.

We haven't spoken this morning, except for when he asked me if I was okay to leave at seven thirty. But I've felt his eyes on me every second while in his presence.

God, how I've felt them.

I gather myself and head into my office.

Vanessa won't be in today. She's still unwell, so I suggested she take the rest of this week off. Her replacement is good at her job, but she's no Vanessa. Even when Vanessa is off her game like she has been lately, she's still the best assistant I've had. I'm anticipating a hectic day, so not having her here will only increase my workload.

"Oh, good," Lara says, coming into my office as I sip my first coffee for the day and scroll emails. "You're in." She sits across from me. "We just got this proposal through for you to do a reality TV show, and while I'm guessing it's probably not something you'd normally consider doing, and while I'm not even sure I'd want you to, I'm intrigued by it and am wondering if it might be a good thing for the brand."

She's right about me not normally considering a reality show, but I'm always open to hearing about anything she thinks might be good for my brand. "Give me your thoughts on it."

She runs me through the details of the proposal, highlighting the fact I'd apparently have equal input into what makes the final cut. Another key point in her mind is the fact the producers are more interested in filming my work life than my personal life.

"I've forwarded you the proposal," she says. "Take a read and see what you think."

"I will, but I have to be honest and say I don't think it's for me." Not while I'm married to Jameson, anyway. There's no way he'd agree to this.

"Yeah, I know, but I'm thinking this might help the launch of Adeline + Pearce next year. I think the show's planned release might coincide well with that."

"That's a good point. I'll put some thought into it." Any extra publicity Jenna and I can generate for the launch of our new company would be good.

She stands as a string of notifications hit her phone. Tapping it, she takes a moment reading whatever just came through. Then, looking at me, she says, "Jameson let the team down this morning." She holds her phone up to show me a photo of him and me on the sidewalk earlier. "Tell him to do better tomorrow."

I shoo her out of my office without responding to that. I then get to work for the day, working a solid ten hours filled with meetings with my designers; signing off on the replacement Mario found for the designer who quit yesterday; meeting with Jenna to go through the wardrobe she's styled for my next month of red carpets and social functions; and doing an interview with *Vogue*.

I've just finished the interview when a text comes through.

Jameson: I'll be home around nine.

I stare at my phone.

I almost fall off my chair.

Like, literally.

He has never texted me.

Not once.

Adeline: Did you send this yourself or is this Shantel texting on your behalf?

Jameson: Shantel never uses my phone.

Adeline: So, you figured out all by yourself how to send a text?

Jameson: Smartass.

Adeline: Right. Just testing to see if this really is you. Thank you for the confirmation. Also, feel free to come home later.

He doesn't reply to that, but I don't expect him to. Mind you, he's started surprising me by doing things I don't expect, so who knows anymore. I'm quite stunned to have received not only a text from him, but also an update on his plans.

I work solidly for another hour before leaving the office. Max picks me up and stops at Brenda's shop on the way home so I can grab a bacon, egg, and cheese bagel. I'm craving carbs today and a bagel always hits the mark for me. Brenda's excited to see me again and insists on giving me a glazed donut for Jameson.

By the time I arrive home just after six thirty, I'm exhausted.

"Good evening, Mrs. Fox," Jeff greets me when I step out of the elevator.

I smile. "Good evening, Jeff."

He doesn't say anything else. He simply welcomes me home and allows me the space to begin winding down for the night. Jeff is a quick study of character and has quickly picked up on the fact I don't like people doing things for me all the time.

I change into leggings and a pink T-shirt, throw my hair up into a ponytail, and make my way into the kitchen. Since I don't have to go out tonight or entertain, I've decided to bake. It's one of my favorite go-to's for stress relief and relaxation. There's something about measuring ingredients and creating something from scratch that makes me feel good. Tonight, I'm baking Chocolate Bourbon Pecan Pie cupcakes with Butter Pecan Frosting.

I've just gathered all the ingredients when Natalie arrives.

"Hey," I say with a smile as she places her bag on the table. "I thought you had a date tonight."

She joins me at the island. "He canceled at the last minute. Something about his sister needing his help."

"Are you disappointed?"

"Yeah, but I get it. And I like that he's the kind of man who'll cancel a date to help his sister, you know?"

"Absolutely."

She eyes all the ingredients on the countertop. "Big day, huh?" Natalie knows what baking means.

I give her a look. "Big week."

"Okay, what's happened that I don't know about?"

I release a long breath. "What hasn't is more the question."

"Jesus." She rolls up her sleeves. "We better get to work. I need to hear everything. Do not leave a single thing out."

We spend the next hour baking and talking through my week. Since we've caught up most nights, she already knows a lot of it, but I don't leave a single thing out that she doesn't know.

She's not surprised to hear I slept with Jameson. I mean, I'm not surprised it happened either. I just wish it hadn't, and not only because I don't like the man. It's already changed things between us, and I'm left wondering what it will mean for the year ahead and our ability to succeed with this marriage.

Sex always muddles things in my experience. And since this relationship is already muddled, I don't think we have room for any more.

"So, where does that leave you guys? Do you think maybe you'll add sex to this marriage? It could be a solution to the no-sex rule MA has insisted on."

I stare at her. "You're not joking, are you?"

"No."

"Has an alien taken over your body? Jesus, you know what I think of MA. I can't fuck that man ever again and certainly not for a full year."

"Oh, sister, you can. You really can. It's not like it would be a hardship."

"Trust me when I tell you it would be."

She nods like she's just decided something. "Right, I see how we're going to handle this."

"How? What do you mean?"

She circles her finger in the air at me. "We're using denial. I'll support that for a little while if you need me to."

A text comes through for me.

Mario: Are you free for a call?

Adeline: I'm baking.

Mario: Makes sense. I'll FaceTime.

A FaceTime call comes through, and I prop my phone against a container on the countertop. "What's up?"

"I wanted to talk through some design ideas I just had with you."

Mario is a creative genius who gets ideas at all hours of the day. I'm used to him calling me during one of his creative bursts, sometimes at three in the morning. I always take these calls from him and have been known to walk away from other important things to do so. One of my skills is to prioritize well, and I'm very aware that Mario's brilliance is integral to the success of my business, so prioritizing him is key.

"Shoot," I say.

We spend the next forty minutes going back and forth over his ideas. Mario is in full visionary flow tonight. Electric with the way he moves from one idea to the next. I bake my way through the conversation, my mind and body lit with the energy I'm drawing from him. Natalie joins us. She often does because I'm often with her when he calls in this mood. She helps balance us out. Mario brings the artistic flair; I bring the business smarts; Nat brings the end consumer's thoughts.

We're in the middle of a lengthy discussion over one of Mario's ideas when Jameson strides into the kitchen. He runs his gaze over me, over Nat, over Mario on my phone, over the kitchen island that is now a mess of flour, sugar, cupcakes, and cooking utensils.

Without a word, he finishes his inspection, turns, and exits the kitchen.

Natalie and I barely acknowledge him. We're too engrossed in our discussion with Mario.

The three of us talk for another ten minutes until

Mario declares it's time for him to get back to work. I know that means he'll likely stay up all night designing and planning.

"Don't come in tomorrow if you work all night," I say.

He gives me the look I often receive when I'm trying to nurture him. It's half eye roll, half admiration. "Don't tell me what to do. You know I can't stay away."

I grin. I adore my team. "I've found a new coffee place. I'll pick you up a latte on the way to work in the morning."

"Good. And you'll keep me supplied all day, right?"

"Done. Now go. And try to get some sleep."

After I end the call, Nat says, "I'm gonna go too, babe. I need my beauty sleep. Ryan just texted that he wants to have breakfast tomorrow."

Jameson comes back into the kitchen as she says this. He's changed into black running shorts and a fitted, black tank.

Um, someone needs to burn these items of clothing.

They're indecent. Lewd. Improper.

Nat looks at him. "When a man says he wants to have breakfast after only dating for a week or so, that doesn't mean actual breakfast, does it?"

Natalie has dated more than any woman I know. She doesn't need Jameson's help, so I can only put this question down to her having some fun with him.

He glances briefly at me before looking at Nat. "I prefer to be clear with my intentions."

I concur.

And is it suddenly very hot in here?

Jameson might have many faults, but I don't doubt a

woman always knows where she stands sexually with him.

"Right," Nat says, grabbing her bag off the table. "I'll wear breakfast attire, then." She comes to me with a hug, whispering against my ear, "Have fun living in denial land, sister."

After she leaves, Jameson moves to the island where I'm about to frost the cupcakes. Eyeing them, he says, "These look good."

It's horrifying how much I like him saying that.

But I put it down to that tank he's wearing that fits far too perfectly, stretching across muscles that shouldn't be allowed to exist. I also put it down to the fact the tank doesn't cover arm muscles that should never, ever be on display.

When he reaches out to take one of the cupcakes, I smack his hand away. "Don't you dare."

His eyes meet mine. "You baked them for show?"

"No, I baked them so I could leave the day behind."

"And we're not going to eat them?"

"They're not ready yet."

"They look good to me."

"They need to be frosted."

"I don't give a fuck about frosting."

He reaches again to take one, and I push his hand away with extra force this time. "You will regret it if you take one. And believe me, you will give all the fucks about frosting once you taste it. Now, go and run. Or do whatever it is you do in those shorts."

His lips form the beginning of a smile, but it doesn't fully eventuate. "I'm coming back for one of those cupcakes."

I watch him walk out of the kitchen.

My core somersaults after him.

I tell her she can somersault as much as she wants, and dream about sitting on his lap, but that she will never get her way again.

After Jameson leaves and I find my wits again, I frost the cupcakes and clean up the kitchen. Jeff tries to help but I don't let him. I like working in the kitchen. Cleaning up after I bake is all part of the process for me, and always leaves me feeling satisfied that I've seen a project through to the end.

I make myself a cup of tea and take it and a cupcake to the table. One bite is enough to tell me this is my absolute favorite cupcake I've ever tasted. It's all chocolate and bourbon and gooey pecan pie with the most delicious creamy brown sugar frosting.

I leave one out on a plate for Jameson, hopeful it will keep his asshole side locked away for the night.

I then go into the bedroom to take a shower and do some of my crossword before having an early night.

My gaze is drawn to a box sitting on my pillow as I walk toward the bed. When I reach it, I realize Jameson meant it when he told me he was going to buy me a new perfume.

A box of Molecule 01 sits waiting for me on my pillow.

I take it into my bathroom and open it. I've heard of this perfume but never smelled it. It's apparently the anti-fragrance fragrance. Very minimalist.

I want to think "fuck him" because fuck him for thinking of himself here. So he's attracted to my favorite perfume; that doesn't mean I shouldn't wear it.

However, the part of me that loves trying new

perfumes can't stop herself from opening the box and spritzing some on.

Goddamn him.

I fucking like it.

A lot.

I shove the bottle back in the box and put it at the back of the top drawer.

I'm never wearing it.

In fact, I'll double down on only wearing the perfume he takes issue with.

Yes, I am now officially that woman.

The one who finds herself doing things she never imagined doing.

Like finding ways to frustrate the one man she shouldn't frustrate.

Because a frustrated Jameson only leads to trouble.

The kind of trouble I know very well I should avoid.

13

Adeline

Natalie: You survived a week of marriage to MA!

Adeline: Technically, I'm on day ten.

Natalie: I stand corrected. You are a warrior princess. How was he this morning? Did he subject you to a kiss this morning when he dropped you at work? Or did he fuck you before leaving for work?

Adeline: I told you, I'm never having sex with that man again.

And I'm doing well with that declaration. It's been five days since I let him touch me. *Let*, not begged. I refuse to acknowledge the begging I did.

Natalie: I see we're still in denial. How much longer are we going to play pretend?

Adeline: You are the worst best friend. How's Ryan?

Natalie: I fucked him twice this morning. He's good.

Adeline: Ugh. Go away. And no, Jameson didn't drive into work with me today, so no kiss was endured.

"Adeline," Vanessa says, popping her head into my office. "Douglas is here."

"Thanks."

Adeline: Gotta run. My money man is here.

Natalie: Good luck!!!

"Douglas," I greet my CFO.

He takes the seat across from me. "I see we're being formal today."

"Well, you requested a meeting formally, which is so fucking odd for you, so I thought I should run with it."

Douglas has worked with me for four years. We have quite an informal relationship these days after he helped me build my company into what it is today. I have a lot of respect for this man. He's never led me wrong. His super formal email last week requesting this meeting threw me a little. It's so out of character for him.

He smiles as he crosses his legs. "Yeah, it was odd, wasn't it? Sorry about that."

"Jesus, can you hurry up and get to the point. Please tell me you aren't resigning."

"Fuck, no." He slides a folder across the desk to me. "Take a look at that."

"Is it bad? I don't need any bad news today, so if it is, come back tomorrow and see if I'm ready then."

He laughs. "It's not bad, Adeline." He lifts his chin at me. "Open it."

I do as he says and find a financial report inside. I skim it and then eye him. "Is this saying what I think it's saying?"

"Yes."

Excitement slides through me. That feeling that sits low in your stomach like electricity waiting to be freed. "Fuck." We've been waiting a long time for this.

"You see why I wanted to do this in person. Formally."

I lean back in my seat and inhale deeply before exhaling. Ever since Jameson took my first company from me, I've been working hard to rebuild. Douglas came on board and guided me in a way I'd never been guided. Chatoyer, my first company, was hugely successful, but I believe a lot of that was luck. Sure, I made good business decisions, but I believe they coincided with luck. This time around, with my second company, I've made extremely sound business decisions that required no luck to work. And I didn't get ahead of myself even when I wanted to. Douglas made sure of that.

One decision he's made me patiently sit on for years is branching out into retail outlets overseas. We have stores in the States, and they do very well, but we don't yet have stores in any other country. I'm dying to open a London store, and then a Paris store, and then stores across Europe.

"So, it's time for London?" I ask.

He nods. "It's time for London."

That electricity swirling inside me, desperate to escape, practically explodes out of me. I stand and do a dance on the spot. I'm laughing like an idiot when I look at him and squeal, "We're going to London, baby!"

He stands. "I fucking love you, woman."

I throw my arms around him in a hug. After I squeeze the hell out of him, I say, "Right, back to work. I want this to happen ASAP."

After he leaves, I text Natalie with the good news, share it with my inner circle here, and ask Vanessa to plan a meeting to go over this tomorrow. Thankfully, I have two hours free in the morning to fit it in.

I find it difficult to concentrate after Douglas's good news, but slowly make my way through my to do list.

I'm halfway through my list when Shantel calls.

"Hey," I say after Vanessa puts the call through. "Please don't tell me you're calling to let me know Jameson has added a last-minute dinner to my schedule for today."

She laughs.

This is a joke between us now after I called her last Thursday to apologize to her for being less than friendly when she called me about that dinner. We had a great conversation, discussing Jameson's tendency to forget that people have things going on in their lives that he should take into consideration. She was half joking. I was not, but she thought I was. Shantel thinks I'm the dutiful wife. I'd love to be able to have a conversation with her in which she knew I wasn't really her boss's wife. I'd love to hear the real stories about working with him.

"No," she says. "No dinner tonight. I'm calling to thank you for the gift you sent over. I freaking love it all. Thank you!"

"Oh, that's great! I'm glad it arrived." I sent her a gift basket of my latest beauty release.

"I never know what products to try, so this is perfect."

"If you ever want me to hook you up with a beauty consult, let me know. I'd love to do that for you."

A call from Jameson's mother comes in on my cell. "Shantel, I'm sorry, but I have to take another call."

"No worries. I just wanted to personally say thank you. I did think about sending Jameson home with instructions to say thank you, but I couldn't be sure he'd remember."

I laugh. "I understand. Men have the worst memory for this kind of stuff."

"His is one of the worst, but I'm sure you know that," she says before saying goodbye and ending the call.

I switch to Reese's call. "Hi, Reese."

"Adeline, darling. I'm so glad I caught you."

I adore how excited she sounds to talk with me. I think Bill was right when he said Reese is a gift from God. "What's up?"

"I'm calling to find out if you're allergic to any food and if there's anything you don't like to eat. I'm planning our Christmas dinner and want to make sure you have everything you love."

My thoughts all slow down, falling over each other.

I feel like a deer caught in headlights.

Christmas is two weeks away. Jameson hasn't mentioned a dinner to me, but I should have realized his mother would plan a family dinner. She holds Taco Tuesday each week, after all.

I don't celebrate Christmas like a lot of people do. It wasn't a big part of my childhood. In fact, my mother wasn't usually around on Christmas Eve or Christmas Day. She was off busy with the latest man she was sleeping with. Sabrina and I were left to fend for ourselves. And as far as presents were concerned, I can only remember three Christmases I received gifts from my mother.

"Um, well, I don't really like cranberry sauce." I

struggle to come up with anything useful for her because my brain has stopped working. "And Christmas pudding. I'm not a fan of that. But honestly, you don't need to go to any trouble for me. I'll find something to eat."

"Nonsense. Everyone deserves to have their favorites at Christmas. Do you like turkey?"

"Yes."

"Pumpkin pie?"

"Yes."

"Are there any vegetables you prefer or any you don't like?"

She's being so patient with me while I'm barely volunteering any information. Not because I don't want to, but rather, because her kindness is overwhelming me. I'm not used to it from family.

"I'm not a fussy eater, Reese. The only things I don't like are what I've already told you. And for future reference, I never eat fish. But I eat everything else. And I really love chocolate, so if Jameson ever tells you I'm annoyed with him, you could suggest he bring me chocolate. It might help him buy his way back into my heart." I have no idea why I tell her this about chocolate, but I sense she'd love to know this kind of thing, so I do.

She laughs. "I'm making a note of it, darling. Thank you for this information. I'll let you get back to work now. And if you want to come early tomorrow night, I'd love that, but I know your work keeps you busy, so not to worry if you can't leave early."

I already know I'm going to try to leave work early tomorrow so I can spend time with her. I'm so drawn to this woman.

I hang up from her and call Jameson.

He answers almost immediately. "Hi."

Jesus, why must his voice affect me the way it does?

He's said one word to me, over the phone, not even in person, and my body is all "Hello, Sir."

It's gotten out of control since I had sex with him.

The worst of it all?

I now want to sit in his lap more than I want to put him in a coffin. Even when he's pissing me off, I'm imagining hurting him while he's naked.

And he's only slightly less of an asshole than before he fucked me, so it's not like the sex caused a one-eighty for him and his treatment of me. I should not be thinking about that lap of his as much as I am.

"Your mother just phoned me," I say.

"And?"

"And she asked me if I'm allergic to anything or if there's anything I don't like to eat at Christmas."

I'm almost certain I hear him exhale one of his frustrated breaths. "Is this story going anywhere?"

"Yes, it's going somewhere. You could have warned me that your family does Christmas dinner."

"Warned? You say that like you need to prepare yourself."

"I do need to prepare myself."

"Why?"

I remind myself that Jameson doesn't know anything about my childhood. That he's not aware I only have bad memories of Christmas and don't enjoy this time of year. "Don't worry about it, but—"

"No," he cuts me off, "tell me."

"No, it doesn't matter in the scheme of things."

"Adeline," he says, his voice filled with gravel and

determination, and a little bit of frustration. "Tell me what it is about Christmas dinner that you need to prepare for."

I know by the tone he's taken that he has no intention of letting this go. If I don't answer him now, he'll just come looking for the answer tonight. "We didn't do Christmas in my house growing up. Mom wasn't even home most Christmases. It was just me and Sabrina. No presents, no food, no nothing. So, I'm not big on it. And I never celebrate it." I pause. "I need to prepare for your mom's level of excitement."

He's silent for a moment before finally saying, "We never celebrated it either when I was a kid. My father didn't allow it. Since his death, Mom goes all out. But she won't expect you to participate if you don't want to. I'll let her know it's not your thing."

I'm surprised he shared that with me. Jameson is not an open book to anyone. The world barely knows a thing about him.

I'm also surprised he offered me an out for Christmas with his family.

"Thank you," I say. "But there's no need to tell her that. I'll be fine."

"Adeline," he starts, but I cut him off.

"No, really, I'll be okay."

"You may change your mind when I tell you that she has a whole range of Christmas traditions that are about to begin."

"What do you mean 'about to begin?'"

"There's the tree, the baking, the shopping, the ice-skating. That's just some of it."

Goodness.

"Right, tonight, we're going over all this. I don't care if you have work you have to do, you're allocating some time to me so I can start preparing for all this."

"I won't be home until late tonight."

"What time?"

"I don't know. Ten, maybe." I swear I can see him raking his fingers through his hair like he does when he's irritated with me. But for once, I hear only a trace of his impatience.

"Ten it is. Don't be late."

"Fuck," he mutters, but I ignore that. If it's the last thing he does tonight, he will be giving me the information I require to make it through this Christmas.

We end the call and I get back to work. Mario has requested we spend an hour together this afternoon to go over some designs the team has been working on, so I have to get through a stack of other work to fit that in.

It's a hectic Monday and I'm thankful that Jameson and I don't have anything to attend tonight. We've been out every night since last Thursday. And while I originally thought the weekend was going to be a quiet one, we ended up attending lunches as well both days.

To say the last four days have been a whirlwind for me is an understatement. But that could have more to do with the fact my *body* has been in a whirlwind. Spending all that time with Jameson has me on edge.

While he hasn't acted on it, he hasn't hidden his desire for me. I'm not sure Jameson is the kind of man who could do that even if he tried. He runs on pure masculine energy. It lives and breathes in him. One look at the man and it's impossible not to sense his power, strength, and virility.

It doesn't help that he's started giving me more consideration. I mean, that was what I wanted, but now that I have it, I'm finding it hard to ignore my attraction to him.

It's a mess of epic proportions. A mental mess I don't have time for because work is busier than ever.

The gossip that was all over social media last week seems to be dying down, thankfully. However, we're busy preparing for fashion week amongst other things, and I'm full steam ahead with my plans to open a London store.

No one has time for Jameson Fox when they're busy trying to get through life.

Yet, here I am, dealing with him.

He has dialed back his morning kisses, though, opting for the cheek kiss instead. And this morning, he had to leave early for work, so there was no opportunity for any form of invasion. I'm not counting on this lasting. All it will take is for Bill to show an ounce of suspicion, and Jameson will resume full invasion mode.

I leave the office just before seven, taking some work home with me to complete after dinner.

Wesley, Jameson's chef, surprises me with pizza for dinner. He asked me last week what my guilty pleasures are, and I included pizza on the list. Since Jameson won't be eating dinner at home tonight, Wesley decided it was the perfect night for one of my favorites.

I take the pizza to the sofa and turn the television on. If tonight is for guilty pleasures, I'm indulging in some *Vampire Diaries* too. A little Damon is good for the soul.

I'm lost in Damon's eyes and some of the best pizza I've tasted when Jameson's deep voice makes me jump and sends pizza flying to the floor.

"Have you ever heard of not sneaking up on a girl?" I mutter as I attempt to save the pizza. I look at him as he crouches to help me. "And what are you doing home so early?"

"I finished up earlier than expected." He places pizza on my plate, his hand brushing mine, causing a whole new round of trouble for me.

I pull my hand back. I do not need that in my life tonight.

Jameson doesn't miss any of this.

His brown eyes meet mine, flaring with the same heat that is filling every inch of me. "How was your pizza?"

I stand. "Wesley certainly knows his way around a pizza."

"That's good to know."

"What do you mean? You've never tried his pizza?"

"No."

I stare at him in shock. "You're kidding, right?"

"No."

How this is even possible is beyond me. I'm so stunned that I shove the plate of pizza his way and say, "Try it." I point to the pieces that didn't end up on the floor. "Eat those. They weren't ruined by you."

Amusement flickers in his eyes, right along with more of that heat.

He's all black suit and muscle and eyes I want to get lost in.

I'm unable to stop the way my body curves toward him and my skin comes alive.

I'm also unable to stop myself from picking up a slice of pizza and forcing it upon him. "I assure you you'll like it."

My gaze is pinned to his mouth as he takes a bite.

I enjoy him eating the pizza more than I enjoyed eating it myself.

I imagine him eating other things while I watch him eat that pizza.

I don't try to hide any of this from him.

When I find his eyes again, they're focused intently on mine. "Christmas," he says roughly.

I swallow all the things on the tip of my tongue and nod. "Yes, Christmas."

"You should expect a family discussion tomorrow night. And an invitation to go in search of a tree with Mom this week. She'll insist we get one too."

"Right." I begin constructing a list in my head of all the things I must prepare for. "What else? You mentioned ice-skating."

He takes another bite of pizza and nods. "Yes. Can you ice-skate?"

I want to say no, but I'm not good at lying. Also, I think I want to go ice-skating with his family. "Yes. When will she want to go?"

He chuckles and it's like I just heard a chuckle for the first time.

On what planet does Jameson Fox chuckle?

And since when did I find that sound sexy?

"The question is not when, but how often," he says, and I'm struck by the warmth in his voice. If anyone had told me Jameson had that in him, I wouldn't have believed them.

"So, you do all these things with her?" Surely not. I just can't imagine it. I feel like this really might be the dumbest question I've asked him to date.

"Yes."

I stare at him. "Really? You're not bullshitting me?"

"No, Adeline, I'm not bullshitting you. I do many things for my mother that may surprise you."

He's right about that.

The Jameson I know doesn't do anything for anyone that he doesn't want to do.

~

THE WEEK FLIES BY. Besides work, we attend Taco Tuesday at his mom's, a film premiere on Wednesday night, and a dinner party on Thursday night.

I only think about the coffin I need for him three times this week.

I think about his lap a whole lot more than I want to.

He doesn't invade me daily with kisses; he doesn't order me around; he only treats me like a child twice; and he only tries to force one social function on me before recalling the red rule we now have. Since I already had a function highlighted in red the day of his event, he declines the invitation. It seems Jameson Fox can compromise when he wants to.

Friday arrives, along with an exhausting list of tasks for the day. At the top of that list sits my sister who I've been going back and forth with for days while she's tried to get money from me. Today's texts begin arriving just after 7:00 a.m.

I'm tired after arriving home close to midnight last night. Jameson's dinner party ran late while he talked property with the men there. I sat through hours of mindless gossip with the wives. It's one of my least favorite things to do, but I did it for Jameson because I knew last night was important for him. He thanked me on the drive home, which was a welcome surprise.

Texting with Sabrina while tired doesn't go in my favor. Feeling so used doesn't help either. I wish I didn't feel this way. After living my entire adult life being used by her for money, I'm unsure why I ever hope for change. But I do. I still live with that hope and desire. She and I don't have a mother who will ever be there for us; I want us to be there for each other.

She finally wears me down me while we text during my drive to work.

Sabrina: Why are you being such a bitch about this? It's not like you don't have the money. Mom needs the cash. Just give it to her.

I stare out the car window while swallowing my hurt.

There's only one person on this earth who has the power to make me question myself the way I am now. My sister.

I don't believe I'm being a bitch, but she makes me doubt that every time she accuses me of it.

She's right; I do have the money. However, is that the point? I don't think so, but maybe I'm wrong. Maybe I am being awful to her by thinking she's lying to me.

"Adeline."

I turn at the sound of Jameson's voice and find him watching me with a frown. "Yes?"

"What's wrong?"

"Nothing."

"You've been on your phone all morning looking upset. Don't tell me there's nothing wrong when there clearly is."

If my brain wasn't so focused on Sabrina, it would zero in on the fact he's paying attention to someone other than himself.

I don't zero in on that. I'm far too upset at the moment to do that. And since I am this upset and could cry, and since the last person I want to cry in front of is Jameson, I say, "I'm fine. I've just got a lot on my mind today."

His impatience flares. "Fine means anything but that. Talk to me."

"Don't tell me what to do. I'm not in the mood this morning."

"I can see that. And God help my balls, but it's more than obvious to me that you're not okay. Since I know you like talking about your problems, start talking."

I bite down on all the things I want to say about what he just said. "You really have a way with words, and I'll say it again, it's no wonder you've never married."

"Adeline," he growls, and I know from the way he's watching me like he's thinking about physically extricating the information from me that he doesn't intend on letting this go.

I glare at him. "It's my sister."

He lifts his brows, waiting for more, nowhere near satisfied with those three words.

This man.

"She wants money. She always wants money. I'm not feeling like giving her any." I pause. "Is that enough for you?"

He ignores my attitude. "You pay all her bills?"

"I give her money, yes. And yes, it's enough to pay all her bills."

"And she comes looking for more?"

"Yes."

"How often?"

I hate discussing my family problems. With anyone. But definitely with Jameson. "You don't need to concern yourself with my family problems, Jameson."

He goes back to watching me like he's contemplating physical extraction. "I have concerned myself with *you*. And along with you, comes your family. How often does she ask for more?"

"Oh my God, you are insufferable." I hate that his questions are making me feel powerless, inadequate, incapable. Less than. I want to get out of this car and away from him and everything he's forcing me to confront. "Every month, okay? Sometimes every damn week."

My words rush out of me, falling into all the gaps between us.

The air in my lungs does too.

It's been trapped for so long that I didn't notice it. It just felt normal. Like air should overfill your lungs to the point where it's hard to bring more in.

And then, goddamn him, tears blur my vision.

I look away.

Out the window.

And try to suck some of that air back in.

I just want to go back to my normal.

I know how to exist in my normal.

I don't know how to be without all that air and all those words locked up tightly inside me.

I've never told anyone how often Sabrina uses me or how much she demands. Not even Natalie. I simply write checks, hand over cash, and push my feelings aside.

It's my dirty shame.

I can't get anyone to love me.

Not my mother.

Not my father.

Not my sister.

Not my ex-husband.

Millions of strangers around the world might follow me, but they don't love me. Not the way I want to be loved.

"Adeline," Jameson says, his voice firm, but smoothed around the edges.

"Don't," I say, my voice cracking. "Just leave it."

I hear his suit rustle against the seat before I feel his hand against my cheek.

He turns my face to him. When he sees the tears tracking down my face, he curses. "You can't keep doing this."

I wipe my tears. All my fight is gone. Now, I just want to curl into a ball and hide from the world. "There's nothing else I *can* do."

He scowls. "You're not a quitter. Don't start that shit now."

And just like that, his words and the way he says them, fire me up. That is, after all, Jameson's superpower. Firing me up. "Don't say shit like that to me when you know nothing about the situation."

"I know all I need to know about the situation. People like your sister don't stop. All they do is come knocking faster, sooner, all the fucking time. And just because she's your sister, doesn't mean you should say yes. Your family should be the last people on earth who use you like that."

He's right. I know he is. But this is something I've struggled with since I first started earning money.

I feel guilty that I make so much money while Sabrina and Mom have nothing.

It doesn't matter that they do nothing to help themselves.

It doesn't matter that I know I worked my ass off to get where I am.

It doesn't matter that I know this isn't down to luck.

I give, and give, and give, and still, it doesn't change anything.

I love my sister, but she doesn't love me.

She pretends to, but really, she hates me for having "boobs and an ass that bring in cash and men", her words, not mine. I want her to be happy, and I want her to love me. Unfortunately, I rely on money to help me get those things because she doesn't allow me into her life any other way.

I don't want to tell Jameson he's right. I never want to utter those words to him. So, instead, I say, "I'm taking care of it. You don't need to concern yourself about me in this way."

He looks at me like he doesn't know what to do with me. He does that for what feels like a long time. Finally, he says, "Stop giving her money. She's a grown woman. She can look after herself."

Thankfully, Max pulls up outside my office and I'm spared more of this conversation.

Jameson and I do our daily dance of pretending to be in love when he helps me out of the car and brushes a kiss across my cheek. Today, though, he settles his arm around my waist and doesn't let me go as soon as he's finished with his kiss.

Keeping his face close to mine, he says, "You deserve to be treated better than how Sabrina is treating you." His eyes search mine for the longest minute. "Don't ever forget that."

He may as well have kissed me because his words bewilder me as much as a kiss from him does.

Letting me go, he strides back to his door, and with one last glance, he gets in the car.

I'm unsure which part of all this does it, but I suspect it's that last glance he gives, that he never gives, that tips me over the edge.

Jameson Fox just rearranged the inside of my brain and I'm not sure I want to put things back where they were.

14

Jameson

I step out of the elevator that's brought me up to Adeline's office and am met by her assistant. It's only the third time I've been here, and I'm struck again by the understated elegance. Adeline has decorated with cream and muted pinks and greens. Instead of flash and glitz, she's chosen carefully placed flower arrangements and artwork. It all works well to give an air of style and sophistication that aligns with her brand.

Vanessa lets Adeline know I've arrived, and I'm shown through to her office. It's as elegant as the waiting area. The only added element is a chandelier above her desk.

"You're late," she says, straightening from where she was bent over her desk, and turning to face me.

My eyes are all over her body after walking in on her

bent over like that. I don't bother to remove them. I'm not sure I could even if I wanted to.

She's wearing a red dress that's stuck to her curves and made for my downfall.

I watch the rise and fall of her chest as she takes me in.

We've been playing this game for a week and a half now, ever since I fucked her. She would never admit it, but she likes my eyes on her.

Frowning, she says, "Why aren't you dressed?"

We're attending a black-tie birthday party for one of my business acquaintances. I was due here to collect Adeline twenty minutes ago but was delayed at the office going over Paulina's latest update. After she left, I changed into a clean suit, so I have no idea what Adeline's referring to.

"I'm dressed."

"You're half-dressed. Where's your bow tie?"

"Fuck knows." I detest bow ties and either misplaced mine or left it at home this morning. "Are you ready?" She looks ready, but she's not giving me the impression she's about to make a move.

Her lips press together for a brief moment before she lets out a breath. "You can't go to a black-tie event without a bow tie, Jameson."

"I can fucking do whatever I want. Now, can we please leave?"

"Do you really not know where it is?"

I shove my fingers through my hair. We're already late and I do not want to be any later. Bill is attending this party and I want to discuss the Brown deal with him tonight. "Adeline," I growl.

"Come with me," she says, giving me a look of exasperation.

She then brings those curves and that fucking perfume she refuses to stop wearing my way. I follow her out of her office, hoping like fuck that whatever she's planning won't take long.

She leads me into what appears to be a clothing and prop storage room and rummages around in boxes for a couple of minutes. It's hell on my dick having her bent over like this again.

Finally, she stands and turns to me, holding up a bow tie. "Come here."

Wanting this over with, I do as ordered.

"The next time we attend a black-tie event, make sure you come dressed," she says as she moves in close and gets to work securing the bow tie in place. "This wasn't listed in my wife duties."

"I can think of other things you've done that weren't on that list either and I don't recall you complaining about them."

The blush on her cheeks hits me low in the gut.

Fuck.

She finishes with the bow tie and meets my gaze. "There. We can go now."

The fact I'd rather stay here and bend her over her desk doesn't escape me.

The other thing that doesn't escape me is the fact I've never allowed a woman to have any hand in dressing me, and fuck if I didn't like Adeline taking charge.

As we walk down to my car, I attempt to push all the thoughts of what I want to do to her out of my head.

I don't succeed.

Hell, I haven't succeeded for the past week and a half.

Adeline is stuck on a loop in my brain.

Surviving her is proving difficult.

THERE ARE MORE people at the party than I anticipated, and while I don't enjoy big parties, Adeline is in her element. She talks with everyone who wants a conversation. Takes photos with everyone who wants them. Laughs at every joke even when I know she doesn't find it funny.

The fact I can read her like this surprises me, but it shouldn't. We may not be a real couple, but some days I think we're more aware of each other than if we were because we don't bother to put on a show for the other. Our love might be fake, but nothing else we do is.

Half an hour into the party, Adeline takes a sip of her wine and looks around the penthouse. "I need the name of their event planner. This party is gorgeous."

I glance at the black and gold everywhere, and the glittery decorations. There's not one ounce of minimalism in sight. "It's over the top."

"Of course, you think that. Let me guess, you'd skip the decorations."

"I'd skip the fucking party."

She rolls her eyes as my friend, Owen, joins us. He grins as he hears what I say. "It's a bit much, isn't it?"

Adeline smiles at him. "It's never too much, especially not for a birthday party."

He turns his grin to her before looking back at me.

"Make a note of that, my friend. Your wife wants you to go all out for her birthdays."

Owen isn't aware our marriage is fake, so Adeline keeps up the charade. "Thank you, Owen. I appreciate that. I'm counting on you to remind him when my birthday comes around. The same goes for half-birthdays."

"What the hell are half-birthdays?" Owen asks.

Adeline widens her eyes at him in what I know is fake shock. The relaxed state of her body reveals her good mood. "You're not being serious, right now? You don't celebrate half-birthdays?"

He laughs. "I'm guessing they fall six months after your actual birthday?"

"Yes, and they require the same level of celebration as the actual birthday. You should both take note."

Owen looks at me. "Were you aware of this when you asked her to marry you? It seems like a dealbreaker to me."

Before I can answer, Adeline says, "No, he wasn't aware. I kept it from him so he wouldn't question his decision to ask me to marry him. You both discovered half-birthdays are a thing today."

I watch her as she continues to talk with Owen, thinking about the difference in her tonight compared to how she was on the way to work this morning.

Without meaning to, I ripped her mask off this morning.

Underneath the strength, and grit, and fierce independence of Adeline is a whole other woman. She showed herself to me when I could see it was the last thing she wanted to do. And while I doubt she's happy she opened up, I respect the hell out of her for it.

"I'm stealing Adeline for a bit," Owen says as I spy Bill coming my way.

I take a sip of whiskey and nod as they leave.

Bill gets stopped by a couple on his way to me, and instead, I'm joined by a woman I've never met.

She smiles at me like she knows me. "Jameson Fox. It's good to meet you."

"And you are?" There's something about her I already don't like. Fuck knows what, but my gut is rarely wrong.

"I like a man who cuts straight to the chase." She smiles. "Robin Johansen. I work with SLY Media and would love to get your thoughts on the reality show it looks like your wife has signed on for."

I throw some more whiskey down my throat.

This is the first I've heard of this, and I doubt it's true.

Adeline is well aware of the terms of our marriage contract. Terms that state she won't agree to any activity that will potentially harm the marriage. And since a reality TV show could harm the fuck out of our marriage, there's no way in hell she'd sign on for it.

"I don't have any thoughts I'd like to share."

"Surely you must have something you'd love our followers to know about it. Like, will you appear in the show much? Will we finally get to know the man behind Fox Enterprises?"

There's a reason I avoid parties as best I can, and it's people like this woman.

I abhor gossip and anyone involved in spreading it.

"I have nothing your followers would be interested in.

And in future, I'd suggest you check your facts before talking about things you know nothing of."

Without another word, I leave her and make my way to Bill who has just extricated himself from the couple who delayed him.

"Where's Adeline?" he asks, glancing around the room.

"Owen dragged her away."

Adeline and I haven't seen Bill much this past week since he came over for dinner. He's been distracted with work and went to Vegas for a few days. By the expression on his face, he's eager to see us together.

I spend some time talking with him about the Brown deal. We've just finished going over some key points when Adeline joins us.

Sliding her arm around my waist, she smiles up at me before looking at Bill. "Did Jameson tell you that he learned about half-birthdays tonight?"

The look on Bill's face is how I suspect I look at half the things Adeline says. She has a way of never saying what you think she will. "He did not."

Her smile grows. "I'm getting the impression you've never heard of them either."

She goes on to explain to him what they are while I get lost in her perfume and her touch. By the time she's finished with her explanation, I've got my arm around her waist.

When my hand drops to her ass, she gives me a look that says I'm pushing it.

We're in the middle of that look when Bill is drawn into a conversation with a passerby.

I bend my mouth to her ear. "When do you anticipate you'll begin wearing that perfume I gave you?"

"Never."

"So, I should go ahead and have Jeff remove all your perfume from your bathroom?"

"You should not. Unless, of course, you wish harm to your balls."

Fuck.

"I like activities that involve risk."

"I'd suggest you run a full risk analysis for this activity. I think the likelihood of a threat occurring and its impact will be too high even for you."

"We need to talk."

"We are talking."

"Not here."

She turns to me. "Now?"

I nod. "Yes, now." I take hold of her hand, and without waiting to get Bill's attention to excuse us, lead her away from the main party, down a hallway, and into the library that's empty.

Closing the door behind us, I say, "When were you going to tell me about the reality show?"

She frowns. "Huh?"

"I had a woman asking for my thoughts on the show you've supposedly signed on for. She particularly wanted to know if I'd be appearing in the show often."

Her confusion clears and she shakes her head. "Jesus, Jameson, I haven't said yes to that show yet."

"Yet?" I back her up against the wall, my attention split between our conversation and the way she's affecting me.

"I'm not thinking about saying yes." She puts a hand

to my chest as my eyes drop to hers. “What are you doing?” That question comes out breathlessly. She’s just as affected by me.

“I’m trying to ascertain if I need to be concerned about you signing a contract you shouldn’t.”

Her hand presses hard against my chest. “First, you damn well know I’m not an idiot who’s going to sign anything like that without consulting you. And second, I wasn’t referring to our conversation when I asked you what you’re doing.”

“I’m aware.” I trace my gaze down over the swell of her breasts.

“Take your eyes off me.”

“You don’t want my eyes off you.”

“I thought you were done making assumptions.”

“I am. This isn’t an assumption.”

“It really is.”

I curve my hand around her neck as I bring my eyes back to hers. “Let’s test that.”

I finish moving into her and drop my lips to hers, demanding the kiss I’ve wanted ever since I last had her mouth.

Her hand against my chest presses hard again, but her other hand makes its way to my waist where she grips my shirt.

The moan she makes as she kisses me tells me everything I need to know.

“Fuck,” I growl into her mouth as I shift my hand from her neck to her hair. I bring my other hand to her breast, cupping it, while grinding my cock against her.

Our kiss is as desperate as our desire for each other.

I’ve never wanted a woman the way I want Adeline.

She rocks her hips against me, searching for the friction we both need.

"Oh my God," she says, tearing her mouth from mine and looking at me wildly. "Why do I want this so fucking much?" She madly reaches for my belt and undoes it. "You are the last man I want to have sex with and yet"—she unzips me and reaches for my dick—"you've somehow convinced me to fuck you again. And here at a party, of all places."

She's barely got me in her hand when I take charge and spin her around. Yanking her dress up, I rasp against her ear, "From where I'm standing, it's not taking much convincing."

She presses her cheek to the wall and her ass back against me. "Just fuck me already."

I crouch behind her and tear her panties off. I've got my mouth and hands to her ass before I even know what I'm doing. She's like a fucking drug.

"Spread your legs for me," I order as I run a hand down the back of her thigh.

She complies instantly and my eyes are drawn to her parted lips.

She's so damn wet I slide two fingers inside easily.

"Oh, God," she moans, arching her back and pushing her ass closer to my face.

I fuck her with my fingers while bringing my tongue to her. The moan she releases when I lick her is louder than the last one.

I thought I was hard before; now, I can't think straight I'm so fucking hard.

Letting her go, I demand, "Turn around."

She turns, her eyes finding mine as she hooks a leg over my shoulder.

I take hold of her ass and pull her cunt to my mouth.

I then eat her until she's making the kind of noise that no one at this party will mistake.

I stand, needing to be inside her while she's making that kind of noise.

She doesn't let me down when I thrust inside.

She wraps her arms and legs around me and cries out for the entire fucking world to hear.

It doesn't take either of us long to come tonight. That's thanks to too many days of not giving into the need we both have.

Adeline's breathing hard and fast by the time we're finished. Her hair is a mess, her face is flushed, her eyes are wild.

When I pull out, she reaches for her clutch. Locating tissues, she hands me some and we clean up before dressing.

"If I start wearing your perfume, do you think you might stop doing that?" she asks as she fixes her hair.

"You don't want me to stop doing that."

"I really do."

"Have you argued with every man you've been with as much as you argue with me?"

She opens her mouth to say something but snaps it closed just as fast. Then, getting another wild look in her eyes, she says, "I'm going to the bathroom to clean up properly. You're going to get me a drink and then you're going to stop looking at me for the rest of this party."

Before I can reply, she's pushed me away, opened the door, and exited the library.

Christ.

I want her again already.

I leave the room and head back out to the party.

Owen gives me a knowing look as he drinks his whiskey. "Can't say I've ever known you to disappear for sex during a party. You're usually only focused on work." He raises his glass. "Thank fuck for Adeline. The woman who's managed to loosen you up."

Hudson has arrived and stands next to Owen, watching me with interest. I didn't tell him I fucked Adeline last week. He gives me a look that says this is no surprise to him.

When Owen is drawn into a conversation behind us, Hudson murmurs, "If Bill had doubts before, I don't think he does now. Nice work."

I'm about to respond to that when I catch sight of Adeline coming our way. Gone is the wild, untamed look that was strewn across her face when she left me. In its place is apprehension.

"What's wrong?" I ask when she reaches me.

"I have to leave." She pauses. "My mother is at your place."

I take hold of her arm and nod. "Okay."

She frowns. "You don't have to leave."

There's no way I'm letting her go home to her mother alone. Not after how upset she was this morning over her sister.

I eye Hudson. "Can you let Bill know we had to leave?"

He nods. "Will do."

"Jameson," Adeline says as I direct her out of the party. "You can stay."

I keep hold of her as we continue walking. "Is your mother okay?" As far as I know, we weren't expecting her.

"Yes." She shrugs out of my grip and stops walking. "Are you ignoring me intentionally or have you gone deaf?"

I stop and look at her. "I'm coming with you. End of story."

"Why? I don't need you to come with me."

"I am well aware of that."

She stares at me for a good, long moment. A moment in which I get the distinct impression she really doesn't want me with her when she sees her mother.

"I'll give you and your mother space when we get home," I say. "But I am going home with you."

"Fine," she finally says before walking ahead of me and muttering something about bossy men and coffins.

It's the second time I'm sure I've heard her mutter about coffins. I've no fucking idea what she's referring to. I'm just glad she's not arguing with me anymore.

Although, arguing with Adeline is fast becoming a preferred activity of mine.

I'm beginning to think I'm losing my mind because I'm almost certain I don't want her to stop anytime soon.

15

Adeline

"It's good to see you've finally found a man who can look after you," my mother says after I give her the guided tour of Jameson's penthouse. She takes a moment to run her eyes over me and frowns. "Have you put on weight? I'm sure you didn't look this puffy at your wedding. You need to be careful now that you're married. You can't afford to add too many pounds. Jameson won't like that."

I still remember the first time my mother suggested I go on a diet. I was nine. The boy who lived next door had taken a liking to me and Mom pulled me aside one night and offered to brush my hair. Since she rarely did anything like that for me, I thought it was the best day of my life. I hung on every word she said to me that night.

Unfortunately, every word revolved around how I could keep a boy interested.

I learned from an early age to watch my weight.

And I kept learning well into my adult years to watch it some more.

All thanks to my mom.

She was the one who encouraged me into modeling. Some might say pushed rather than encouraged. And she's still the one telling me to watch my weight.

These days, I don't watch it. I watch my health instead.

I eat well, I exercise, I meditate, I sleep.

I do all the things that are good for me, including eating cupcakes and bagels and anything I damn well want when I want. And I love the curves I now have.

However, I don't think it matters how old a girl gets, or how confident; her mother has the power to cut her down with just a few words. And right now, I feel cut down. Not because I believe what she's saying, but because a daughter doesn't want to hear these kinds of things from her mother. Mothers should only tend with love.

"Jameson won't care," I say.

Her gaze shifts beyond me as I hear Jameson's voice. "What won't I care about?"

I close my eyes for a second and inhale a breath.

He told me he'd give me and Mom space. I should have insisted on a timeframe for that space. His idea seems to be fifteen minutes. Mine would be hours.

"Adeline's weight gain," Mom answers him, looking quite happy to involve him in the conversation. The thing about this? She actually thinks she's helping me.

Jameson comes to stand behind me, snaking his arm

firmly around my waist and resting his hand on my stomach. Keeping up the marriage charade for Mom. A good idea because I have no doubt that if she discovered the marriage wasn't real, it would only be a matter of time before my sister shared that information with someone who would pay for it.

"What weight gain?" he asks, sounding genuinely confused.

Mom motions her hand at me. "The weight she's gained since you married her. I was just reminding her that getting married doesn't mean a woman can take her focus off looking good for her husband. There's no extra security simply because you're married."

It's not often I'm embarrassed, but I am now.

I'm embarrassed to hear my mother say these things. Women have come too fucking far to still believe this kind of garbage.

"Mom," I start, ready to educate her, but Jameson cuts me off.

"Frances, what Adeline weighs is her business, not mine. And as far as security in a marriage goes, that's not what marriage is about."

Mom is the kind of person who hardly hears a word others say. Her conversations are mostly one-sided, so it doesn't surprise me that she pays little attention to what Jameson says. She looks at me after he finishes speaking and says, "You should come for a walk with me in the morning. It'll help with this."

I'm about to tell her what I think of that when her phone rings. Her face lights up when she sees who's calling. "It's Peter," she says to me like that means something. She then answers the call, sounding like a giggly schoolgirl, and brushes past me and Jameson to take the call.

Jameson moves his mouth to my ear and murmurs, "She's something else," before letting me go.

He can't possibly know what those three words mean to me, but when I turn to him, I get the sense that maybe he somehow does. It's in the way he's watching me with care, like he understands how I feel after that conversation.

I brush it aside.

I don't want to talk about how my mother makes me feel. Not with Jameson.

"Which bedroom can she sleep in?" I ask.

"Whichever room you want."

"Okay, thanks."

"She can stay as long as you want," he says as I head toward the hallway.

I look back at him. "You may regret that."

He doesn't say anything further; he just watches me silently.

I'm so thrown by him that I almost stumble in my hurry to escape the confusion of it all.

And good God, I can still feel him everywhere.

Inside me.

Outside me.

All around me.

I need a shower and a million hours by myself to figure out this entire situation with him.

Half an hour later, I finally make it into the bathroom. That's after sorting Mom out with a bedroom, finding out that she's here so she can have a break from Sabrina who is apparently driving her up the wall, and agreeing to help her find a new dress tomorrow for a date she's having with Peter when she gets home.

I take a bath instead of a shower. A long, hot, bubble bath in the floating tub in my bathroom that overlooks Manhattan. I'll give it to Jameson; I love this bathroom and will miss it when my year here is up.

When I leave the bathroom an hour later, the anxious energy my mother always stirs up is still there but lessened. I grab my crossword book and phone, and crawl into bed. I send Natalie a text to check in on her, and when I don't receive a reply, I find a crossword to do.

I'm deep in thought trying to figure out a clue when Jameson strides into the bedroom. He slows when his eyes land on me. "Your mother has everything she needs?"

I nod. "Yes."

"Good."

His hands go to the buttons on his shirt and begin working their way down it. The top one is already undone. It's perpetually undone on Jameson. I think one of the reasons why he wears a suit better than any other man is because he has his own style. Undone buttons, exposed skin, rolled-up sleeves, and ties that are often loosened like he wants nothing more to do with them. Jameson might not have been born into a suit-wearing world, but he's firmly in it now. And he lives in it exactly how he does everything: in his own way.

I'm mesmerized by his fingers as they work those buttons. So much so that he's undone the entire shirt before I realize I've watched the whole show. When I drag my gaze back to his face, he's watching me with a look that says he's feeling all the same things I am.

I've never orgasmed as fast as I did when Jameson fucked me tonight. He might be clueless when it comes to many things with a woman, but he knows how to deliver an orgasm. The only thing I'm thinking while sitting here watching him undress is how much I want more of those orgasms.

However, that's my body doing all the thinking, so I push her aside and take back control.

"You need to do that in the bathroom," I throw out, ignoring the fact that even I can hear how turned on I am.

He keeps his eyes on mine as he removes his shirt.

"Jameson." The thread of need in my voice can't be missed, but I'm unsure if it's the need for him to stop or the need for him to start that's more urgent.

He reads me perfectly. I know he does by the way he takes a moment analyzing me, determining his next move. It's quite unlike the Jameson I know. That man would just take what he wants without regard for what I want. This Jameson, this new one I'm slowly meeting, takes my wants into consideration.

Finally, his nostrils flare, and with one last glance, he walks into his bathroom.

I let out the breath I was holding.

We can't have sex again.

It's messing with the way I think about him.

Jameson stole my company from me.

He's an asshole who only cares about himself and treats me like a child.

I hate him.

Those are the thoughts I need to hold onto in order to survive this marriage.

Yet, the only one of those thoughts that feels completely accurate anymore is the fact he took my company. The others are in tatters and as much as I try to put them back together, I'm floundering.

We really can't have sex again.

A text sounds and I grab my phone, grateful for the reprieve from the mess in my head.

Natalie: Just got your message. Are you okay? Did you know your mom was coming to stay?

Adeline: No and no.

Adeline: And I had sex with Jameson again.

Natalie: So, we've moved on from denial?

Adeline: No. I'm never doing it again.

Natalie: It was that bad?

Adeline: It was fucking awful.

Natalie: Right, so definitely still deep in denial. Got it. Why'd your mom come to town?

Adeline: Who knows why my mother does anything? She said she needed a break from Sabrina.

Natalie: Do you need me to come over? I could source Nutella rolls and bring them to you.

Adeline: No, I'm in bed. I'm going to have an early night.

Natalie: How many crosswords have you already done?

Adeline: None. I'm stuck on a clue.

Natalie: You know Google is a thing, right?

Adeline: You know I don't cheat.

Adeline: Enough of me. Tell me how you are.

Natalie: I'm confused by Ryan.

Adeline: Why?

I wait for her reply, but it doesn't come.

Adeline: Nat?

Natalie: Sorry, gimme ten minutes.

I go back to my crossword, finally figuring out the clue I was stumped on. I work through four more before getting stuck again.

Jameson comes back into the bedroom while I think about it. He's wearing black pajama pants and nothing else.

Sitting on the edge of the bed, he checks something on his phone.

I stare at his back, willing my core to shut the hell up while I inspect every muscle on show.

When she refuses, I drag my attention back to my crossword.

I'm busy doing everything I can to focus on clues that shouldn't be this hard when he shifts to sit with his back to the headboard and his legs stretched out in front of him.

"That must be some clue," he says.

My head snaps up and I look at him. "Huh?"

"I've never seen you frown so hard."

I unscrunch my face. "What's a coil that's an electrical gizmo? Starts with 'T'."

He only takes a second. "A Tesla coil."

Jesus, I knew that.

I scribble the answer into the crossword and move to the next clue.

When it also stumps me, I look at Jameson again. "Emergency sorting process?"

He glances up from his phone and thinks for a moment. "Triage."

"Ugh," I mutter as I fill in the answer. I then close the

book and place it on my nightstand. "I give up." I knew that answer too. My brain has obviously decided she's done with today.

Jameson puts his phone down and studies me. "Did you speak with Sabrina today?"

I don't want a thing to do with that question.

And most definitely not if he's asking.

"I think we should go back to ignoring each other."

I expect his impatience to bristle. Or his annoyance to flare. Or something other than what he gives me. *Anything* but what he gives me.

"I hope she's aware of what she has in you."

How can it be that Jameson sees me better than anyone?

I swallow my heart that decided sitting in my throat seemed like a better idea than staying in my chest. "The only thing Sabrina is aware of is herself," I say softly, wondering how he's managed to draw these words from me.

"So, she's like your mother."

I find myself smiling at that. I like Jameson's no-bullshit approach. "Yes, she's a mini-Frances. Although, she can be quite aggressive, whereas my mother is much calmer about things."

"I picked up on that at the wedding."

That surprises me. As far as I knew, Jameson paid no attention to me, my family, or my friends that day.

"Mom likes to say that Sabrina is like our father while I'm like her."

"Do you remember your father?"

"No. I have some memories. Fragments, really." I

pause. "I remember things that don't feel good, so I don't spend time lingering, you know?"

"Yeah," he says roughly, like he knows exactly what I mean.

My phone sounds with a text.

Natalie: Sorry! Ryan came over. Question: what the fuck does it mean when a guy you thought was into you doesn't initiate sex? I've never had this before and it's confusing AF.

Adeline: I've not had that either. Maybe he's tired?

Natalie: This isn't just tonight. Almost every time we've had sex has been because I've started it.

Adeline: But he's into it? Like, he wants to fuck you, right?

Natalie: God, yes.

Adeline: Google is your friend.

Natalie: Is MA there? Go ask him for me.

Adeline: I'm not asking MA about anything that has to do with sex.

Natalie: How much do you love me? Seriously, I need a man's perspective on this.

Adeline: UGH.

I look at Jameson. "What does it mean when a guy you've just started dating isn't initiating sex?"

I knew this was a bad idea before I asked the question. Now, I know it was a really bad idea. Jameson and I can't discuss sex without thinking about fucking each other. That much is clear from the heat that's come to life in his eyes.

"He's not fucking her?"

Jesus.

I can't go on.

I press my thighs together.

"He is. And he's into it. But she has to get it started."

"He wants more than just sex from her."

"So, he's just taking it slow?"

He nods.

I go back to my phone faster than my hands are ready for, fumbling with the damn thing in my haste.

I don't look back at Jameson, but I have zero doubt he knows exactly what's happening right now.

Adeline: You and me are in a war. Never ask me to ask MA about sex again.

Natalie: What did he say? And for the record, you don't have it in you to stay in a war with me. I complete you. You can't be in a war with your person.

Adeline: He said Ryan wants more than sex. He's taking it slow.

Natalie: Oh.

Adeline: I mean, it makes sense.

Natalie: Yes. I think MA might be right. I can't believe I didn't put that together.

Natalie: Okay, I'm gonna go and beg for some sex. You should think about doing the same xx

Adeline: I have one word for you. War.

I put my phone on the nightstand, push the bed covers off, and walk into the bathroom. I need some space from all the muscles and bare skin sitting next to me in bed. Not to mention the desire vibrating off both of us.

I moisturize my body. For the second time tonight.

I brush my teeth. Again.

I contemplate running away.

Jameson is nowhere to be seen when I go back to the bed twenty minutes later.

It's disturbing how disappointed I am by this.

I'm only further disturbed when I'm lying in the dark an hour later, still thinking about how I wish he was here.

When he slips under the covers fifteen minutes later, I level up to a whole new status of disturbed.

Sleeping next to Jameson for the last couple of weeks has been difficult. There have been some nights where I've had less than a few hours of sleep. I've gone to bed angry with him some nights. Frustrated with him, others. But mostly, since the first time we had sex, I've spent the night desperate for his touch. Tonight, I want it more than I've ever wanted it.

I lie quietly for many long minutes. Probably ten, but it feels like a thousand.

I don't move.

I'm not even sure that I breathe.

And then, unable to stop myself, because I need to do something to escape the images of sex with him that are on repeat in my head, I say, "Thank you for saying what you said to my mother about my weight tonight. I know you were doing it for the marriage, but I appreciate you choosing to say that."

A few moments pass before his deep voice moves over me. "I didn't say that for the marriage."

I still.

Not that I can get much stiller than I am.

And then I do something I never thought I'd ever do.

I roll to face him.

His bed is massive, which I've been glad for, but right now, he feels too far away.

He's lying on his back, and he turns his face to mine when I roll over.

I pull my legs up to my chest and rest my hands under my head on the pillow. "What was your father like?"

"Fuck." The word falls harshly from his lips instantly. I feel every drop of heavy in his response. Every ounce of pain. He looks up to the ceiling for a long minute before scrubbing a hand over his face.

I can't tell if he's going to answer me or not.

Another minute passes and I decide he's not going to.

"You don't need to tell me," I say. "I just—"

He looks at me. "You don't want to know what my father was like." His voice is jagged. Filled with bruises and cuts and wounds that I sense sit deep in his soul.

I think he's right.

I don't think I want to know what his father was like.

I map the angles of his face. It's dark, so I can't make out the fine lines, but I can see the shape of him. It occurs to me, though, that I don't need light to know where the lines sit. Jameson and I might not be married in the true sense, but I've studied him so closely over the last three and a half months that those lines are committed to memory already.

"How many times has your nose been broken?" I ask, thinking about the fact he was a fighter at one time in his life. I suspect it's been broken at least once because its alignment is slightly out. It's barely noticeable, but I noticed it the other day.

"Twice." He pauses for a long beat before adding, "By my father."

I know Jameson's father died when he was eighteen, so this means his broken noses occurred while he was still a child. He was absolutely right that I don't want to know about his father.

We lie in silence for a long time, watching each other.

This man is the biggest puzzle I think I'll ever meet.

What lies on the surface is nothing compared to what lies beneath.

Yet, everything on the surface is there only because of what lies beneath.

I have an overwhelming desire to do something I never saw coming.

I want to break through his surface.

I want to move past the shallows and find the real Jameson.

16

Adeline

I'm onto baking my second batch of cupcakes when Mom joins me in the kitchen just after 6:30 a.m.

"Goodness," she says, eyeing them. "You're not planning on eating any of those, are you?"

"She'll get a few," Jameson says, coming in after Mom. "There won't be many left after I get to them."

I could grow used to having him around while she visits me. He has this way of coming in at the exact right moment of a conversation when I need help.

I smile at him, trying hard not to drop my gaze to his muscles that are on full display after he spent the last hour and a half in his gym. I fail, but I actually don't care. And judging from the way I find him watching me, he's on board with it too.

"Well," Mom says to him, "you can afford to eat as many as you like."

I only just stop myself from rolling my eyes. Honestly, she's too much with all this diet talk. Not to mention her distinctions between what's appropriate for a man versus a woman. Trying to shift the conversation, I ask, "What time do you want to go shopping today?"

"Oh, no, I can't go today. We'll have to do it tomorrow. Or Monday."

I frown. "I thought we'd made a plan to go today."

"Yes, but I spoke with Marla last night and she invited me out to lunch. Her boyfriend has a friend she thinks I'd get on well with. He wants to meet me."

I stare at her.

Stunned, when I shouldn't be.

Of course, she's abandoning me in favor of a man. She's not even abandoning me for a friend; she dislikes Marla and only contacts her when she comes to town in the hope she'll introduce her to men.

Jameson grabs a drink from the fridge and comes to stand next to me. I barely notice him. My mom has my full attention.

"I can't go tomorrow or Monday."

She waves me off like she doesn't care. "No worries. I can go by myself. You can just write me a blank check."

"No, I'm not writing a blank check."

I don't know if it's my tone or what I've said that causes it, but she blinks and looks at me like I've just said something hurtful to her. "I need a dress, Adeline."

The guilt and shame that usually stops me saying no to her is no match for the hurt and anger coursing through me. "You have plenty of dresses." I should know because I bought them for her.

"I want a new one for this date."

I swear I hear Jameson grunt beside me. When he makes a move like he's going to leave the kitchen, I place my hand on his arm and stop him. I don't want him to leave.

"Well, I'm not paying for it," I say.

"You're punishing me because I can't go shopping today."

My anger sparks like lightning cracking across the sky. It's not that she *can't* go. "I don't punish people, Mom. That's not my style."

"It feels like punishment," she says, sounding like a child.

How can a mother be like this? When did her ability to nurture, to care, to love, disappear? Did she ever even have that ability?

"I'm hurt, Mom. Hurt that you're so easily discarding me so you can go out and find a man to sleep with. And as for not wanting to write you a blank check, it's not my responsibility to pay for your life."

"I never said it was your responsibility, Adeline. But I do think it's nice for a child to help her parent when she can."

And just like that, she shows my hurt and anger out, and welcomes my guilt back in.

I'm in the middle of dealing with that guilt when Mom gives me one last look that expresses her disappointment and walks out of the kitchen.

I watch her go, lost for words. So lost that I don't even

have any for Jameson when he says, "She's a piece of work."

Yes, she is, but I'm struggling to acknowledge that because my guilt is spiraling through me, reaching down deep to the little girl inside me who desperately wants her mother's love and approval. I know that little girl exists in all of us because my therapist has taught me about her. I've done a lot of healing work on my inner child, but I know it can be a life-long process. I know I've still got a lot of work ahead of me.

"Adeline," Jameson says. "She's wrong."

"I know, but she always has a way of messing with my thoughts."

He studies me before finally saying, "You need to finish these cupcakes and then get dressed. I'm taking you out for the day."

My brows pull together. "Where? Why? I thought you were working today."

"It can wait."

"Your work can never wait." It's true. This man is always working. More than me. And I thought I worked a lot.

His trademark impatience makes an appearance. "Do we need a discussion every damn time we plan something?"

"Don't you snap at me. I'm just trying to figure out where you're going with this. And yes, I like to be involved in making plans."

"I need to do some Christmas shopping. You can help me."

"You do your own Christmas shopping?" I'd have

taken Jameson for being the kind of man to have Shantel shop for him.

"For my mother and brother, yes." He reaches for a cupcake. "I'll be ready to leave in an hour."

I let him take the cupcake. It turns out Jameson has a sweet tooth and I've decided I like him eating what I bake. He devoured most of the cupcakes I made last week and a lot of the lemon cake I baked late Tuesday night after we arrived home from Taco Tuesday with his family.

As he leaves the kitchen, I call out, "Just so you know, telling me you'll be ready to leave in an hour does not mean I'll automatically be ready to leave in an hour."

Honestly, that man needs someone like me to teach him how to exist in the world. One day, the woman he marries for real will thank me.

17

Jameson

I'm unsure what possessed me to bring Adeline shopping. What I assumed would be a simple trip to choose two gifts has turned into a fucking huge undertaking. Thank Christ I've already bought Bill's gift. If not, we'd be here for another two hours while she ensured I bought an assortment of gifts he doesn't need like she's done for my mother and brother.

"What about this tie?" she asks, holding a navy tie up for me to inspect. "I think Hudson would look good in this one."

"A tie is a fucking tie. It's perfect." I take it from her and add it to the collection of gifts she's accumulated while we've spent hours walking through this mall. Even my security team whose faces always remain blank masks appear exasperated with this expedition.

"A tie is *not* a tie." She looks horrified by that statement. "Do you need me to explain the intricacies of ties to you?"

"Fuck, no."

She reaches for the navy tie, frowning as she glances between it and another one on display. "I don't know. I think maybe this red one might be better."

I grab the red one, the navy one, the black one, and the fucking dark green one. "We'll take all of them."

Her eyes come to mine. She's less than impressed with me. "Why are you being difficult about this?"

"I'm not."

"You are."

"Jesus," I mutter. "I needed two gifts. *Two*. And here we are with more than twenty things. I'm not the one making this trip difficult."

Her eyes widen. "You think *I'm* making it difficult?"

"No, I don't think it, I fucking know it."

I catch sight of people stopping to watch us argue, and I note their phones capturing all of this. As Adeline opens her mouth to continue arguing, I pull her to me and bring my lips to hers, silencing and kissing her all at once.

Her gasp of surprise is followed by that sound that tells me just how much she likes my mouth on hers. And instead of trying to keep me away like she does whenever I kiss her, she grips my shirt and pulls me closer, devoting herself to the kiss.

When I end it, she keeps hold of my shirt and gives me more of her attention in a way I fucking like. "Kissing me in the middle of an argument will not make me forget what we were discussing."

She might look like she's still arguing with me; hell, she might think she still is, but she's not. Adeline has put down her weapons today.

She was quiet when we left home after her mother did a number on her this morning. I had to work to get her to talk. Not a strength of mine, but I managed to get her to move past that bullshit and immerse herself in shopping. Once she did that, I saw her lack of arms.

She's spent the past three hours dragging me from shop to shop, talking about everything from the gifts she thinks my family might like, to the designer she's recently hired, to how she's concerned her assistant is in the middle of a crisis, to questions about Shantel, to her stress over some fashion show she's got coming up.

Throughout all that, she gave me her special brand of battle, arguing with me over things no one argues with me over. Testing every last shred of patience I possess. But she did it differently than she usually does it. Gone is her hostility. In its place is a ceasefire that feels a lot like foreplay.

"I have no doubt nothing could make you forget what you were arguing over," I say as she lets me go.

"You will thank me for helping you select these gifts when your mother and brother fall in love with them." She looks at something behind me. "And now, you should buy me lunch. I see a place that looks good, although I don't think they'll have Nutella rolls."

I've never known anyone who craves Nutella like Adeline. She's asked Max to stop at Brenda's coffee shop almost daily to pick up Nutella rolls. Not that she always ends up buying some. There's been a few times where she's simply stared lovingly at them before ordering only a latte. I've wondered why the hell she made us stop in the first place, but after spending time with her mother, I now understand. Her mother has a lot to fucking answer for.

I pay for the gifts and follow her to the noisy food court she's set her sights on. I can't remember the last time I came to a mall. It's not something I particularly enjoy, and while we blew past my time limit for shopping hours ago, I can't deny I'm enjoying watching Adeline now.

She's radiant, alive in a way I haven't seen yet, as she walks through the crowd in the food court. She's not oblivious to the people who recognize her, but she's not paying them the kind of attention she's spent the last three and a half months paying the public. It's almost like she's forgotten her job. Not that I think being available twenty-four-seven is her job, but I know she does.

Something catches her attention, and she turns to me with excitement, grips my forearm, and says, "Oh my God, tell me you love Korean chicken."

"I've eaten it once."

"Did you like it?"

"I don't remember much about it."

She squeezes my arm and I feel it low in my gut. "We need to fix that. Now."

With that, she glides her hand down my arm to take hold of my hand and drags me to the Korean chicken.

Twenty minutes later, we're sitting on stools at a long high table with about fifteen other people, eating our chicken. Thank fuck we've got two of my security guys with us because Adeline has drawn a lot of attention at this table.

My preference was to take our food and eat in the car. She wouldn't hear a word of it. "This is fun," she insisted. Clearly, our ideas of fun are vastly different. I put one of my security men next to her and the other across from her. If I could get ten more of them here in the next five minutes, I would. Either that or shut the entire fucking mall down so she's safe. I don't doubt she wouldn't hear a word of that either.

"Oh, God," she practically moans as she eats a piece of the sweet, tangy Korean popcorn chicken we're sharing. "This. Is. Divine."

I've lost count of the number of women I've shared a meal with, but not one of those dining experiences was like this one.

The women I've dated would never eat in a food court in a mall. They wouldn't talk and laugh with strangers sitting around them. And they sure as fuck wouldn't eat crispy chicken that cost thirteen bucks.

Adeline's as at ease here as she is at a black-tie event.

She finishes her mouthful and looks at me expectantly while I eat. "Stop keeping me in suspense. Do you love it?"

"It could be sweeter."

"Seriously? That's all you've got for me?"

"I like it." I drop my gaze to her mouth. "I like watching you eat it more, though." I'd bring her here every day for this experience.

The rise and fall of her chest draw my attention as she feels the effect of my words. Hell, her entire body is feeling my words and I'm having difficulty sitting here, amongst this crowd, keeping my hands to myself.

She lowers her voice. "We're changing the subject

before you do that thing you do that gets us in trouble."

My lips twitch as I find her eyes again. "That thing I do?"

"Yes, that thing. You know very well what I'm referring to."

"I think I'd like to hear you say it."

"You would think that."

I angle my body toward hers, shifting so her knee is between my legs. I place my hand on her hip. "It's suddenly occurred to me that we're in public."

More of that rising and falling of her chest happens as her cheeks stain with that blush my dick fucking loves.

She's aware this hasn't just occurred to me.

She also knows where I'm going with this.

I bring my hand up to her face and thread my fingers into her hair as my mouth finds hers. The noise around us dies the second I taste her. Adeline has that effect on me. When she's in my arms like this, it flips a switch in my brain that no one has ever flipped. It hushes the world, the demons, the bullshit.

My tongue slides over hers and I deepen the kiss. I lose myself in my want. In my need for this woman that is only intensifying every day.

One of her hands grips my thigh while her other hand comes to my chest, clutching my shirt. She gives me the sexy noises she never fails to give me when I kiss her.

Kissing isn't usually something I dedicate a great deal of time to. With Adeline, the opposite is true, and not just because it's proved useful to validate our marriage in public. Since the first time I kissed her like this on our wedding day, I've wanted my mouth on hers.

She has her own special brand of kiss in the same way

she has her own special brand of everything.

Her body fits mine in a particular way when she kisses me. Like all her hollows fit with my lines. Like she was made to sink into me.

Her mouth surrenders to me. Even when everything else in her is fighting me, her mouth doesn't know how.

She gives herself to me completely. Her body, her attention, her everything.

This kiss is no different.

Not even a busy food court can stop her from falling into it.

When she pulls her lips from mine, I'm given that wild look she reserves for me while she pushes me away. "You need to eat your chicken."

"No, I need to get you out of here."

She tries to reposition our legs so hers isn't between mine. When I stop her, she gives me another wild look. "Jameson, we're in the middle of a shopping mall. There are a million people around us, watching and taking videos. I know we're all about putting on a show for them, but now is not the time to do"—her eyes drop to our legs—"*this*."

I roughly grab her chin and angle her face back to mine. "I agree." I jerk my chin at her. "Grab your shit. We're leaving."

That bewilders her but I'm off my stool and have her off hers before she can catch a breath. I gather the bags of gifts we've bought and guide her out of the food court. When I find a clothing store that has what I'm looking for, I lead her into it after telling my security team to wait outside for us.

"You dragged me away from my chicken for more

shopping?" she says from beside me as I yank a dress from the rack.

I walk her to the fitting rooms, take a number card from the attendant, and wait in line.

Adeline looks at me like she thinks I've lost my damn mind.

I have.

But I'm about to find it.

I see the moment she solves the clues.

Pink colors her cheeks again and her breathing picks up.

"I'm not fucking you in a fitting room in this store." Her attempts at bossiness fall flat. We both know that's exactly what she's going to do.

"Yeah, you are."

"Stop telling me what to do." She reaches for the dress. "And give me this. Jesus, Jameson, no one would believe I'd wear this."

It's busy in the store I chose. Fuck knows if it's a popular women's store, but I'm getting the sense it is. There's a long line waiting for the fitting rooms and many of the women are staring at Adeline. Some are snapping photos of us.

I eye the dress I pulled from the rack. She's right; even I know she'd never wear that. It's purple and looks to be shapeless.

I lean in close. "Do you think anyone here believes you're trying it on?"

My question gets my desired response.

Fuck, she's sexy when she's in this state of turned-on denial.

We reach the front of the line and when the next

fitting room becomes free, I guide her into it, ignoring her hands that are trying to smack me away. Her efforts are weak at best, so I have no trouble getting her where I want her.

I discard the dress and pull her to stand in front of me in the mirror. Circling my arms around her, I reach for the button on her jeans. Her eyes hold mine in the mirror as I flick it undone.

When I move to the zip, she puts her hand over mine. "I'm not fucking you here."

I bring my other hand to her jeans. Cupping her pussy, I bend my mouth to her ear. "Stop denying this. You want me as much as I want you."

She grasps my forearm. "I do, but I don't have sex in shops. Especially not shops that refused to stock my first ever collection."

I keep my mouth against her ear while rubbing her through her jeans. "They wouldn't stock your dresses?"

"No." She presses herself into my hand, searching for what she wants while biting her bottom lip. "And it hasn't escaped my attention that you got them to when you stole my company."

I don't have a thing to do with Chatoyer on that level, so I'm unaware of who stocks that company's products. "I'll pull their contract."

Her fingers dig into me. "Don't be stupid. They're a huge contract for you."

"If it will move me closer to getting inside you, I don't give a fuck."

Her sharp intake of breath shoots more need through my veins.

"Consider it done," I growl. I dip my mouth to kiss her

neck, adding some teeth as she tightens her hold on my arm even more.

When I'm done with her neck, I find her eyes again. "We need to renegotiate our contract." I slide her zip down. "Going forward, I'm going to fuck you daily. More than once. Sometimes in public. And you're only going to argue with me over it enough to ensure I fuck you so you have difficulty walking afterwards."

She opens her mouth to speak but loses that thought when I find her clit.

Her back arches and her eyes close while she lets me take control.

I circle my finger over her nub, dropping my gaze to her cunt in the mirror. Needing to see it, I say, "Push your jeans down."

Her eyes open. "No. I told you, I'm not fucking you in here."

Fuck.

My mouth finds her ear again. "Good girl."

Defiance mixes with heat in her eyes, and before she knows what's happening, I've stopped what I'm doing, I've taken hold of her hands and have them pinned to the mirror above her head while pressing her against it.

Grinding my dick against her ass, I promise her, "This will be rough. I'm too fucking hard for it to be anything else."

She rocks her hips against me, moaning as I shove her jeans and panties down.

I undo my jeans and free my cock. "Tell me you want me."

"You know I do." She presses the crack of her ass back into me. "Hurry up already."

"Fuck," I rasp, getting my mouth on her, kissing her neck. She has no idea how she affects me.

I take hold of my cock and line it up with her cunt. She's wet enough to take me in one hard thrust, and a second later, she's moaning loud enough for the entire store to hear.

Keeping her to the mirror, I fuck her with an intensity I've never known. She consumes every one of my senses, demanding complete submission. I might be in control here, but it's at Adeline's pleasure.

We chase our release together, completely in sync.

Adeline comes, her pussy squeezing around me.

I thrust harder as pressure builds at the base of my spine, my hips driving faster into her.

Fuck.

My muscles tense.

I let go of her hands and grip both her hips.

The pressure gathers.

Everything tightens.

I thrust one last time, jerking, and coming hard.

Adeline moans again as I empty myself into her.

I grip her harder and drop my mouth to her shoulder.

We're quiet for a few moments.

Then, she says, "I think you'll need to buy that dress." After I pull out and turn her to face me so I can claim another kiss, she says, "And don't think I've forgotten your promise to pull this company's contract. I'm holding you to that."

We clean up, buy the damn dress, and finally leave the mall.

I struggle to keep my eyes off her while I walk her to the car.

I also struggle with that on the drive home.

I'm already working out how I'm going to fuck her next.

My mother interrupts these thoughts when she texts us. She's started a fucking group chat with us and Hudson this week. Hudson and I don't contribute much, but Mom and Adeline bombard the group with texts daily.

Mom: Can you all get to my place earlier tomorrow? Nine instead of ten?

Adeline's face breaks out in a smile as she reads the message. "I adore your mother." She goes back to the text before glancing at me again. "I'm telling her yes."

"I have no doubt."

Adeline: Yes.

Mom: Adeline, would you like to stay and make a gingerbread house with me after we're finished with the tree? I know the boys won't want to, but I thought we could have a girls' afternoon. If you're not busy, that is.

Adeline: I would love to.

She looks at me, her face sex-flushed and happy. "I love how she refers to you and Hudson as boys. I don't think that will ever grow old."

"Because?" She's mentioned this before. I've no idea where her fascination with this comes from.

She gives me a pointed look. "Because you are far from a boy, Jameson."

Christ.

Everything about this woman is sexual.

The way she moves.

The way she looks at me.

The way she speaks.

Her scent, her eyes, her lips.

Her fucking nose of all things.

I can't look at, listen to, or touch her without thinking about fucking her.

She goes back to texting with Mom for a while.

I grab my phone and try to distract myself with emails.

I'm halfway through replying to one when she says, "Did your mother work while you were growing up?"

I nod. "She was a housekeeper at a hotel."

"Did she enjoy it?"

That's a question with many answers. I give her the most honest one. "She enjoyed the time away from home."

I've barely spoken of my father since he died. There's a good reason for that. Just thinking about him dredges up rage I've done my best to bury.

I tried to fight it out of my system for years, and that helped to some extent. These days, I simply avoid thinking or talking about him. Adeline's questions about him this week have caused me extra time in my gym.

She reads me well and nods without asking anything else about that. Instead, she says, "When did she stop working?"

"A year and a half ago. Her back wasn't good for years, but she refused to quit work. She wouldn't let me or Hudson help her. She's stubborn, but we finally convinced her to quit her job and let us buy her a condo. She does some work for me, but not by my choice."

"What does she do?"

"We set up a foundation to help single parents. She

helps run it."

Her eyes soften. "I don't think I knew about your foundation."

"We keep it separate. There's no reason to tie it to me. Hudson and I just ensure they have what they need. Mom plays a big part in steering their mission."

Adeline has me neatly boxed as the asshole who stole her company. I can see this new information is messing with that box. She doesn't say anything further about it because she receives a text that redirects her attention.

We spend the next ten minutes on our phones, at which point she says, "I think I'm going to have to fly to London next week for a few days."

"For work?"

She nods. "Yes, I'm finally in a place where expanding our retail stores into the UK and Europe makes sense. My COO wants me to go with her to check out potential sites. We're looking at leaving on Tuesday and should be home by Friday. I'm sorry if that clashes with things I've agreed to attend with you."

There's nothing on next week that's of any real importance, so I'm not concerned. "Take my jet."

Adeline dislikes taking anything I offer. Her independence flares now. "No, we can fly—"

"Take the jet. It's just sitting there. I'm not using it next week."

I can see her warring with herself over this, but in the end, she says, "Thank you."

"You should prepare yourself for my mother to bombard you with requests for your time when you return. I'm almost certain she was planning to get you out ice-skating daily next week." Being the week before

Christmas, Mom would have had her out there at least once. I know she'll be hopeful that Adeline can spare some time next weekend for it.

She smiles. "Consider me prepared. We're absolutely going ice-skating at least once." Her smile morphs into a grin. "I want to see you fall on your ass."

"I never fall on my ass."

Max pulls the car into my garage as Adaline rolls her eyes. "How boring."

I grab all the bags of gifts we accumulated once the car is parked. I'm following Adeline to the elevator when Hudson calls. "I'll be up soon," I tell her.

"What's up?" I answer the phone as the elevator slides closed with Adeline in it.

"Adeline's got a problem and it's not a small one. I'm just calling to find out where you two are so I can come to you and detail it."

"We're at home. What's the problem?" Hudson is one of the calmest, most logical, rational people I know. If he says she's got a problem that's not a small one, she's got a fucking problem.

"One of the factories she uses to manufacture her clothes in Asia is a sweatshop that uses child labor. The workers are also forced to work in unsafe conditions."

Adeline's brand regularly promotes the fact they don't use sweatshops. She's built her company on that promise.

Hudson continues, "This isn't one of her main factories. The work was subcontracted out through a supplier that couldn't meet demand. I'm not sure she's aware of this." He pauses. "I'll be at your place in about forty minutes. I'll email the information through so she can go through it before I get there."

18

Adeline

"I wasn't aware we were using that factory," I say to Hudson after he runs through the information he emailed when Jameson and I returned from shopping. I could vomit. And not just because this is bad for my company, but because this is humanity at its worst and I do everything in my power to ensure my company and myself are never involved in hurting fellow humans.

He nods. "I figured as much."

I reach for my phone, ready to call my team in on this.

"This isn't public knowledge," he says.

"No, but it won't take long for that to happen," I say.

"If you can get ahead of it, you might be able to stop that from happening," he says.

If there's one thing I've stood firm on from the day I went into business, it's been my integrity. I've always vowed honesty and transparency. I'm not about to stop now.

I shake my head. "No, I'm not getting ahead of it. I'm taking charge of it."

"How?" he asks.

"I'll pull our work from that factory immediately and release a statement regarding it."

Jameson steps in. "That could potentially wipe billions from your value."

I look at him. "I'm aware."

He doesn't say anything further, which I appreciate; my mind is made up.

I call Douglas and Kimberly, my COO, and fifteen minutes later, the three of us Zoom.

Kimberly agrees with me on my plan of attack. Douglas crunches numbers and comes back with his analysis that we can weather a storm if it eventuates. We then work through the afternoon and into the night reviewing our supply chain. After hours of digging into this, pulling our team in to help, we identify issues we didn't know we had, including the unapproved subcontracting of work. Just before 10:00 p.m., we finish work, ready with our plan for tomorrow.

I step out of my office, mentally drained and physically exhausted, and go in search of food. Jeff offered me dinner earlier, but I didn't want to stop to eat. Now, I'm starving.

Jameson is in the kitchen when I get there. "I was about to come looking for you," he says. "Are you hungry?"

I nod as I run my fingers through my hair, brushing it off my face.

He lifts his chin at the table. "Sit. I'll get your dinner."

"I can get it."

He gives me a look of pure Jameson. Frustration and impatience all rolled into one. "Sit."

"Why can't you just let me look after myself?"

More of that look. *A whole lot more of that look.* And then, he comes to me, takes hold of my hips, spins me around, and walks me to the table. Sitting me down, he orders, "If that ass leaves that chair, there will be hell to pay."

"I hope your next wife is a real ballbuster," I grumble as he goes back to the island.

"I don't intend on having any more wives after you."

I watch him get my dinner. "Really? You don't want to marry and have a family?"

"No."

As far as my team who did the research on him could ascertain, Jameson has never been married or engaged. The longest relationship they could find lasted a year, and he hasn't had many that got past the three-month mark. It seems Jameson doesn't do love.

He brings me a plate of chicken, rice, and salad, and as he puts it in front of me, he says, "I don't need another ballbuster. Not when I've already had one."

I watch him fold himself into the chair next to me. "I'll assume you're referring to a previous girlfriend."

His lips quirk but he doesn't respond to that. "How did things go with your plan?"

I eat some chicken. "I think we did well, considering what we're working with. Douglas is apprehensive about the decision I made, but he knows it's the only decision I will make." I pause as I think about the question I've had on repeat in my head since Hudson came to me with this. "Why was Hudson digging into my company?" God help Jameson if he's planning on stealing another company from me.

He looks at me knowingly. "Hudson handles my risk assessment and management. I asked him to keep abreast of any risks that threaten you."

I frown. "Why?"

"Because you're my wife."

"I'm not your actual wife, Jameson."

"That is true, but that doesn't mean I shouldn't protect you." He leans in close. "And before you tell me you're quite capable of protecting yourself, I am more than aware of that, but it doesn't hurt to have someone else looking out for you too."

His phone rings, and he leaves to take the call.

I watch him go, stunned at what he's just told me.

I'm quickly pulled from thinking about him, though, because Kimberly texts me to confirm our trip to London next week. We go back and forth on that, deciding to still go ahead with it even though we'll also be busy with the potential fallout from the statement we'll release tomorrow about our supply chain.

I finish eating dinner and take a shower before doing a little more work and crawling into bed at midnight. I text with Natalie for five minutes when she checks in to see how I am after working all night. I'm placing my phone down from that when Jameson comes into the bedroom.

"Did you hear from your mother?" he asks as he walks toward his bathroom.

"She texted. She's staying out tonight." With the man she just met.

He scowls. Blink, and you'd miss it, but I see it.

He then goes into his bathroom and showers.

I lie in bed while he's in there thinking about the sex we had today. And the promise he made me before he fucked me. The 'renegotiation of our marriage contract'.

It's shocking how happy I am about the new terms.

It's also shocking how much I enjoyed him fucking me in a fitting room.

By the time he emerges from the bathroom, I've moved back to thoughts of my company and the mess I have to get it out of.

"You won't sleep tonight, will you?" he asks as he slips under the bed covers.

I roll to face him. "I'll try." God knows I need it. Every muscle in my body feels like it's just climbed Mount Everest. But Jameson knows as well as I do that it's my brain I won't be able to switch off.

"Come here."

Who would have thought two words could affect me the way those two do?

"No."

"Adeline." The vibrations of his deep voice collide with the command he's issuing, causing a pulse of need in my core.

I reach up and flick the light off, putting us in darkness. "I'm not coming over there."

Before I know what's happening, his hand wraps tightly around mine and he pulls me across the bed to him. He manhandles me, bringing me to straddle him.

Bewildered, I place my hands to his bare chest and look down at him. I find it difficult to concentrate on anything but his hard dick that I want to do filthy things to, number one being to rub myself shamelessly all over it right now.

He switches the light back on and takes hold of my thighs. "I'm going to get you to sleep. And you're not going to argue with me."

I attempt to bring air into my lungs. It's kind of hard when he's got me on top of him while saying things like that and looking at me like he wants to devour me. "You told me to argue with you."

His eyes.

Oh God, those eyes.

I swear they do this thing where the color shifts from brown to black to brown again.

My vagina likes it a little too much.

Especially when his jaw does that thing it's doing now where it reveals all the things he's not saying.

"I didn't tell you to argue with me."

I can't stop myself; I rock my hips.

Jameson hisses and grips my thighs harder.

"I distinctly recall you telling me to."

"I told you to tone your arguing down."

I rock against him again. "That wasn't how I interpreted it."

"Interpret it that way now."

I move my hands over his chest as I drop my gaze to his tattooed arm. The fact I've started to find his ink hot is perplexing. In no scenario should I be into this eyesore that covers his arm. He's got a wolf on there, along with mountain peaks, tree branches that look like they're from a scary movie, wings, and a whole lot of swirls and other patterns mixed in. The only tattoo I like is the rose that covers the back of his hand. It's also got other patterns mixed in, but mostly it's a black rose and I find it quite beautiful.

"Who was the rose for?"

He finds my eyes. "My mother." He begins working his way down the buttons of my silk pajama top.

We watch each other in silence while he strips my top from me. I decide I'd like him to undress me like this daily. The sex we've had up to now has been fast and rough. This is slow and sexy, and I like it a lot.

He skims a finger under the top of my pajama bottoms, his light touch blazing heat over my skin. "Is there anything you won't do during sex?"

I keep hold of his eyes. "Sometimes you surprise me, Jameson." I wouldn't have expected him to ask about my sexual preferences; I'd have expected him to simply make his clear and wait for me to accept or reject.

His hand delves deeper, his fingers searching out my clit. "You have me boxed in a box I don't fit into."

I place both my hands to his chest and arch my back as he wakes my body up. "You put that box together for me all those years ago."

He circles the most amazing circles over my clit.

I'm adding circles to our contract.

"I made a business move, Adeline."

I join in on the circles, circling my hips. "It was hostile. We didn't want you."

"You made that clear when you all resigned."

"That was supposed to deter you." It was the defensive strategy my management team instigated when he swooped in. It failed. I took my team with me when I built my new company.

He stops with the circles and gives me two fingers. It's the best thing he's done all night and I clench around them, trying desperately to bring them in deeper, harder, faster.

His gaze drops to my body as he finally reaches deeper inside me. Roughly. And fuck me, how did I never know I prefer it rough? "I wanted you to stay, but I wanted the company more."

"You took advantage of me when I was down. That's a shitty thing to do."

"Fuck," he says, thrusting those fingers in faster, "it's business. And besides, I didn't know you were down."

I reach for the headboard, resting my hand against it as I lean forward and fuck his fingers. "That's not how I do business."

Jameson's other hand comes to my breast. "It should be."

"And there you go"—oh, God, the way he's pinching my nipple is everything—"thinking your way is best." I press my hand harder against his chest as I use it for leverage. "Not everyone wants to do business your way."

"No," he says, pinching my nipple harder, "but most do. Most, except you."

I secretly like the frustration lacing his words.

Secretly, because I will never tell another soul that I find his frustration hot these days.

My vagina, though, she's an audacious bitch. She has no qualms letting Jameson know all the things she finds hot.

She contracts and clenches and practically throws

him his very own party to say 'Good job, Sir.' By the time this orgasm is finished with me, he'll have zero doubt that she really likes his fingers, his frustration, his everything.

My orgasm moves straight into another one.

Wave upon wave, it doesn't end.

I close my eyes and ride it.

Every cell in my body feels it.

Pleasure like I've never experienced.

I get lost in it.

Clenching, reaching for more, *needing* more.

God, how I need more.

Jameson does his growling and cursing thing, but I am lost. Completely and utterly ruined by the orgasms he's giving me.

And then, he's got me in his hands, he's flipped me onto my back, he's got our pants off, he's on top of me, and he's slamming his dick inside me, all while making those sounds he makes that my vagina is here for.

He grips my hands and pins them to the bed with my arms spread wide, and he fucks me like it's the only mission he has in life.

I press one foot to the bed, wrap the other one around him, find his rhythm, and take everything he's got to give.

And holy fuck if he doesn't figure out how to ruin me some more.

He comes right after me, pressing my hands harder into the mattress while his orgasm takes over.

He drops his head to my shoulder for a quick moment before pulling out of me. He lets go of my hands but keeps his to the bed while he looks down at me. "I need a list of what you won't do."

Right now, I don't have the ability to even breathe; I

certainly don't have the ability to deal with his methodical, ordered way of doing things.

"I'm not giving you a list. Jesus, that's not how I do sex."

His eyes shift from brown to black and back again. "I'll take that to mean everything's on the table."

"Everything is most definitely not on the table."

He works his jaw. "Adeline."

I put my hands to his chest and attempt to push him away. He's too strong for me, though, and I barely move him. "Get off me."

"Not until we finish this conversation."

"It's finished. You can put in the work to discover my preferences."

"This conversation isn't for me to discover what you like. I'm more than happy to learn that for myself. This conversation is for me to know what not to do."

"I'm not into pain. You can do anything but hurt me. And just so we're clear, your dick would hurt me if you tried to fuck my ass, so no anal."

His eyes search mine like he's trying to get a read on me. "I would ensure it wouldn't hurt."

"There's no way it wouldn't, Jameson." Surely, he's aware of just how big he is.

He takes that in before finally nodding and moving off me to walk into his bathroom.

I leave the bed and go into my bathroom to take another shower.

Jameson made good on his promise to help me sleep. I'm already nearly there.

Multiple orgasms, it turns out, are the key.

I make a note that I'm going to have to find a man

who's just as talented at delivering them as Jameson is after I divorce him.

I CALL an emergency board meeting Sunday morning, and after getting their agreement, I release the statement regarding my supply chain. We then quickly move onto the damage control part of the plan I put together with my team.

Unfortunately, this means I have to skip Christmas tree shopping with Jameson's family. It also means I miss out on making a gingerbread house with Reese. That might be my biggest disappointment of the day.

One: I've never made a gingerbread house. I've also never taken part in Christmas activities like this.

And two: I won't be married to Jameson next Christmas, so this was my one chance at spending this time with his mother.

She sends him home in the afternoon with Nutella Swirled Meringue cookies. He's tightlipped when I ask him how she knows I love Nutella. I refuse to share them with him, but he threatens to skip my orgasm tonight if I don't, so I relent and give him one. We both know there's no way he's skipping my orgasm, though.

He fucked me before hitting his gym this morning and he fucks me again before I go to bed.

Jameson leaves me after we have sex to go and do some work, but before he goes, he asks me about my mom. She returned just before lunch, packed her belongings, told me she'd come visit again soon, and left.

I look at him while he puts his shirt on. He took a

quick shower after sex and came back into the bedroom without that shirt on. It's disgraceful how much I never want him to wear a shirt again.

"I think she's gone home. But maybe she's gone to stay with that guy she just met." I shrug. "Who knows with Frances."

He watches me carefully. "You would have preferred her to stay longer?"

It strikes me that out of all the men I've dated and had relationships with, including my ex-husband, none of them have dug into my relationship with my mother like Jameson is. That's possibly because I've given strong 'don't bring it up' vibes, but I did that with him too, and he chose to ignore all those vibes.

He's chosen to take a shovel and do the digging for me.

"I would have preferred to have a mother who wants to spend time with me."

The other thing that strikes me about him? I never have to say very much. He understands without a million words having to be said. And I know by the way the lines on his face settle differently with the new information that he understands perfectly.

He runs his fingers through his hair after putting that shirt on, and with a nod at what I've said, he asks, "Do you want a drink or anything?"

This moment feels unlike any after we've had sex. Asking me about my mom, asking if I want a drink. I don't know what to do with these things. These aren't moves that belong in the Jameson Fox sex playbook.

It's confusing and I need it not to be.

He's not getting me a drink.

"No, thank you. And if you're thinking of stealing another meringue cookie while you're in the kitchen, you should stop that now. The rest are mine."

He gives me an amused look. "We'll see."

And then he's gone, and I'm left in a state of "what the fuck?"

I'm sleepy after having sex with him and am hopeful I'll sleep like a baby, the same as I did last night.

As I snuggle against my pillow, I decide Jameson's bed is the most comfortable bed I've ever slept in.

And I make a note to buy one for myself when I move back home.

MONDAY HITS LIKE A SLEDGEHAMMER.

She comes in fast.

She comes in hard.

And she comes in ready to decimate.

Jameson nailed it when he said my decision to be transparent about the factories my company has worked with could wipe billions off my company value.

I erased just over one billion yesterday. Douglas is confident more will be wiped out today.

I spend time this morning on a call with investors, trying to allay their concerns. I assure them we'll move through this and be stronger for it.

It's a difficult sell, though. Social media and the tabloids are ablaze today with more bullshit about me. This time around, it doesn't focus on my family, thankfully. However, it concentrates on whether I'm the right person to lead the company now. There are numerous lies published about my personal life that all tie to an overall narrative that I'm not fit for the job anymore.

Jameson is brought into it.

He is my husband, after all, so they point out he must know all about my shady dealings.

I was ready to answer calls from investors about the company.

I was not ready for this.

And all I can think is I took my fucking eye off the ball somewhere along the line.

Again.

This stirs up too many memories and bad feelings from when I lost Chatoyer to Jameson.

I lost that company because I was busy trying to save a marriage that should never have been a thing in the first place, let alone be saved.

When Jameson calls me just after lunch, I snap at him. Not because he's done anything, but because he's twisted up in all my feelings of failure from five years ago. "I'm busy. If you're calling to order me to do something or be somewhere, I don't have time for it today." It's completely unfair to him; he hasn't done any of those things recently, but why else would he be calling?

Full points to the man. He doesn't go near my bad mood. He doesn't pull out his impatience. And he doesn't call me out. He simply says, with more patience than I thought he had in him, "How are you?"

Those three words slow all my jittery, irrational thoughts down.

They cause me to release the air trapped in my lungs.

"I hate this day."

"This day will end at some point."

"And then it'll be tomorrow, and I'll probably hate it too."

"Tomorrow will also end at some point."

I release more air. "Are you always like this in the middle of a crisis?"

"Like what?"

"Like this!" I wave my hand in the air even though he can't see it. "So calm and logical." How do men do this? It irritates me. Mostly because I want to be calm and logical right now and I'm finding that harder with each passing moment. "Although," I mutter, "it makes sense. You're always so damn methodical."

"I don't let the bullshit get in the way."

"I don't let the bullshit in," I say with indignation.

"I never said you do."

"You implied it."

"Fuck," he curses. "Don't twist my words."

A text comes through from Douglas who needs to go over some figures with me.

"I have to go." I pause. "Thank you for checking in. I'm sorry this is affecting you too."

"You know I don't give a fuck about any of that."

"I know, but you will if it affects your company."

"It's not going to, Adeline. Don't blow this up in your mind. You'll take a hit. You'll rebuild. End of story."

"That's not what you said the other day."

"What the fuck did I say the other day?"

"You pointed out that this would wipe billions off my value."

"I didn't say that because I thought you couldn't rebuild."

And just like that, he steals something from me.

Something *else* from me.

Something I'm not sure I want to let him steal.

I know from the way his voice lost its hard edges that Jameson didn't tell me my company would lose value in case I wasn't aware of that fact.

He said it because he was concerned for me.

Worried about me.

And now, he's called me because of that worry.

"I have to go," I say. I do have to go, but I also need space from this conversation.

We end the call and I gather myself for the conversation I'm about to have with Douglas. God knows what news he has for me now.

While I wait for him to arrive, my mind loops back to Jameson.

I'm going to need that sliver of my heart back that he just stole.

When I divorce him, I'm taking it along with my company.

There's no way I can allow him to keep either.

~

TUESDAY DOESN'T HIT any easier than Monday.

On top of that, Vanessa calls early to let me know she has to take the week off to help her mom who is in the middle of a divorce. The timing for me isn't ideal, but I feel for her and her mother. I'll make do without her.

"You're flying out at eleven?" Jameson says after he fucks me in my bathroom. He's referring to my flight to London this morning.

I'd just finished showering when he returned from his

gym all sweaty. After he caught sight of me in my towel in the bedroom, he was like an animal, all over me. Well, animal is excessive, but honestly, I was clean, I wasn't looking for sex, and there he was, unable to stop himself.

I was unable to say no.

My vagina, after all, has it bad for him.

When I smacked him away and told him he was too sweaty for me, he forced me back into my shower and fucked me in there.

I meet his gaze in the mirror as he moves behind me at the vanity. "Yes, eleven."

"Call me when you arrive."

"Okay." I'm unsure why he wants a call, though. His flight crew will keep him updated, I'm sure. Jameson's people have their eyes and ears everywhere. I'm under no illusion he doesn't know where I am at all times, and what I'm doing.

He drops me at work with a kiss for the world to see. He's started them up again this week. I'm not complaining.

Douglas goes over the half billion wiped from the company overnight when I arrive at the office. Lara details the social media storm we're still in. I work on thinking like Jameson would.

I do okay at it, but I will never be a Jameson Fox. I just don't have that in me. I will always be led by my emotions, even in business. And I decide that's okay. That's what makes me, me.

I've kicked ass in my life, and I will continue kicking ass.

Kimberly and I board Jameson's jet just before 11:00 a.m. and fly to London. I don't leave behind the things troubling me, but I do find the change in scenery refreshing.

I call Jameson when I arrive at the hotel. It's almost 8:00 p.m. for him and I hear that he's distracted by something.

"Everything okay?" I ask, kicking my shoes off.

"Yeah."

Yeah, no, he's definitely distracted.

"What's going on? I can hear it in your voice. You're off."

He's silent for a moment. And then, he blows out a breath. I imagine him doing something with his hair. Probably pushing his fingers through it like he's trying to control it in the same way he controls everything. "The woman I hired to guide us through fixing our hotel business is giving me hell."

A laugh bubbles out of me before I can stop it. "Oh my God, that is the best thing I've heard all day."

He sounds less than impressed by that. "I'm glad you find it amusing. I do not."

I wedge my phone between my shoulder and my ear so I can free my hands to undo my jeans. Shimmying out of them, I kick them aside with my shoes. I breathe out with relief as I do this.

"What are you doing?" Jameson asks.

"I just took my jeans off. They were slowly killing me."

"Fuck." The curse drops from his lips with rough, hot energy, slamming into me with the same kind of heat I know he's feeling from that one word.

"Right, back to your woman who's giving you hell," I

say, breathlessly. I'm going to have to take care of myself after this call now.

"No," he says, switching us to a FaceTime call.

His face fills my screen, and my vagina instantly lets me know she is here for this.

"Take your hair down," he says, his voice all gravel in a way it wasn't a minute ago.

"No."

Approval flares in his eyes. Right before he growls, "Adeline."

I pull a chair across from the bed and set my phone on it, propping it up so it's at the height I want it.

Standing in front of the phone, I turn to face the bed. I bend over and place my hands on the end of the bed.

Jameson says something I can't quite make out, but I can hear it in his voice that he's enjoying this.

Looking back at the screen, I say, "What do you want me to do?"

"I want you to take your fucking hair down." More of that gravel and need all rolled into one.

I smile sexily at him.

I don't take my hair down.

I mean, I didn't ask him what he wanted me to do in order to obey his directive.

Instead, I arch my back and sway my hips from side to side.

I then reach a hand back and hook my fingers into my panties.

I slide one side down to reveal one cheek.

My underwear hits the floor a few moments later.

I continue swaying my hips, giving him a show.

I then lean forward, drop to my forearms, and bend

even more. So Jameson can see everything he wants to see.

Glancing back at him, I note the look in his eyes and the movement of his upper arm.

"Show me your dick."

"I should give you a taste of your own medicine," he says, but he doesn't. He angles his phone down so I can see his hand working his dick.

My hand goes instantly to my clit.

Fuck.

It's like I can feel his dick even though it's nowhere near me.

This isn't going to last long.

I can get myself off in minutes if I want.

I can also drag it out if I want.

Right now, I'm not sure I'd be able to slow myself down even if I tried.

"Show me your cunt," he orders, and I sag a little against the bed as a wave of need hits.

I turn and sit on the end of the bed.

I spread my legs wide for him, feet up on the edge of the mattress.

And I push a finger inside while continuing to rub my clit with my other hand.

"How close are you?" I ask.

"Close." It's practically a grunt. A course, crude, deeply masculine sound that calls to my feminine core in ways only he ever has.

I orgasm.

I close my eyes as every muscle I have contracts, spasms, tenses.

It's intense.

It's bliss.

It's everything I need right now.

And then Jameson's coming.

I hear him before I see him.

When I open my eyes, I watch him lose himself. It's one of the hottest things I've done. Sitting in a hotel room in another country and still affecting him this way? We need to do this again.

"Tomorrow, you'll take your hair down for me."

"Tomorrow, you'll get what you're given."

He brings a glass to his lips and takes a sip of what I presume is whiskey while we both recover.

"I'll let you go so you can get back to figuring out how to handle that woman who's giving you hell," I say, moving off the bed to grab my phone. I bring it closer to my face so I can see him better.

"Did you hate today?"

My breaths slow as I stare at him through the screen. "It wasn't as bad as yesterday," I say softly.

"Good."

"Goodnight, Jameson."

"Sleep well," he says, and then he's gone, and I'm left with an ache I know I'm going to have to take care of before I can think about sleep.

I'm also left with a whole lot of something else my heart knows it shouldn't be feeling.

Goddam that man.

19

Adeline

My trip to London is a success. Thank fuck, because not much else this week feels like a success. And while I'm usually good at not letting things get to me, this is getting to me.

Analysts downgraded my company to 'hold' from 'buy' on Wednesday. Jameson assured me that won't last. Douglas did too. It didn't escape me that I listened to Jameson maybe a little more than my CFO.

Kimberly and I shortlisted a few sites in London for our flagship store there. We also identified other sites in the UK to consider for stores outside of London. It was a hectic trip, not just because we had a lot of sites to tour, but also because we spent a lot of time putting out work fires.

I have no idea why the fake stories about me have

amped up this week, but it feels like someone has it in for me. And that's not a thought I've ever had. I'm used to social media and the waves that the good and bad come in, but this is next level. There's no good to be found and I can't help but wonder if someone is targeting me.

My team is stressed. They're not saying that to me, but I can hear it every time we talk. I've had to double down on remaining calm and strong in the face of everything. They need that from me. Hell, I need that from me. But by the time I board Jameson's jet to fly back to New York on Friday, I'm beginning to crumble.

"Call me on your way home," he says as I buckle myself in for the flight.

I'm tired, so I don't have the energy to keep my thoughts to myself. "Surely your pilot will check in with you. Or your security guys. Or Max. Why do you need me to update you on my whereabouts?"

"Adeline," he says in that bossy voice of his that makes me think of the last time he used it on me. *Last night.* I finally let my hair down for him last night. "Call me."

"Fine," I mutter. "I have to go." I watch as the plane door is armed.

We end the call and I check my emails one last time before putting my phone away. I then pull out my laptop and go over reports Douglas has sent through, as well as reports from my other executives.

The flight is around seven hours but feels like seventy.

We arrive in New York just after 1:00 p.m. and I call Jameson once Max has me on the way to my office.

"You're going to the office?" he asks.

"You know I'm going to the office." Someone would have told him already.

"You need sleep."

I sigh. "I know, but I also need to get through a lot of work before I can even think about sleep."

"Have you heard from Vanessa?"

There's something about the way Jameson remembers the things I tell him. The things that are important to me. He may suck at remembering to share information about social engagements he's added to his calendar, but he's good at remembering the little things that are big to me.

"She called me this morning. She's taking another week off. It's Christmas, after all, and I think her mom needs her."

A text comes through, and I check it.

Reese: Darling, are you home now?

I smile. "Your mom just texted."

"I hope you're prepared for tomorrow. I've warned her you'll likely be unavailable for ice-skating this weekend, but you should expect her to drop by for a quick visit. She's worried about you."

Warmth floods me. It fills every space in my body. Even the spaces that are resistant to letting in anyone or anything that feels warm. "I'm going ice-skating. I'm not letting these fuckers stop me from that."

"There's the Adeline I know," he murmurs.

I release a long breath as I stare out at the city passing me by. "It's been a long week. I don't think I've ever felt this unsettled and unsure. But you were right that day you said I'm not a quitter. I'm not. I will never just lie down and give up."

"Good," he says, and it feels like he needed to hear that from me. Like that was the whole reason for this call.

We end the call and I go back to Reese's text.

Adeline: I just got in. I'm on my way to the office.

Reese: I'm glad. How are you?

Adeline: Tired. Looking forward to tomorrow.

Reese: If you can't make it, I'll be sure to send more cookies home with Jameson for you. I baked Vanilla-Butter Sugar cookies yesterday. Jameson already ate five of them, but I saved some for you.

And just like that, Jameson's mother causes tears to well in my eyes.

I haven't heard from my mother since she left last weekend. I don't even know if she's still in New York or back home. And not for lack of reaching out to her. She hasn't bothered to return any of my calls or texts.

And here's Reese texting me, asking Jameson how I am, worrying about me, and saving me cookies.

Adeline: Thank you, Reese. This means the world to me. I'll see you tomorrow xx

Reese: I'm looking forward to it, darling xx

An hour later, I'm knee-deep in work at my office. I sit through a three-hour meeting with my top executives, and we go over the UK and European expansion plans. We also go over where the company stands after this week and strategize the way forward. Mario catches me after I leave the meeting, and we spend an hour working on fashion week prep.

I work by myself after he leaves and I'm starting to think about food at around 8:00 p.m. when Jameson strides into my office carrying bags of takeout.

I look up from my laptop and blink at him. My eyes

are sore from all the computer work I've done today. "Hi." I watch him place the takeout on the coffee table in front of my sofa. "I wasn't expecting you."

He eyes me. "Shantel checked in on you. She insisted I deliver you food."

I frown as I push my chair back and stand. "What do you mean that she checked in on me? I haven't heard from her."

"She called your assistant who told her you haven't eaten since you got in."

I watch as he removes his suit jacket, sits on the edge of the sofa, and begins loading two plates with Korean chicken. I am here for that chicken.

"You're wearing a three-piece today," I say, walking toward him. The only time I've ever seen Jameson in a three-piece suit was on our wedding day.

He glances up from our food. He doesn't respond to what I've said as his gaze drops to my body. Like he was distracted on the way to opening his mouth to speak.

"You almost never wear a three-piece." I take the seat next to him.

My eyes are all over him in the same way his are over me.

I can never go past his forearms when he's got his shirt sleeves rolled up. Which is always, so that's a lot of not going past those arms.

"I had a board meeting today," he says, still distracted. His gaze appears permanently fixed on my legs, which are visible thanks to the short leather skirt I'm wearing. Since it's winter, I haven't been wearing skirts. I'm only wearing this one because it's a new design we're considering, and I was testing it this afternoon.

"I'm not taking this skirt off. Or taking my hair down."

He finally gives me back his eyes. "I don't need the skirt off or the hair down for what I want to do."

Jesus.

I jab my finger at the food. "Finish serving our dinner. I'm hungry."

The look he gives me tells me he plans to revisit this, but for now, he goes back to the food.

We eat and discuss our afternoons. He shares with me that his biggest rival in the hotel industry is fucking with him, his words, not mine, and that he's spent time today with Hudson figuring out how to fix that once and for all. Those were not his words, but I read between the lines and come to that conclusion.

Jameson is not a man I would want as my rival in business. I have no doubt he, Hudson, and Gabriel don't hesitate to take care of their rivals when necessary. In whatever way necessary.

After he finishes sharing this, he says, "Bill wants to have dinner with us tomorrow night. I told him you may be unavailable."

"No, I think I should be okay for dinner. Are we going out or will he come over?"

"What would work best for you?"

I stop mid-bite of chicken and stare at him. "Okay, who are you really?" At his pulled-in brows, I elaborate. "This"—I motion between us—"isn't how you prefer to do things."

His eyes remain steady on me. "No, but I've learned it's how you prefer to do things, and since I'm also learning that my life is a lot fucking easier if you're happy, this is how we do things now."

"Right, so for future reference, in case you change your mind and decide to find another wife after me, skipping the bit about your life being a lot fucking easier if I'm happy would have made that a good talk."

His impatience flares. "Can we get back to the conversation?"

I'd enjoy it to no end to not get back to the conversation, and to stay with this one instead, but I don't push him. "Staying home would work best for me."

He nods. "We'll stay home."

We finish our meal, keeping the conversation light. I get the impression Jameson has had a long day, and I don't have the energy for anything more than light. We talk about Christmas which is two days away. I mention the cookies his mom made that he ate five of, telling him that if he touches the ones she gives me, he will live to regret it. We also discuss the logistics of tomorrow and getting to the ice-skating rink after lunch.

It feels positively like married-couple life.

If I wasn't so tired, I'd inspect that thought a lot more, but since I'm exhausted, I don't.

When he stands and lifts his chin at me, I frown.

"We're going home," he says, packing up the takeout.

"I've got more work to do."

"You can do it at home."

"I don't want to do it at home."

He straightens and gives me that pure Jameson look. "You're doing it at home. I'm not leaving without you." When I give him my pure Adeline look, he doubles down. "Up. We're going. And if you continue arguing with me, I'll put you over my knee."

If I had the energy, I'd continue arguing with him.

Sadly, I don't.

SATURDAY IS BUSY WITH WORK, ice-skating, dinner with Bill, and more work. I'm so busy I struggle to catch my breath. This means that I wake super tired on Christmas Eve. We've got dinner with Jameson's family tonight at his mom's. Being this tired is the last thing I want today.

"Did you hear back from your sister or mother," Jameson asks, joining me in the kitchen for breakfast after working out and showering.

"Yes." I watch him from where I stand at the island as he moves to the fridge. "Sabrina will come for lunch tomorrow."

He grabs the milk and looks at me. "And your mom?"

"We won't see her." I try to inject indifference into my voice. By the look on his face, I fail.

When he opens his mouth to say something, I shake my head and cut him off. "No, we're not doing this. She's not coming. End of story."

I go back to spreading jam on my toast.

I'm in the middle of doing that when Jameson moves behind me, places his hand to my hip and brings his mouth to my ear. "Not end of story. You're hurt. Don't hide that away."

My breathing slows down as my brain attempts to get a handle on what is happening here. "Jameson, don't."

He turns me to face him. "Don't what?"

"Don't do *this*. It's confusing. You're not my husband when it's just the two of us. You don't need to act like one."

He works his jaw. "I'm not acting like a husband. I'm acting like a man who gives a fuck about the woman in his life. You may not be my wife, but that doesn't mean I can't worry about you. I am not the man you have in that fucking box, Adeline, so please don't treat me like him."

He's right; I do treat him like that man in the box. Not all the time, but whenever I get confused, I revert to thinking he's the Jameson I thought he was. That's not fair to him.

"I'm sorry," I say softly. "I hated you for so long and had such a vivid idea of who I thought you were that it's hard to let that Jameson go."

"Let it go. I won't tolerate it much longer." His eyes are dark like the reaction I've inspired.

I nod. I didn't realize he felt so strongly about this.

"I've got some work to do this morning," he says, moving to the coffee machine. "I was thinking we'd leave for Mom's around two this afternoon?"

"I'll be ready."

He looks at me. "That works for you?"

I smile. "Yes." He really is trying here.

"Okay."

He makes his coffee and takes it with him when he leaves to go to his office.

I release a long breath when I'm alone. I then reach for my phone to send Natalie a text.

Adeline: I want to go back to denial. It was easier there.

Natalie: It really wasn't. You don't recall how assholey MA was back then?

Adeline: At least I knew what the fuck was going on.

This new place I'm in is messy and confusing and OMG how am I going to survive eleven more months of it?

Natalie: Just have sex all the time. Confused about something? Fuck him. Hate him over something? Fuck him. Feeling weird about something? Fuck him.

Adeline: How are you even a therapist? Is this the advice you hand out all day, every day?

Natalie: I'm seriously contemplating it. World peace, here we come.

Adeline: Okay, but I actually need your real advice now. Tell me what to do.

Natalie: Right, so this is the part where I remind you that most people don't go around pretend marrying people. I'm not actually skilled in handing out advice for how to make it through a year of a fake marriage. But once you complete your mission, we'll pow wow and figure out a game plan for next time, 'k?

Adeline: We are in another war. Just FYI.

Natalie: I complete you. Just FYI.

I skip breakfast.

I'm not hungry. Not after that conversation with Jameson.

This isn't how it was supposed to go.

I was supposed to hate him for the entire year, succeed at staying married to him, and get my company back.

It was going to be hard, but I was going to do it.

This place we've come to now? I'm beginning to think it might be harder to survive.

Yes, I like that Jameson is more considerate of me now.

Yes, I like that I get to have sex with him.

Yes, I like the ease of being with him.

Yes, I like that I get to spend time with his family.

But him stealing slivers of my heart along the way?

That was not what I signed up for.

I need to remind myself that he's only in this for what he will get out of it at the end.

And that's not me.

It's Bill's company.

20

Jameson

"How's Adeline holding up?" Hudson asks after Christmas dinner.

I eye her talking with Mom and Bill as I drink some of my whiskey. "She's exhausted but hanging in there." She's hanging in there better than many others I've seen in the same position.

"It was a gutsy move going public like she did."

It was. Gabriel, who came to Hudson with the information, advised us he could handle the situation for her quietly. The chance would have existed that it could still blow up for her, but knowing Gabriel's skills, the chance would have been low. However, the thing I've come to know about Adeline is that she wouldn't have wanted the situation handled in that way. I didn't mention it to her because I know she would have said no.

She's not only made of grit and determination; she's held together by the kind of honesty and purity I rarely see.

Bill catches my eye, and after excusing himself from Mom and Adeline, comes our way. Hudson leaves us so we can talk alone.

"Marriage is good for you," Bill says while watching Adeline laugh at something Hudson says.

"Yes." He's watched us closely tonight, still looking for a sign this marriage isn't what he's being led to believe it is.

"I'm happy for you, Jameson."

Something in his voice draws my full attention. The doubt I've heard for months appears to have almost disappeared.

"From the moment you came to work with me," he continues, "I've watched you fight against this. Against being happy. You haven't allowed yourself the chance at it." He eyes Adeline again. "Adeline makes you happy, and that's all I've wanted for you."

I look at her.

Bill's right; she's brought something into my life I didn't have before. Even with all her arguing, and fighting to keep that wall up between us, she's changed my life for the better.

I don't work as much as I did before.

I look forward to coming home at night.

I think about others more.

Hell, I even breathe differently. Easier.

"Life is better with her in it," I say, meaning every word. This isn't all for show anymore.

"As it should be." He takes a sip of his drink. "I start radiation in two weeks."

"Good. You'll let us know if you need help with anything?"

He nods as Adeline joins us.

She slips her arm around my waist and looks up at me. "I'm sorry to interrupt, but I think you need to take me home. I'm almost falling asleep."

"Yes," Bill agrees. "That sounds like a good idea. You're exhausted."

I gather the presents my family gave us as she says goodbye to Mom.

"I want you to get as much sleep as you can tomorrow, darling," Mom says before hugging Adeline.

I watch as Adeline returns the hug. She's building a close relationship with Mom. It gives me pause, because these two are emotional women. I fear it will hit them both hard when our divorce goes through. Adeline will be prepared for that; Mom won't be.

"Jameson," Mom says. "Do not eat Adeline's chocolate that I gave her. You have your own."

I eye Adeline with amusement before looking back at Mom. "I might like cookies and cake, but that's nothing compared to Adeline's chocolate addiction."

Adeline smacks me playfully. "Hush. That's our secret."

I lift my chin at her. "Let's get you home."

She gives Mom one last kiss and thanks her for a wonderful Christmas dinner, pulls Hudson in for a goodbye hug, and says farewell to Bill. She then follows me down to my car.

"There's something sexy about watching you drive a car," she says from the passenger side when I slide in behind the wheel. "I'm glad you gave your staff some time off."

I drive us out of the garage and into traffic. "It's a shame you're so exhausted." It's not often I drive, or that I have her alone in a car. I'd like to make the most of it.

She shifts in her seat, angling her body my way. "Does your mind have filthy thoughts running through it twenty-four-seven or just when you're with me?"

I reach for her hand and bring it to my dick. "These days, they never stop."

She removes my hand. "You're right, it's a shame I'm so exhausted. I can think of so many things I could do right now if I wasn't so tired."

"Fuck," I curse, curving my hand around the back of her head and pulling it toward me as I stop the car at a red light.

She smacks my hand away. "I'm not sucking your dick in this weather."

"We're not out in the weather."

"You're driving in it. Honestly, Jameson, I know your mother would have taught you about safety."

I look at her. "You know I'm good with risk." I drop my eyes to her chest that she's done a good job of covering today with a high-neck sweater. I've spent half the fucking night thinking about removing that sweater.

"Stop ogling me and watch where you're driving. The light's green again."

I focus on getting us home safely. She's right that this weather isn't the best to be driving in.

We chat about dinner on the drive. Adeline gushes about the food Mom made. She goes into detail about each dish, telling me exactly what she loved about it. I've never discussed a meal in this way, and while I wouldn't usually have the interest or patience to sit through a review like this, I don't check out of this one. I'm almost certain she could spend more time going over it and I'd stick around for that.

She then tells me she loves the watch Mom gave her for Christmas and the gift certificate Hudson gave her for one of the most popular spas in New York.

Adeline may not have been ready for a Fox Christmas two weeks ago, but she handled it in style. And if the happy glow on her face is anything to go by, she enjoyed it.

As I pull the car into my garage, a text hits both our phones. I assume it's from Mom in the group chat she insists on. But Adeline reads the messages and laughs before saying, "I think I adore Shantel."

I park the car and cut the engine. "Why?"

"She's discovered a clash in our schedules. She says she'll do her best to rearrange your thing because it'd be sad for you not to attend my thing, which is a party in a club that she knows you're absolutely dying to go to."

Jesus.

Shantel knows I detest nights out at clubs.

These two will be the death of me. This isn't the first time Shantel has rearranged my schedule in favor of Adeline.

Adeline replies to the text before frowning. "Why is she working today?"

"That's not by my choice. She doesn't have family in New York, so she tends to work over Christmas."

She looks horrified. "Why didn't we invite her over? You should call her and tell her to come over tomorrow."

I arch my brows. "Tell, not ask?"

"Well, that's your preferred way of doing things."

"She's not coming over."

"Why not?"

"You're sleeping tomorrow. Nothing's getting in the way of that. And besides, Shantel likes spending Christmas by herself. She's not a fan of being with people unless she absolutely has to."

"I could sleep in the morning, and she could come in the afternoon or evening."

"No, no one is interrupting your sleep. Now, get your ass out of the car and upstairs. I'm putting you to bed."

"I don't have the energy for your style of putting someone to bed."

"I'm not fucking you."

"So, you're literally putting me to bed like I'm a child?"

I curse.

I get out of the car.

I walk around to her side and open her door.

I pull her out of the car.

I back her up against it.

I thread my fingers through her hair.

"One of these days, you'll do what I say without argument," I growl before crashing my lips down onto hers.

I kiss her deeply and thoroughly, something I've been thinking about doing for far too many hours.

I grind my dick against her. There's no way I can't. I'm hard as hell for her and will have to take care of myself after she goes to bed.

She moans into my mouth, sliding her tongue over mine, begging for more from me.

I give her more, losing myself in it.

When I finally let her go, she grips my shirt and keeps me close, not ready to let me go yet. Her eyes are sparkling, her breaths are coming fast, her body is alive. "One of these days, you'll realize I'll never stop arguing with you."

I keep her in my arms for a minute, taking her beauty in, taking her essence in.

No woman has ever held my attention like Adeline does.

I was aware of that during our engagement period, but I assumed it was because I was focused on getting us to the wedding day and then getting us through the year of marriage. I assumed she was in my thoughts so much because of my ultimate goal.

She fought her way through those three months like she was put on this earth to fight with me. And I don't doubt she'll fight with me until the very last day of our marriage.

I also don't doubt that she'll keep my attention all that time too.

I tighten my hold on her. "Don't ever change. Not for me. Not for the world. Not for anyone."

I let her go and collect our gifts and the food Mom insisted we bring home.

Adeline attempts to help me.

I refuse her help.

She argues with me over it.

I tell her to get her ass upstairs.

She's still arguing with me over the fact she'd rather

do things for herself when we step out of the elevator in my penthouse.

Jeff meets us as she launches into a new argument. "Sir, you have a guest."

We weren't expecting anyone, so I'm wondering who when Adeline's sister joins us. She looks to Adeline first before bringing her eyes to mine. "Surprise!"

The first time I met Sabrina, I was struck by how different she and Adeline are. Not just in looks, but in personality.

Where Adeline is classy, sincere, and confident to her core, Sabrina isn't any of those things.

She's loud and rude. Disrespectful to her sister. She lacks belief in herself and compensates by treating others badly. She's critical and judgmental, especially of Adeline. And if my gut isn't wrong, she's deceitful.

Sabrina is always looking for how she can get more out of others.

She's a taker, and I have no time for parasites like her.

"Sabrina," Adeline says, clearly surprised to see her sister. She hugs her and moves through the motions of welcoming her, but I see the stiffness in her body, the wariness. "I thought you were coming tomorrow."

Sabrina shrugs. "I wanted to come today. Is it a big deal?"

Adeline quickly shakes her head. "No. I'm so glad to see you."

Fuck, I've never heard Adeline like this.

Filled with nervous energy.

She's walking on eggshells with her own fucking family.

Sabrina shoots a smile my way. "So, what's the plan for tonight? Some drinks? Some fun?"

"Your sister's tired. She's going to bed," I say in no uncertain terms.

Adeline touches my arm, giving me a small frown. "Jameson," she murmurs. Then, looking back at Sabrina, she says, "I'll get some wine. We'll catch up."

I want to tell her she can do that tomorrow, after she's rested, but I keep my mouth shut.

Adeline heads into the kitchen ahead of Sabrina who gives me a look that can only be interpreted as sexy.

I leave them to it and go into my office.

I've been in there working for an hour and a half when Hudson calls.

"Have you seen?" he asks.

I lean back in my chair. "Seen what?"

"Check your messages. I just sent you a link."

I open my messages and find his. The link takes me to a *New York Times* article detailing the drop in my company's share price this week. It mentions sensitive information regarding the work Paulina is doing for me and the reason for that. Information that hasn't been made public. It also touches on my marriage and Adeline's plummeting share price.

"Who the fuck gave her this information?"

"Gabriel's looking into it." He pauses before saying what I already know. "This isn't good, brother."

He's right. It'll likely stir investor concern.

"I'll make some calls. Put their fears to rest." I rake my fingers through my hair. "Tell Gabriel to work fast. Whoever did this needs to fucking go."

After our call, I'm angry enough that I know I won't

sleep unless I work some of this anger out of my system, so I change into my gym clothes and head into my gym. Adeline isn't in the bedroom, which tells me she's still with Sabrina.

I work out for just over an hour, and when I walk into the kitchen afterward to get a drink, I run into Sabrina.

"Oh, hello there," she says, her eyes all over me, her voice far too sexy to use with the man she thinks of as her brother-in-law. Moving toward me, she takes a sip of the wine she's holding. "Is this a thing for you?"

I pour myself a glass of water. "Is what a thing for me?"

She motions her hand up and down at my body. "Getting all hot and sweaty at midnight."

This conversation is pointless, so I don't bother answering her. "Where's your sister?"

She moves into my space and trails her long, clawlike fingernails down my chest. "We don't need her."

My first instinct is to remove her hand from my body and tell her to get the fuck out of my penthouse. My second is to consider Adeline in this decision. It's an odd fucking occurrence that I even have a second instinct because that's not how I normally function.

I remove her hand. "Why are you here, Sabrina?"

Doubt flashes in her eyes. That, and the way her body also loses some confidence, leads me to believe she's not used to being told no from men. "I'm here to spend time with Adeline for Christmas."

"How much cash do you need?"

Now, anger flares across her face. "I don't need anything."

"I don't believe you. Tell me, do you ever plan to stop

bleeding money from your sister? Or is that just your job now?"

Her lip pulls up in a sneer. "Fuck you. You know nothing about me."

"I know you're always asking Adeline for money."

"Well, she has it and I don't."

"Plenty of people don't have it. Those people get their asses to work. They don't sponge off their family for life."

"You don't get to come into our family and tell us how to live. You're only married to Adeline, not me and Mom."

"And as such, it's my job to protect her. From where I'm standing, you two are the ones she needs the most protection from."

Pure anger is coursing through her. I know that because every pore in her body is screaming that at me now. "You just fucked up your chance of enjoying some fun on the side that no one would have ever needed to know about."

"I don't need fun like that in my life, Sabrina."

"Every man needs fun like that in their life." A scheming look passes through her eyes. "And you know what? Just because we didn't get to have some, doesn't mean we didn't do anything."

I follow her line of thinking perfectly, and the dislike and distrust I had for her before this conversation only grows. "I advise you not to travel down that path. It won't end well for you."

"It's a win-win for you, Jameson. You pay me to keep my mouth shut about something we both know you would have said yes to, and Adeline will never hear me asking for money again. And look at that, you get to protect your precious wife."

Fury hunts its way through my body, looking for an out. "Get the fuck out of my home and don't ever come back here again."

She takes her sweet time following that directive, and while she's standing there glaring at me, Adeline's voice sounds from the kitchen doorway. "What's happening here?"

I lift my face to look at her while Sabrina clutches my shirt, presses her body to mine, turns to face her sister, and says with fake breathlessness, "Oh my goodness, Adeline, this isn't what it looks like. I swear."

The biggest difference between these two women? Adeline is an intelligent woman while Sabrina is not.

Disappointment flares in her eyes. "Sabrina," she says softly, not one ounce of fight left in her for the relationship I know she wants with her sister. "Don't."

Sabrina clings to false hope while pushing me away. "I told him no, Addy. I would never do that to you. *Never*."

Adeline comes to us, her eyes firmly on Sabrina. "Jameson didn't try to fuck you. We both know that, so just stop. This isn't going to be another one of your schemes to get money."

Anger consumes Sabrina's entire body. "Fuck you both with your bullshit about me scheming to get money! I have bills to pay. For me and Mom. And I don't have boobs or an ass like you to help me do that."

Adeline slaps her.

Wild and furious.

I didn't see it coming and fuck if I don't support it.

"I will not be made to feel bad for the body I have anymore. But you know what I have that I use more than my boobs or my ass? A brain." Her eyes burn with the kind of anger and hurt that she'll feel long after tonight. "You have one of those too. You're just too lazy to use it."

"God, you are so fucking high and mighty," Sabrina seethes, holding her cheek. Then, stepping close to Adeline, she spits out, "Mom says you're just like your father. He must have been a real fucking asshole."

Adeline blinks, her chest stilling like she's no longer bringing air in. "What did you just say?"

Sabrina gloats, pushing her shoulders back. "You think you know everything. You think you know better than everyone else. You don't. You didn't even know we don't have the same father. You're too busy trying to get people to look at you and follow you that you don't pay attention."

"Who is my father?"

"I don't know. And I don't fucking care. As far as I'm concerned, we're not even real sisters. You're a bitch and I hate everything about you." Sabrina looks at me after spewing that bullshit. "You deserve her. Fuck you both."

With that, she storms out of the kitchen and a minute later, I hear the elevator open to remove her from my home.

Adeline looks like she's been hit by a weapon. Stricken in the worst possible way: by a loved one.

I pull her to me and wrap her in my arms.

She sags against me, holding on with a desperate need.

We don't speak. There are no words for what just happened.

She holds me and I hold her, for a long time.

Finally, she lifts her head and looks up at me. Tears stain her cheeks. "How can someone be so hateful?"

I cup the back of her head. I want to tell her she has to let her sister go, that she can't keep that hateful energy in her life, that she'll be stronger without her, but I don't. Adeline doesn't need that from me. She needs something entirely different. "I don't know. I honestly don't fucking know."

Her eyes search mine for the longest time. Time I give her. I'll give her whatever she needs to get through this. "I'm sorry she dragged you into this."

"You've got nothing to apologize for. That was on her, not you."

"I know, but you're a good man, Jameson. I hate that she did that to you. I hate when innocent men get pulled into shit like this."

Being called a good man by Adeline settles deeply inside me. She's battled against letting me in for so long, thinking of me as the asshole who took her company from her, that I wouldn't have expected this assessment from her.

"I appreciate you not buying into her bullshit."

"Well, for one, I've reached the end of the line where her bullshit is concerned. But mostly, I don't think you're the kind of man who cheats. Not that we're in a relationship, but still, I think you have more respect for me than that."

"We're in a relationship, Adeline. It might not be your usual kind, but you're the only woman in my bed. And you're right, loyalty is my greatest requirement in a relationship." I pause before asking, "Do you want to talk about your father?"

She grips me a little harder, a little tighter, like she needs me. "I don't know." Those three words are more of a whisper than anything else. I hear all the agony behind them.

Deciding she needs some space and some time alone with her thoughts, I say, "I'm going to take a shower. If you want to talk after that, we can."

"Thank you."

I'm in the shower five minutes later and Adeline is in bed. I don't know for sure, but I suspect she's pulled out her crossword book.

My first instinct while I think about her is nothing like any I've had before.

I want to have this shower and then pull her to my side of the bed, wrap her in my arms again, and help her sleep simply by lending her my strength.

My second instinct is more in line with the way I've always lived my life.

I want to remove her sister from her life.

I won't, but fuck, I want to.

21

Adeline

I lie in bed and listen to Jameson's shower running. It's a distraction from the mess in my mind after Sabrina's bombshell.

My father is not who I thought he was.

For my entire life, I've thought one thing, but it's not true. Something else is true, and I don't even know what that is.

My heart is beating fast.

And then slow.

It's in my chest.

And then in my throat.

My sister hates me.

Real, raging hate.

Because I have boobs and an ass that she doesn't.

Or maybe because I have money and she doesn't.

I thought we were close when we were kids, but now I think I didn't know anything.

I *don't* know anything.

I suck air into my lungs.

A lot of it.

But there's no room for it.

Nowhere for it to go.

I'm pretty sure my lungs are about to explode.

My heart too.

And my throat feels like it's being roughly stitched closed.

Hacked together.

The stitches are so tight.

I can't breathe.

I sit up and press my hand to my chest while taking big, dragging gasps.

And still, *I can't breathe*.

I push the bed covers off and get up.

I need to stand.

I need to walk.

I need air.

Oh, God, I need to bend over.

I place my hands on my thighs and bend.

My head goes funny.

All light and fluffy.

I'm going to pass out.

I reach for something to steady me, but there's nothing near me.

My hand connects only with air, and I stumble forward.

And then, strong arms circle my waist.

I'm pulled back against a hard chest.

And the voice I've come to associate with care, and safety, and protection fills all my senses.

"I've got you."

I place my hands over his at my stomach. "I can't breathe." My words come out in between gasps for air.

"Yes, you can."

"I can't, Jameson." I really can't.

"Stop talking and focus on your breathing. Count to five slowly as you take each breath."

I do as he says.

I'll do anything he says if it'll get air in my lungs.

I breathe in slowly, counting to five.

"Good," he says in the most calming voice I've ever heard. "Now, let it out slowly. Count to five."

I do that too.

I do it all again.

And again.

Jameson keeps me in his arms the entire time.

I have no idea how long it takes to feel like I'm not going to die, but it seems like the longest time of my life.

When I finally turn in his arms and face him, I say, "I never want to do that again."

He nods.

"That was a panic attack, wasn't it?"

"Yes."

"Have you had one before? How did you know what to do?"

He takes a moment to reply, like this isn't something he wants to talk about. "Mom used to have them. When Dad was on one of his rampages."

Jameson's face is like stone. He really doesn't want to discuss this. I know that just from one look at him.

"Thank you," I say softly. "I hate that you know how to deal with a panic attack, but I'm grateful too."

He studies me for a moment. "Do you want to talk?"

"I want to call my mother." I didn't realize this until right this second, but I need to ask her about my father, and I don't want to wait until the morning.

Jameson lets me go so I can do that.

I sit in the bed and call her.

She doesn't answer.

I call her again.

It takes me five attempts to get her to answer.

"Adeline," she says, clearly grumpy that I've called at this time of the night. "I was busy."

Busy is code for sex. She's used that code since I was seven. I didn't know exactly what it meant at that age. I just knew she had a man in her bedroom, and that they were making a lot of noise. Busy to me meant making noise.

"Who's my father, Mom?"

She's silent for a moment, and then—"You called me at this hour of the night to ask me that? Surely, this could have waited until morning."

A lifetime of hurt rushes up. It's a raging torrent I couldn't stop even if I tried. "Who. Is. My. Father? Tell me! And don't give me any bullshit. I'm done with every last bit of your bullshit. You will act like a fucking mother for once and give me this information."

I hear her sigh.

I don't care about that sigh or how she's feeling.

In this moment, for the first time in my life, I care only about how I'm feeling.

"Fine, if we must do this now," she says, "your father's name is Mike."

"Surname?" It snaps out of me. I've never felt more impatient in my life.

"Mike Carroll. He was a singer. I met him at one of his shows. We were together for a year. He died while I was pregnant with you."

My heart beats hard against my chest. "He's dead?"

"Yes, Adeline," she says snappily. "He died in a car accident."

My father is dead.

He didn't leave me, walk out on me, not want to know me.

He died in a car accident before he even had the chance to meet me.

Tears well in my eyes.

"What was he like?" The words tumble out of my mouth in the same way my emotions tumble out of my heart.

She sighs again. "He was a good man." She might have sighed, but her voice has now softened like she's remembering something good. "He was kind, and thoughtful, and he loved me more than anyone ever loved me." She pauses and I get the impression she's lost in her memories. "He wanted you so badly. He wanted a big family."

I wipe the tears streaming down my face. "Why did you let me believe Samuel was my father, Mom?" I'm so angry with her right now. And hurt. And unbelievably sad.

"I had no choice, Adeline."

My anger cracks like a whip. "You had a choice, and

you chose to lie to me. Don't lie to yourself now. Be a mother for once in your goddam life and be honest."

"If you were a mother, you'd understand. I had to make hard choices."

"Oh my God, Mom, just stop! Tell me what the hard choices were. Help me understand."

"Samuel wasn't a good man. I tried to shelter you from that and take it all myself. You don't know what I went through with him. He came along just before you were born and was there for me when I needed help. When I needed someone to get me through the days and the nights of you. He made me put his name on the birth certificate."

"But after he left, why didn't you tell me the truth?"

"Oh, Adeline, there was no need. You thought he was your father. Your birth certificate said it. Why go and stir things up that don't need stirring?"

I will never understand my mother.

Never.

And I decide right now that I'm not going to try anymore.

Taking a deep breath, I say, "Where is my father buried?"

"Why on earth would you want to know that?"

"Because I want to go and see him," I snap. "Tell me where he's buried. Tell me his date of birth. And tell me anything else about him that will help me find him. And then you can get back to being busy and I won't ever disturb you while you're busy again."

She sighs some more, but she gives me everything I've asked for.

When I say goodbye, I do it with a heavy heart.

I don't think I want my mother in my life anymore.

I don't think I *can* have her in it anymore.

I don't think she's good for me.

"Come here." Jameson's deep voice cuts through all my thoughts and feelings from the other side of the bed.

I look at him. "No."

His eyes darken. "Come here."

"No, I'm not in the mood." I'm really not, and I'm unsure why he thinks I would be.

"Adeline."

I wipe the tears that are still falling down my cheeks. "Are you kidding right now? You've witnessed everything I've gone through tonight and you think you can fuck me and make it all better?" I push the bed covers off angrily and leave the bed to go into the bathroom to wash my face.

I've just splashed water on my cheeks when Jameson fills the doorway.

I glance at him. "Go back to bed. I don't want to talk to you."

"I'm more than okay with that," he growls, coming to me. "But I'm not okay with you sleeping on your side of the bed by yourself when you've just had your heart ripped out."

He flicks the tap off, dries my face, lifts me into his arms, carries me to his side of the bed, lies me down next to him, wraps his arms around me, and orders, "Go to sleep."

The man spoons me.

Spoons.

And I let him.

I also let him steal another sliver of my heart.

I SLEEP LIKE A BABY.

For many, many hours.

My mind finally decides it's time to give in, to stop keeping my thoughts churning every second of the day and night, and allows me to rest.

I also think having Jameson wrap me in his arms helps.

I wake just before 9:00 a.m., which is a sleep-in like I haven't seen since my early teen years.

Jameson is in his office when I get up. I find him in there after looking in the kitchen for him.

"You're awake," he says, looking up from his desk when he hears me.

I eye the reports spread out in front of him. "You look busy."

He nods. "I've got a lot to get through before we fly to Vegas."

I frown. "Why are we flying to Vegas? And when?"

"We'll leave as soon as I finish going through these reports, which will likely be in two hours or so."

I move further into his office. "Okay, but why?"

"To visit your father's grave."

I frown some more. "Today?"

His impatience flares. "Adeline, we're wasting time. Let me get through these reports—"

"No." I put my hand up to stop him as I stand across from him at his desk. "I've woken up to you bossing me around about visiting my father's grave, a man I only just discovered exists last night. I'm still trying to wrap my mind around that, let alone wrap it around getting on a plane and going to visit his grave. You're going to have to give me a minute."

It's his turn to frown. "You don't want to go today." It's not a question. It's more of a 'fuck, I didn't consider that' statement.

I have an overwhelming desire to go and sit on his lap, put my arms around his neck, and tell him I'm grateful for everything he's doing. But I don't. That feels a lot like something I'd do if this was a real relationship. It's definitely not something I should do in a fake marriage.

Instead, I give him a smile. "I hadn't considered it, but now that you've suggested it, I think I'd like to go." I pause before softly adding, "Thank you."

"Jeff prepared Nutella rolls for you."

Warmth fills all my spots that usually keep everything out while protecting me from things that will only end up hurting me. "You asked him to make me Nutella rolls?"

His gaze settles on me in a way it hasn't already. A way I really like. It's the kind of gaze that makes me feel safe, and protected, and cared for. "Yes. I imagine Nutella will be high on your list today."

And there goes another sliver.

I go in search of the Nutella rolls and eat more than I should. I don't regret one mouthful.

I then shower, dress, and pack for our trip.

We leave New York at midday and arrive at Jameson's Vegas hotel just before 3:00 p.m. I've never stayed in one of his hotels and am immediately impressed.

It's luxury and sophistication that isn't over the top with its cream and gold design.

"You need to do everything you can to keep whoever designed this hotel," I say as we step into the private elevator to take us up to the penthouse. His security team have gone ahead of us, so we're alone.

"You approve?"

Usually, I would say my approval means very little to him, but today, I hear something in this voice that tells me maybe it does mean something. "Yes. Very much so."

His eyes tell me I didn't misread him.

He likes that I approve.

And I like that he likes it.

Holy fuck, why is my heart starting to feel like it's missing too many slivers?

"Do you want to rest before we go to the cemetery?" he asks, opening the door of the suite for me to enter.

I stop for a moment when I step inside. The penthouse is exquisite and takes my breath away. I'm looking at floor-to-ceiling windows that give a spectacular view out over Vegas.

I walk into the suite, looking at the view for a few moments before turning back to Jameson. "No. I want to go now."

He takes our bags into the bedroom, and I look around the penthouse.

It's endless marble and opulence with a cantilevered pool on the terrace that makes the most of the view, a sauna, a massage room, a gym, dining for twelve, a twelve-seat bar, a walk-in steam shower, two bedrooms, and jetted deep-soak tubs that are calling to me.

"I'll bring you back here in the summer," Jameson says when he joins me at the window in front of the pool. "You'll enjoy swimming here then."

I smile at him. "I'd like that."

His phone rings and he curses when he looks at the

screen. "I have to take this," he says before putting it to his ear and striding to the long dining table where he deposits the laptop he's carrying and sits to take the call.

I haven't had a chance to check in on work today. More to the point, I haven't wanted to. This is unusual for me. Kimberly would have called if anything urgent came up, so I took the opportunity to relax on the flight here. I slept for a couple of hours and then read for a little while. Mostly, I thought about my father and how everything I've always thought about my family and my place in it is not true. Toward the end of the flight, I pulled out my crossword book and, with Jameson's help, completed a crossword. He seems to enjoy helping me solve puzzles.

I check my phone now while he's on his call and find an email from Vanessa. I haven't heard from her while she's been away from work with her mom and am surprised to receive this email. It's Christmas Day after all.

My thoughts all slow down while I read the email. She's forwarded information regarding a drop in share price for Jameson's company this week. She also included links to various news articles that sell the narrative that Jameson should be scrutinized due to his marriage to me, because although I was transparent about what I discovered in my company, sentiment is that I was well aware of the factories I was using and only came clean because I had to. The narrative is that Jameson is as dishonest as me and should not be trusted.

I text Vanessa while trying to stop the ill feeling these stories have caused. I've been so focused on my own company that I haven't had a chance to keep up with much else, so I've missed this news.

Adeline: Thank you for sending me that information. How are you and your mom?

Vanessa: I'm good. Mom's doing okay. And I figured that you might not have seen those stories since you've been busy this week and I'm not there to give you the updates I normally do.

Adeline: I hadn't seen them, so I appreciate you forwarding them.

Vanessa: I'll see you in a few days. I hope you're okay.

Adeline: Don't worry about me. Just focus on your mom.

"I'm ready when you are," Jameson says, coming back to me after finishing his call.

We leave the suite and go down to the car to head to the cemetery. I push all the thoughts swirling in my brain about Jameson's company to the side so I can focus on the reason we're here.

My dad.

He's buried in a cemetery about twenty minutes from the Strip. The only things I know about him from my mother are that he would have turned fifty-five this year; he had no family that she knew of; he grew up in Vegas, so she buried him here; and that he was a singer-songwriter, but none of his music was ever recorded.

"What are you thinking?" Jameson asks as I stare out the window during the trip to the cemetery.

I turn to him. "That I want Gabriel to find out everything he can about my father."

"He's already working on it."

I guessed that already but wanted to make sure. "Thank you."

"Have you heard from Sabrina today?"

"No, and I hope I don't." I don't tell him the words on the tip of my tongue because they feel so very wrong to even think, let alone say.

I think I'm done with my family.

But who does that?

Who walks away from the people who birthed them, raised them, grew up with them?

It doesn't feel right, however all I keep coming back to is that I don't feel loved by them, so why would I stay? Being blood-related shouldn't mean a person has to accept being treated badly or not being loved how they should be.

We arrive at the cemetery and Jameson puts his hand to the small of my back as we search for my father's grave. It doesn't take long to locate, and I find myself slowing down as we approach.

Jameson's hand splays across my back as he senses me slowing, and his eyes come to mine. "Do you want to do this by yourself?"

"No."

I look at the grave, taking in the weeds surrounding it. My heart hurts looking at those weeds and I make a silent promise that my father will never know another day of not being cared for.

I glance back at Jameson. "I don't want to be alone right now."

He reaches down and takes hold of my hand. Gripping it firmly, he walks with me the rest of the way.

"Do you think my mother has ever visited him?" I ask after five minutes of standing in front of the headstone, reading it over and over, thinking about the man I never knew.

My question isn't one Jameson can answer. Really, it's not even a question for him because he barely knows my mother. It's simply me thinking out loud. But still, he gives me what I need. "I would hope so. She loved him enough to have a child with him. I imagine she cared for him in her own way."

For a reason I can't even come close to figuring out, his answer makes me cry. I think about my phone call with Mom last night. She sounded different when she talked about my father. Different than she's ever sounded while talking about a man.

I think Jameson's right. I think she did love my dad. And I think she must have visited him. I hope so.

I thread my fingers tighter through his.

We stay for an hour.

Jameson keeps hold of my hand the entire time and lets me talk about everything I need to.

Was my father happy in his life?

What were his dreams?

Did he want to marry my mother?

What caused the car crash he died in?

Did he help my mother choose my name before he died?

I have so many questions that it feels like my mind can't possibly fit them all in.

Jameson patiently listens to every one of the questions I raise. I wonder if he realizes I have so many more that he'll have to listen to over the next eleven months.

When I'm ready to leave, I turn to him and ask one last question. "Do you visit your father?"

His features harden. "No."

I thought that would be the answer he'd give. And I don't expect anything further, but he surprises me when he adds, "Mom does, and for the life of me, I can't understand why."

I contemplate that for a moment, trying to put myself in her shoes. "How often does she go?"

"Once a year, on the anniversary of his death."

"Have you asked her why?"

"No. We don't discuss my father."

"Why not?"

"He has no place in our life."

This man.

He's powerful, and strong, and sometimes made of stone, but underneath all that are wounds that have never been touched, never been looked at, never been tended to.

"No, but he had a big place in your mom's life at one point. Maybe she needs you to talk with her about that. Maybe she visits him seeking closure."

The vein in his temple pulses. "She's had sixteen years to get that closure."

"There's no timeline on grief, Jameson."

More of that vein pulsing. "She had nothing to grieve. We were all better off without him."

"I understand that, but I imagine she might have been grieving other things. The death of your father may have really brought it home to her that her sons would never have a father who loved them. Maybe she'd experienced some denial over that previously or hoped and prayed he'd change. She could have been grieving the loss of her family dreams. She'd invested so much time, and energy, and love into building a family for herself and her sons. It had to be hard to let that go." I search his eyes. "It might help her if you give her the space to share her feelings with you. And it might help you too."

He processes that for a few moments before finally saying, "We'll see." He looks at me questioningly. "Are you hungry?"

"I'm starving."

"Would you prefer to eat in or go out?"

"I don't want to go out." Vegas is too busy for me on Christmas Day. Also, I'm feeling raw; I just want to snuggle in and forget the world exists tonight.

He walks me to the car and twenty minutes later, we arrive back at the hotel. Jameson takes two calls on the drive, and from what I can ascertain, they're both calls from investors with concerns he's working hard to ease.

When we reach the penthouse, he receives another call. Looking at me with apology, he says, "Can you order dinner while I take this?"

"What do you feel like eating?"

"Anything. You choose."

"Okay."

He heads out to the terrace, and although it's cold outside, he takes the call out there. I can't help but think he doesn't want me to hear these conversations. I got that impression while he took the calls in the car, and I'm getting that impression now.

I call the butler and order Pad Thai for dinner. It's one of Jameson's favorites and I've begun to really enjoy eating it too.

He doesn't end up eating with me.

He receives call after call and sits at the table working on his laptop late into the night.

Shantel messages me around 9:00 p.m. to advise she's fixed the clash on our schedule she mentioned yesterday.

Shantel: I'm delighted to let you know Jameson can now attend that club party with you.

Adeline: LOL. I'm delighted at that news.

Shantel: As I knew you would be.

Adeline: Merry Christmas, Shantel.

Shantel: I don't celebrate Christmas but thank you. I've had a great day by myself, although the next time your husband decides it's a good idea to leave town when we're in the middle of a work shitstorm, please tell him that taking a fun trip to Vegas is not a valid reason for this. Also, I apologize now for the fact you'll hardly see him when you get home, but it was unavoidable due to him not being available tomorrow for those meetings. Please don't hold any of this against me.

She thinks Jameson came to Vegas for fun?

I don't correct her. That's not my place.

Adeline: I won't hold anything against you. Glad to hear you had a great day.

After messaging with her, I get in the deep-soak tub in the bathroom. I turn the jets on, lie back, rest my head, and close my eyes.

It's heaven and I think about sleeping in here.

I stay here for an hour or so. After, I moisturize my body, put on my pajamas, and crawl into bed to read for a while.

My thoughts are darting between my father and Jameson. I can't help but wonder about those meetings he pushed so he could come to Vegas. Not to mention, the fact he came when he's got a million headaches at work.

When I'm still fixated on these questions at midnight, I go in search of him.

I find him sitting in the leather armchair in the corner of the living room, working on his laptop. He glances up when he hears me and watches intently as I walk toward him.

His gaze reaches to the deepest parts of me with ease. With heat. With need.

I feel it everywhere.

"You can't sleep?" he asks when I draw close.

I reach for his laptop and move it from his lap to another chair.

"No." I crawl onto his lap, one arm going around his neck while I take hold of his face with my other hand.

His eyes are glued to mine.

"I was missing you," I say as I bring my mouth to his. "I needed this." My mouth closes over his so I can claim the kiss I came for.

That trademark Jameson growly sound vibrates through me as he kisses me back. One of his hands slides over my ass while the other one curves around my waist.

Everything about this feels right.

Everything.

From flying here with him today, to visiting my father's grave with him, to this kiss on his lap.

And the thing I know without a shadow of a doubt is that I want more of this with him. So much more of it all.

When I end the kiss, I keep my face close to his and ask, "How much longer until you come to bed?"

Before I know what's happening, he's standing, lifting me with him, and carrying me into the bedroom.

He deposits me on the floor and drops his gaze to my chest while starting to make his way down the buttons of my pajama top. He works slowly, far slower than we've ever done this. It's like he's mesmerized by those buttons.

"You know you could do this a lot faster by just lifting it over my head, right?" I say as I reach for his buttons. His shirt cannot be lifted over his head unfortunately.

His eyes meet mine again. "I'm enjoying the anticipation."

Those four words curl their way through me in the very best way.

"As you were then," I say while working his buttons, even though what I want to say is 'hurry the hell up.'

His lips curve up in the kind of smile that promises so many good things. "Has anyone told you how fucking sexy you are when you're turned on?"

"No. You should tell me."

He gives me more of that sexy smile as he finishes with my buttons and discards my top. He moves into me, cupping one breast and reaching his fingers into my hair. Bending his face, he brings his mouth to my ear. "You are sexy as hell when you've got my eyes on you."

I can't be sure, but I'm almost certain I moan at that.

The next-level heat that's in Jameson's eyes when he looks at me again tells me that he liked whatever I did.

His mouth claims mine as I strip his shirt from him.

We move from slow to fast.

We're arms and hands and mouths and grinding and holy-hell-I-didn't-think-our-sex-could-get-any-better-but-it-is.

He tears all my clothes off me.

I tear all his off him.

And then, he gets me on the bed, legs spread wide, his mouth to my clit, and I'm arching my back and gripping the sheet and giving him more of those moans he likes.

He gets me close, over and over, and then pulls me back, not letting me find the release I'm desperate for. It's pleasure I both love and hate.

When I can't go on, I grip his hair and demand, "Make me come already."

Jameson likes it when I beg, now being no different. It always inspires him to fuck me with an intensity I can't get enough of.

He lifts his face and moves up my body. Taking hold of one of my legs, he raises it and rests it against his shoulder. Keeping a firm grip on it, he thrusts inside me.

Oh. God.

Yes.

He finds a good rhythm, and I hold on tightly.

I cry out when I come. I've no idea what sounds come out of my mouth; I just know that Jameson fucks me so well that a lot of noise is made. I regret none of that noise.

He comes almost straight after me, staying in me for longer than normal.

When he finally pulls out, he drops a kiss to my lips, lingering there, eyes searching mine, and says, "So damn sexy," before rolling onto his back and pulling me into his arms. Something he's never done after sex.

I lie on my side, curling into him, and rest my head on his chest while tracing circles over his skin.

We lie in silence for a few minutes before I say, "Your share price has dropped."

He takes a moment. "Yes."

"Because of me."

He doesn't take a moment this time. "No, this is because of bullshit that has no place in business."

"Yes, and that bullshit is all because of me."

"Not all of it has to do with you. Someone in my executive team leaked information that has my investors concerned."

"But it doesn't help you to be linked to me, does it?"

"No, but I don't want you to worry about this. I'm handling it." His tone tells me he really didn't want to answer that question.

"Jameson—"

"No," he says so firmly and so finally that I know not to argue with him again. "We're not having this conversation."

I move so I'm straddling him. Bending, I kiss him before saying softly, "I hate that I'm hurting you."

He grips the back of my neck and pulls my mouth back to his. After taking his time kissing me, he says, "This isn't hurting me, Adeline."

I stay where I am, keeping my eyes on his, torn between pushing this and letting it go. In the end, I let it go.

"Thank you for bringing me to Vegas today. I'm not sure I could have done this by myself."

"You could have. You have more strength than any woman I know."

"Sometimes even the strong need to lean on someone, Jameson. I'm grateful I had you to lean on today."

Something about the look in his eyes and the way he brings me back down to the bed to lie next to him, wrapped tightly around him, makes me think he's affected by this conversation in a way he's not used to being affected.

And something about the way my entire being feels cherished makes me think I like this a lot more than I should.

22

Jameson

Adeline: I thought I might drop by your office on my way to your Mom's tonight.

Jameson: Because?

Adeline: You're working too hard and need a break. I can give you a break.

Jameson: I'm already on my way home.

Adeline: You're coming to Taco Tuesday? I thought you couldn't make it.

Jameson: Yes, but we're going to be late to Mom's since I'm coming home to fuck you.

Adeline: I like the way you think.

Jameson: I'll be there in ten minutes. Get yourself ready for me.

Adeline: For future reference, those last five words work for me. You should use them often.

Fuck.

She has no idea how often I want to use those words or ones like them.

A text comes in from Hudson.

Hudson: JRO are targeting our conference accounts. Leroy gave them everything they need to succeed.

JRO Hotels is the rival who is still intent on putting us out of business.

Leroy is the executive who leaked the information to the *Times* last week. I fired him when I returned from Vegas. Clearly not soon enough if he's given our rival the kind of information they need to steal our clients.

Our conference accounts are worth billions. We can't fucking afford to lose any of those accounts.

Jameson: Has Gabriel found anything useful yet?

Hudson: He's just checking something. He'll call you in the next half hour.

I glance out the window at Manhattan as Max drives me home. My thoughts shift from work back to Adeline. Since our trip to Vegas last week, she's consumed my thoughts. At a time when I should only be thinking of work, I've been dedicating hours to her.

She's been moving through her feelings over discovering her mother lied to her about her father, struggling with that. Gabriel gave her the information he found on her father, and she's spent time researching him, the schools he went to, the friends he had, the places he worked at, and any other little thing that was in Gabriel's notes. Every night, I come home to new thoughts she's had that day about him, about her mother, and about her sister. Some nights, I haven't made it home before midnight, and I've found her lying in the dark waiting to talk. And fuck if I don't like that.

Shantel texts me, interrupting my thoughts.

Shantel: You are now the proud owner of *Wanton*. I never imagined the day we'd own a women's magazine but here we are.

Jameson: Schedule a meeting with the editor-in-chief as soon as possible.

Shantel: You are aware of the fact your schedule is already overbooked, right?

Jameson: I don't care. I want a meeting with that editor.

Shantel: Right. Got it. I shall begin work on a new Jameson. One who can get through twice as much work with no extra effort. As you were.

Max pulls into my garage and parks the car. I'm almost at the elevator when Gabriel calls.

"Tell me you've got something that will fucking end this once and for all," I say when I answer. I thought we'd taken care of this fucking JRO problem, but these assholes just keep coming back at me.

"Yeah. Huntington is overstating earnings to their shareholders. He's pocketing millions along the way."

Huntington is the CEO of JRO Hotels. He's a motherfucker I will take great fucking joy in crushing.

"Anything else?"

"I've detailed everything in my email. Also, I finally managed to trace the latest gossip about Adeline. It originated from her sister."

Jesus.

And yet, this doesn't surprise me.

We end the call and I phone Hudson.

"You've read Gabriel's email?" I ask.

"Yeah."

"End this bullshit. Get that information out there." Once the news breaks of the fraud Huntington is committing, it won't take long for JRO to collapse.

"I'm on it."

I step into the elevator after we hang up and turn my thoughts to how I'll proceed with the information Gabriel just gave me about Sabrina. My first instinct is to share it with Adeline. In my opinion, the more information a person has in order to decide on a course of action, the better. However, Adeline is in turmoil over her family. She hasn't heard from her sister since Christmas, and I know she's battling thoughts of removing Sabrina from her life.

Her sister has broken her heart and I'm unsure if I want to break it even more.

I reach the penthouse, and after speaking with Jeff, I stride down the hallway to the bedroom. I find Adeline in her bathroom, leaning close to the mirror at the vanity, squinting at something on her chin.

Moving behind her, I place my hands to her hips and watch her in the mirror. For the life of me, I can't figure out what she's doing with her chin. "What are you doing?"

Her eyes meet mine, widening as she says, "I just found a fucking chin hair." Her eyes widen some more. "I'm thirty. How is this even a thing at this age?"

My lips quirk. "You don't have hair on your chin."

More of the eye widening. "I do." She jabs at her chin. "It's right there. Trust me; you men have no fucking clue about the things women go through. Chin hair!"

I reach my arms around her to find the button on her jeans. Undoing it, I say, "Trust me, I've studied your face enough to know there are no chin hairs."

That quietens her.

I lower her zip and slide my hand into her panties. The sound she makes when I circle her clit is a sound I never want to not hear.

She wraps her hand around my forearm, her grip tightening with each moment I make her wetter.

I push two fingers inside her. "We need to renegotiate our contract."

She bites her lip as I reach in deep. "Why?"

I kiss the side of her neck. "I never want to see you on a magazine cover again without any clothes on." I had Shantel buy every copy she could find of the issue that went on sale this week. The fact the magazine also sells in digital format did not please me.

She bends slightly, drops her head, and places her hands to the vanity to hold herself up. Her breaths are coming faster as she argues with me, "I had clothes on."

My fingers inside her work faster as I press more kisses to her neck, biting her lightly as I go. "You were barely clothed."

She grinds her ass back against my dick. "Don't be dramatic. I'm not renegotiating anything. You'll need to learn to be okay with my skin on display."

I thrust my fingers in rougher. I've come to the place where I won't ever be okay with that. "At some point, you'll run out of magazines who will photograph you with skin on display."

She lifts her head and finds my eyes in the mirror.

"What do you mean?" I know by her tone that she's already connected the dots.

I grip her face and angle it to the side so I can bring my mouth to hers.

I kiss her.

Rougher than I've ever kissed her.

I keep hold of her face when I end the kiss. "I now own *Wanton* and I won't hesitate to buy every last magazine there is if needed."

She grasps my arm again. "You didn't."

"I did."

"Oh my God, Jameson." She moans as she comes, her pussy clenching my fingers, wet in the way that causes my brain to shut down and my body to take control.

"Fuck," I rasp as I tear her jeans and panties down.

I press my hand to her back to bend her over.

I grip her hips.

And I slam my cock inside of her.

I can't do this fast enough or hard enough.

Adeline is all I want.

Being inside her.

Touching her.

Smelling her.

Tasting her.

It's a need unlike any I've ever known.

She fits me so fucking perfectly.

The sex.

The back and forth.

The day-to-day.

All of it.

"Oh, God," she pants.

I drive myself deeper inside her and reach for her clit.

She orgasms.

I keep thrusting.

Then, with one last jerk, I come.

I stay inside her and drop a kiss to the back of her neck before murmuring, "Are you still anticipating that you'll never wear the perfume I gave you?"

I hear the smile in her voice when she says, "Yes."

Fuck.

I want to always do this with her.

I pull out of her and turn her to me. "I will find a way to get you to wear it."

Her eyes smile as she leans in and kisses me. "How long do you anticipate your denial over not being able to boss me into things will continue?"

"I don't deal in denial."

A sexy look fills her features. "You're even in denial over your denial." Her lips brush mine again. "I'm going to enjoy watching your downfall." She pushes me gently. "Now, we have tacos to go and eat, so you need to leave me to get ready."

"You're ready."

She gives me a look that says she thinks I'm a clueless male. "You just fucked me. You're all in me and over me. I am not ready anymore. And"—her eyes widen—"I have a chin hair to remove."

She shoos me out of her bathroom.

She showers and gets ready.

I shower and change while contemplating again whether to tell Adeline about her sister.

By the time she joins me in the bedroom, I've decided not to tell her unless it becomes necessary to.

"Can you please help me with my necklace?" she asks, coming to me.

I take her necklace as she turns around. After I fasten it around her neck, I slide my hands around her waist and lean in close. "You look beautiful."

Her hands come to mine as she breathes out, "Thank you."

I've just kissed her neck when Bill's voice sounds from the bedroom doorway. "Sorry to interrupt, but I need a minute, Jameson."

I glance at him, noting the approval in his eyes.

Adeline steps out of my hold and looks at Bill with a smile. "Be quick or else I'm going to leave for Reese's by myself. I'm starving because my husband can't keep his hands to himself."

With that, she leaves the bedroom.

I struggle to remove my eyes from her ass, but I do.

"What's up?" I ask Bill while we walk into my office.

He discusses a new direction he's considering taking his company in, asking for my thoughts on his idea. We talk about this for longer than the minute he asked for. Instead of being focused solely on him like I normally would be, I'm distracted by thoughts of Adeline and the fact she's hungry.

Bill stops mid-sentence while detailing something I can't quite keep up with. "You want to get back to Adeline." It's not a question. It's an observation. One that is accurate.

I nod. "Yes."

He smiles. "We'll talk about this tomorrow. Are you free for lunch?"

"I'll have Shantel move my schedule around so I am."

As I walk him out, he places his hand on my shoulder and slows me down. "I'm happy for you, son."

I don't process that fully until he tells Adeline goodbye and steps into the elevator. The look he gives me as he leaves tells me everything I need to know: Bill doesn't have any doubts about my marriage now.

Adeline looks up at me once we're alone. "I have to admit I thought you were going too far when you insisted we share a bedroom, but you were right about Bill checking in on that."

"He's not a man to be underestimated."

"I know that now." She takes hold of my shirt. "Okay, you need to get your ass down to the car and take me to dinner. And maybe if you drive, I'll be persuaded to take some risks with you tonight."

~

THE NEXT TWO days are busy with back-to-back meetings. The ones I had to push last week to go to Vegas with Adeline. Late Thursday afternoon, I finish meeting with Ashton Scott and Beckett Pearce, my partners in a hotel and retail development that's given us a great deal of hell since we began work on it. We've recently had some breakthroughs that I'm hopeful signal the end of all the headaches.

"Let's meet again in three months," I say as we finish going over everything.

Ashton stands. "I can't leave Sydney in April, but I can meet there if you fly out."

Beckett looks at his phone. "That works for me. I'll

bring Jenna. She's told me how much she wants to visit Australia."

I pull up my calendar. "I can make it work." I can also turn it into the honeymoon Adeline and I never had. I make a note to mention it to her.

A message comes through from Shantel.

Shantel: Adeline is here. Do you have time to see her? She said she needs about fifteen minutes if you can spare it.

Jameson: Tell her I'll be out in five minutes.

Shantel: Also, dinner is booked for eight. I've emailed everyone the details.

I glance up at Ashton and Beckett. "Our dinner reservation is for eight tonight. Shantel has emailed you both."

We finish up and after they leave, I head into my office where Adeline is waiting.

"You know," she says when her eyes land on me, "I could help you with this office."

"Help me with what?"

She gestures at the room. "With adding some personal touches. Seriously, Jameson, you're not even in this room."

I frown. "You're making no sense."

"I'm making perfect sense."

I arch my brows at her. "You're going to have to enlighten me. And if we could get to the point fast, that would be good." I'm double booked for some of my hours this afternoon. I don't have time for the fifteen minutes she's requested, let alone the extra time we're taking for this.

"Oh, I see impatient Jameson is in the building today."

I do my best to hold my impatience back. "Adeline."

"Fine," she mutters. "I'm just saying I'd like to see more touches of you in here. Maybe a photo of your mom. Or one of you and Hudson. Maybe a lamp that is one you actually like rather than this boring one you've got that I know you didn't choose."

I glance at the lamp.

She's right; I didn't choose it and I don't like it.

I meet her gaze again. "You select a lamp and I'll replace this one."

"No. I'll take you shopping, and you can select one for yourself."

Jesus.

"We're not going shopping."

"We are. I've just decided. We'll find a new lamp and photo frames."

Choosing to ignore that, because this isn't an argument I have time for today, or one she's likely to give up on easily, I say, "Why are you here?"

"I wanted to run something by you." When I give her a look that says I'm waiting to hear it, she carries on. "My London expansion is moving ahead faster than I anticipated, and my team has suggested I should consider spending more time there throughout this process."

"That makes sense."

"Yes." She pauses. "When I say more time, I mean they think I should spend the majority of my time there for the next few months. So, I wanted to run that by you to make sure it works for the marriage."

"You want to move there?"

"Yes. Just for a few months."

I shake my head as I think it through. "No, that won't work."

Her forehead wrinkles. "Why not?"

"Because this marriage only works if we're living together."

"Okay, so I understand where you're coming from with that, but surely the marriage can still work so long as we're seeing each other regularly. I can fly back to New York to visit you, and you can fly to London to visit me."

"It's not enough. Bill won't approve."

"Perhaps we could test that theory. Maybe bring it up in conversation and get a read on him that way."

"We're not testing that theory."

"So, what, we're back to you being the one who decides how things will happen? And I just have to go along with it?"

"No, but we have to come to decisions that make sense."

"This decision makes sense, Jameson. You just need to open your mind to it."

"My mind is open to everything. But Bill has no doubts about the marriage anymore and I'd like to keep it that way. This plan could fuck with that."

"Bill knows our work situations. I don't think he'd blink if I traveled for work."

"You're not talking about traveling. You're talking about moving away for months."

"I'm also talking about building time together into the schedule."

A text comes in for me. I know from the ringtone that it's Shantel. I also know she's prompting me for my next meeting because it's one I really shouldn't be late for.

"It won't work," I say firmly. She needs to listen to me on this. And I need to get to my next meeting.

Her lips flatten. "I don't appreciate you taking that tone with me, and I don't appreciate you not listening to me. This is important and I'd like to find a solution."

"There is no solution, Adeline. We have a clear end goal here, and you signed a contract agreeing to the terms. Let's not fuck this up now."

Her eyes come to life with a cluster of emotions. Anger, mostly, by the look of it. She snatches her purse off the sofa and pushes her shoulders back. "This conversation isn't finished."

"It is." I check my watch. "I have a meeting to get to. Dinner is at eight. I'll be home around seven thirty to pick you up."

"You'll be lucky if I'm talking to you tonight."

She exits my office in a cloud of anger and that fucking perfume I need her to stop wearing.

I can only hope she's come to her senses by tonight.

I loosen my tie and shove my fingers through my hair.

She can't fucking move to London, and not just because of Bill.

I don't want her to leave.

23

Adeline

Jameson places his hand on my thigh and leans in close. "You're being particularly argumentative tonight."

I remove his hand. "And you're being particularly assholey."

We're an hour into his work dinner and I'm ready to leave. Thank God for Jenna, my business partner. She's here because she's married to Beckett, Jameson's business partner. She's keeping me occupied with conversation and distracted from Jameson.

He's right that I'm being argumentative. I can't help myself. I'm so annoyed with him that I want to challenge him over everything. I think I'm looking for an argument I *can* win because I'm not convinced he'll allow me to win my London argument.

I tried to broach it with him again at home before we came tonight. He refused to listen to sense again, telling me he can't see the situation working out well.

I don't understand his reasoning. I can see us making it work and I believe Bill will buy it. But Jameson won't even engage in a conversation about it. I'm confused and frustrated, and those emotions are manifesting as anger that causes me to continue arguing.

"So, Adeline," Ashton says from across the table, "I read something about you expanding into the UK and Europe. When is that happening?"

I reach for my wine and take a sip. "I'm working on it now. I'm hopeful to have our flagship London store open in the next six months."

"And after London?" Beckett asks.

"Paris," I say. "After that, I'll look at other UK sites."

"I imagine that means a fair bit of travel coming up for you," Ashton says.

"I'm hoping not too much. I'm looking at basing myself in London for a while," I say.

"No, there will be a lot of travel," Jameson says, using the tone he takes when he's intent on having the last word on something.

Jenna frowns. "Basing yourself there would make more sense."

"No," Jameson says, his voice getting darker.

I look at him, noting that his eyes have darkened too.

I truly don't understand him right now. I thought we were growing closer. I thought we were in sync with each other. I mean, he took me to Vegas last week to visit my father's grave, canceling meetings to do so. He bought a magazine simply because he didn't like so much of my skin being on display for the world to see.

The last couple of weeks' worth of social engagements and time spent with his family haven't felt like everything we did was just to prove our marriage is real. But he's taken every opportunity today to remind me of our contract.

It suddenly feels like I maybe took my eye off the ball and gave away too many slivers of my heart.

Men aren't like women, Adeline.

My mother's voice slams into me.

They don't feel things like we do.

Oh, God.

I think I fucked up.

I think I've fallen in love.

And I don't think Jameson has.

"No," I say with resolve while a storm of emotions rush through me. "I won't be doing a lot of travel. I'll definitely be moving to London for a while."

Jameson clenches his jaw and I know he's working hard to rein his feelings in. That's a good thing, because I'm ready for a fight, and I don't care who witnesses it. And as much as I rationally know I should do everything to avoid a public fight, I'm not thinking too rationally right now.

A lot of people told me I'd never succeed when I started my business. They told me models only know how to parade around in clothes, not run businesses. When I lost my first company, they came out and said, "I told you so." I've worked hard and put everything on the line to get where I am today. Expanding overseas is the next step, and I don't want to mess it up. I really need to be in London to oversee everything and ensure it succeeds.

I need to protect my company.

Losing my first company nearly ruined me. I won't survive losing another one.

I also won't survive losing my heart.

I swore I'd never give it away again after my first marriage, and here I am doing just that.

Jenna says something about me moving to London, but I can't focus on it. Not when Jameson is looking at me like he wants to order me to do things I don't want to do.

"We'll discuss this when we get home," he says quietly enough for only me to hear, but with enough dark energy for me to know how he feels about this.

"Yes," I agree, just as darkly. "We will."

We make it through the rest of dinner, and I only argue with Jameson over things I really don't care about twice more. I'm that annoyed with him that I can't help myself. And he knows it.

By the time we get to the car, we're grating against each other with the kind of angry friction that doesn't end up in a good place.

Jameson has to take a call on the drive home.

I sit beside him, staring out the window, berating myself for being so stupid.

This was always a fake marriage.

It wasn't built on love.

He has a clear goal and is doing everything to protect that goal.

I came into the marriage with a clear goal, too, but I got lost along the way.

Now, I need to move into preservation mode.

We must look after ourselves, Adeline, because a man will never look after us.

My mother invades my thoughts again and I struggle to remove her from my mind.

When Max parks the car in Jameson's garage, I get out and walk to the elevator without waiting for Jameson. He's still on his call, so I make it upstairs alone. I go straight to my bathroom and close the door behind me. I need a moment to myself.

I get ten minutes alone before Jameson is on the other side of the bathroom door telling me we need to speak.

I open the door and come face-to-face with him. His face is an intense mask of determination as he orders, "That can never happen again."

I stand tall against him. "What can never happen again?"

He jabs his finger in the direction of the restaurant we just came from. "That bullshit at dinner. You spent the night arguing with me over everything."

"You deserved it."

His brows climb his forehead while his nostrils flare. "Why?"

"Because you won't let me win the London war. Hell, you won't even let me have a say in it."

More flaring of his nostrils. "The London war?"

"Yes! The war we're in because you refuse to listen to me when I tell you I have to be in London for my business."

"And you're refusing to listen to me when I tell you why that can't happen."

"No, I'm not! I told you we could discuss how to make it happen. I'm open to compromise, but you're doing that thing you do where you just take over and make decisions for us."

"Someone has to, Adeline, and since you're not thinking straight, it has to be me."

I stare at him angrily. "God, I think I'd almost forgotten what an asshole you can be. Thank you for the reminder."

"I'm not being an asshole. I'm being practical."

"No! You're being an asshole. Trust me on that."

"Fuck." He pushes out a long breath. "I'm not spending the night going around in fucking circles with you on this. I don't have the time to fly back and forth between London to keep up appearances for Bill. And you don't either. End of story."

"You know what, Jameson? I hate the ends of your stories. You can take that one and stick it somewhere very special. I'm not paying any attention to it."

"You *will* pay attention to it," he says like he's telling me another fucking end of story.

"No, I won't."

He's silent for a moment and I watch the storm clouds roll in. Finally, he says, "We have a contract. I suggest you re-read it. You'll find it clearly states why you can't move to London."

With that, he stalks out of the bedroom.

I stare after him, my heart beating wildly.

I'm angry.

I'm furious.

I'm enraged.

But most of all—*worst of all*—my heart is in shreds. Torn apart by the man I should never have allowed to take even one tiny sliver.

He doesn't feel anything for me.

He only cares about our contract.

Jameson claimed my mouth, my body, my soul.

He could keep my heart if he wanted it, but since he doesn't, my heart gets lost and confused and bewildered, and doesn't know what to do or where to go.

She and I have a come-to-Jesus moment.

I sit her down and have a big talk with her.

I tell her how things are going to work from here on out.

I tell her that she must never allow pieces to be stolen again.

I tell her to buckle in because she and I are about to cause a commotion.

One that Jameson is not going to like.

~

"TODAY?" Vanessa says early the next morning when I call her with instructions for what I need from her this morning. "You can't be serious. You've got a full day of meetings. And then a full week of more of the same. Not to mention red carpet appearances and parties to attend. You can't cancel everything and fly to London."

"I can, and I am. And you're going to switch all those meetings to Zoom meetings and rearrange my calendar to make this work." I take a deep breath and exhale it. "I'm moving to London today, Ness. It's happening."

She takes that in, turning silent for a long moment before finally saying, "Okay, so I'm presuming you're taking Jameson's jet."

"No. You'll need to book me a flight. And a hotel."

More silence. "Doesn't he own hotels all over the place that you could stay in?"

"Please book me the hotel I normally stay in. I've got some things to do at home before I come in. I should be in by lunchtime. Put a few hours aside this afternoon for us to go over how this is going to work. And please book me a car to take me from the office to the airport."

She connects the dots that neither Jameson nor his driver will be taking me to the airport. "Right, so it's just you flying to London and you're getting to the airport by yourself. Correct?"

"Correct. I'll also need security while I'm at the airport and in London."

"I imagine you do," she says, also putting it together that Jameson's security won't be with me. Then, softly, she asks, "Is everything okay, Adeline?"

I steel myself.

Tighten my armor.

"Everything is exactly how it should be. Let me know if you have any problems with any of this."

She agrees to do that, and we end the call.

I glance around Jameson's bedroom, taking in the suit jacket he dropped on the armchair last night, his shoes that he didn't put away, and my packed bags that are sitting on the bed.

I told him I had a meeting away from the office this morning. That I wasn't driving into work with him because of that meeting. He didn't question this, and after he left, I packed my bags.

I'm going to London whether he likes it or not.

We'll figure out how to make the marriage work once I'm there.

I can't not do this.

My company and my heart are depending on me.

With one last glance at the bedroom, I leave it to go into my office and pack my things up in there, ignoring the pain slicing down my chest. Soon, that pain will ease, and I'll be able to get on with my life and put Jameson behind me.

24

Jameson

"What do you mean she went away?" I say to Jeff when I arrive home at 10:00 p.m. After his daily update, he asked me when I'm expecting Adeline home from her trip. Apparently, she didn't tell him when that would be. Considering I wasn't aware she was going away, I don't have an answer for him.

His brows pull together. "She left around lunchtime. I gathered from the number of bags she took that she will be gone for a while."

"A while?"

"Yes, Sir. Perhaps a couple of weeks." He appears to be uncomfortable with this conversation, but since he's the only person with the information I need, I continue questioning him.

"And she didn't say where she was going?"

"No."

Fuck.

We argued last night, but I didn't expect this. I didn't expect her to walk out. Because that's what my gut's telling me she's done. She's left me.

"Thank you, Jeff," I say before putting my phone to my ear to call her.

She doesn't answer any of the three calls I make.

I leave messages for her to call me and then I call Trent, the head of my security.

With each passing second, my chest is feeling tighter. My anger is building.

"This can't be good," he says.

I yank my tie off. "It's not. Where is Adeline?"

"Let me check." He turns silent while he checks his system. He takes longer than I expect. Not a great sign. "Adeline cancelled her security this morning. We don't know where she is."

I tear at the buttons of my shirt, ripping a few off while freeing my chest of the material suffocating me. "And you didn't think it important to tell me this?"

He takes a moment before replying. "No. You've never specified that you wanted to be alerted to Adeline making changes to her security detail."

"In future, alert me to any fucking change that hasn't come directly from me. Are we clear?"

"Yes."

"Good."

I jab at the phone to end the call and immediately phone Shantel while wondering why the fuck I don't have Adeline's assistant's number.

She answers straight away. "I'm on my way home, but if you need me to go back to the office for something, I can," she says. "But for the record, this could lead to me being cranky tomorrow since I'll miss an episode of my favorite show and—"

"Shantel." I work hard to contain my frustration but fail. "I need you to get in touch with Adeline's assistant to find out where she is."

I'm greeted by silence before she launches into a monologue. "How do you not know where your wife is? I swear if you've fucked this up, I will throttle you myself. I've had to sit through years of awful, awful women that you've dated, making reservations for dinners with them, and weekends away with them, and dealing with their whiny bullshit. Adeline is a treasure, Jameson. *A Treasure!* Oh my God, it's after ten at night and you don't know where she is! I'm hanging up right now so I can find her for you."

The line goes dead, and I stare at my phone.

Christ.

Shantel has never spoken to me that way. Something tells me I should prepare for more of it in the future.

Fucking hell.

I pace my office while I wait for her to call back. I contemplate phoning my mother to see if she heard from Adeline, but I don't want to worry her at this time of night.

Shantel only takes a few minutes before coming back to me. "Right, I'm getting the jet ready because your wife has gone to London and something tells me if you didn't know she was going there, you need the jet. Pack your bag. I'll text you the flight details as soon as I have them."

She's gone before I have a chance to speak, but I'm already halfway to the bedroom, focused on packing a bag and getting the fuck to London.

My mind races.

I replay our argument from last night over and over, trying to figure out what the hell I said that made her leave like this.

She wanted to move to London.

I pointed out why that wouldn't work.

It was a no-brainer to me.

We can't do anything that will put our goals at risk.

Shantel has the jet ready in a few hours.

I spend those hours pacing.

Thinking.

Going over and over the argument we had.

Figuring out how to convince Adeline not to leave me.

I need my wife back and I'll do whatever it takes to make that happen because I've never felt the way I do now.

It's like there's a gaping fucking hole in my chest.

One that only she can fill.

25

Adeline

I land in London just after 5:00 a.m. to three missed calls and three messages from Jameson asking me where I am. I also have a message from Vanessa letting me know that Shantel called her to find out my whereabouts.

I'm tired after the flight and don't have it in me to call anyone back. I text them to let them know I've arrived safely and then slip my phone in my pocket to avoid it.

I couldn't sleep, so I spent the entire flight ruminating on my marriage and how I'm going to make it through the rest of this year with the state my heart's in.

The only conclusion I came to is that I didn't come this far to only come this far. I've dedicated just over four months to the marriage. I'm not quitting now.

I know I shouldn't have left like I did. I should have

talked with Jameson some more about moving to London. But I wasn't thinking straight when I made the decision. I've never been able to think straight when my heart is hurting. I don't know how people manage to do that; I just don't have that level of compartmentalizing in me. I can't box my emotions up separately and put them away when they're not serving me like I know some people can. I experience them all at once and just make the best choices I can in each moment to protect myself.

I pull my cap down as I get off the plane and make my way through the airport. The security that Vanessa hired find me quickly, guiding me through the maze of people, many who are trying to get photos and videos of me. Social media and the tabloids are still shining a spotlight on me. Jameson and I sometimes struggle to avoid the cameras when we go out, and today is no different. I'm relieved when I finally make it to my waiting car and the safety and privacy it provides.

I go straight to the hotel Vanessa booked. I shower and collapse into bed. I'm taking today off work to sleep and get myself together because it will be full steam ahead from tomorrow.

Sleep claims me until lunchtime. It's not great sleep because my mind won't switch off all the thoughts I'm having about Jameson.

I decide to go in search of food and am in a tiny coffee shop sipping coffee when Jameson calls.

I stare at the screen for long enough that the call ends.

I think I need some more time before I talk with him. I'm feeling too raw to listen to him tell me what he thinks of me leaving New York.

However, I don't want to jerk him around. This isn't a game I'm playing here. I'm just hurting too much for this right now.

I text him instead of returning his call.

Adeline: I shouldn't have left without telling you, but I need some space right now. I'll call you later.

Jameson: Where are you staying?

Adeline: Park Lane.

He doesn't reply after that. I attempt to sit and enjoy my coffee and lunch, but I can't stop thinking about him.

Needing something to distract me, I call Holly, the head of my London team, and tell her I'm ready to start work today rather than tomorrow. She's excited and suggests we spend the afternoon visiting suppliers.

Half an hour later, we meet at her office before heading out.

I'm mostly successful at putting Jameson out of my mind, but I can't deny that he's stuck in my head like he's moved in there for life.

I think about him when Holly and I stop at a coffee shop, and I spot red velvet cupcakes. His favorite.

I think about him when we meet with one of our suppliers. The three-piece suit the guy is wearing reminds me of the night Jameson brought dinner to my office wearing a three-piece.

I think about him when Holly has a long conversation with me about perfume and her idea to introduce a new line into our business.

"So," Holly says at 4:00 p.m., "I was thinking it might be good to have a drink with the team tonight. You know, so that everyone has a chance to chat with you before we begin working together."

"That's a great idea,' I agree.

"Oh, good, because I already mentioned it to everyone and they're excited. They're going to come to your hotel for a drink in the bar. We'll keep it super casual."

We say goodbye to the supplier we've just met with and drive back to my hotel.

"I'm going to head up to my room to freshen up," I say when we arrive. "Do you want to come up?"

"No, I'll wait down here."

I leave her and have just walked into the bathroom in my suite when there's a loud knock at the door. That confuses me because my security guy is outside the door and has instructions not to let anyone in. When the knocking happens again, louder and more insistent this time, I make my way out to the door.

Opening it, I intend on telling whoever it is to calm down. However, I come face-to-face with a furious Jameson who barges into my suite, bringing a wild gush of anger with him.

I close the door. "Right, so just come on in," I throw out, annoyed with the way he just assumes I want him in here.

His eyes meet mine, fury blazing in them as he drops the large envelope he's carrying on the sofa. "I've been trying to find you all fucking day. I'm not waiting outside a second longer."

"And that's *my* fault?" The way he said it makes me think he believes that.

"If you'd keep me updated on your schedule, we wouldn't have this issue." He jabs his finger toward the door. "And as for the security you have working for you, they're fired. They just let me through without a fucking second glance. I'll have my men here soon."

He is far too much.

"You're angry with me for coming to London without telling you. I get it, but don't you come in here and yell at me and try to boss me around. I won't have it."

He works his jaw. "Well, you're going to have to have it, Adeline, because that's what married couples do. They get angry when the other person does something they shouldn't, and they lose their temper. Consider my temper lost." He takes a step closer to me. "And now, we're going to work through it and sort it out."

"We're not a real married couple, Jameson, in case you've forgotten. Although, I really don't think you have. You love that fucking contract so much."

"Fuck," he says, pulling me to him. "You misunderstood me the other night when I mentioned the contract."

I try to smack him away, but he's got a firm grip on my arms. "Let me go! We are not doing this."

"We *are* doing this, and you are going to listen to me."

I press my hands to his chest. "I'm done being bossed around by you."

He slides his arm around my waist and holds me tightly to him. The anger vibrating off him matches the heat that's always there with us. I want to shove that heat away so I can only respond to the anger, but my body can never ignore it. "You will never be done with me bossing you. I won't ever allow that."

"Right, so you're doing the same thing you did when I brought up moving to London. You want to boss me into doing whatever works for you."

"You ran London by me to see if moving here would work for the marriage. I thought through the practicalities. I fucked up, though. I should have told you that me not wanting you in London had nothing to do with the contract and everything to do with the fact I'm a selfish bastard and do not want you living anywhere but with me."

My heart beats faster.

She's running to him.

I do my best to hold her back.

"Well, it's too bad. I'm here now." I stand strong. I cannot give him my heart.

"I can see that. I can also see that you're in the mood to argue with me."

"No, I'm done arguing with you. We don't ever have to argue again."

"Fuck," he rasps, fierce determination raging in his eyes. "We will be arguing until the day I die."

I try again to remove myself from his hold.

And I fail again because he uses his strength to keep me right where I am.

I glare at him. "For the record, we will not be arguing until the day you die because I will have divorced you long before then."

"We will never divorce, Adeline."

I stare at him while my heart starts galloping toward him.

My lungs forget how to manage the normal intake of breath. It's chaos in there while they speed up and then try to slow down and get all out of whack.

"What?" I breathe out.

He finally lets me go and moves to the sofa to collect

the envelope he brought with him. Pulling documents out, he hands me the first one. "Chatoyer is yours. I'm having my shares transferred to you." He hands me the next document. "Black Diamant is yours." He then holds up a copy of our marriage contract. "And this is done. Our marriage is now real." He tears it in half and hands the torn paper to me.

If I thought my lungs didn't know how to work properly a moment ago, they really don't know how to now.

I glance down at the paperwork I'm holding, bewildered by it all. "You own Black Diamant?" They're one of my biggest competitors. I had no idea Jameson owned that company.

"I took the company over when Gabriel identified they were behind the social media smear campaign against you just after we were married."

I frown as I try to make sense of this. "Why would you do that?"

He looks at me like the answer to this question should be clearer than clear. "To stop them fucking with you."

I look at the paperwork again.

I want to let my heart keep galloping his way, but I also want to guard her.

"Why are you doing this?"

He moves into me again. "Because I love you and I don't want anything coming between us and confusing you. I want you to know without a shadow of a doubt that I am in this marriage for you, not a company. And if you need to wipe the slate completely clean by telling Bill it was a lie to begin with, we can do that too. I may have married you to inherit a company, but all I want now is you."

My arms are around him before I can stop them. Not that I want to stop them.

I want everything he wants.

I want to argue with him until the day I die.

I never want to divorce.

And I want nothing between us confusing us.

His mouth crashes down onto mine and I kiss him with everything in me.

I melt into him.

My heart practically forces my chest open so she can climb out and be with him.

With this kiss and that declaration of love and that promise of never divorcing me, Jameson ruins me once and for all.

When he finally lets my mouth go, I keep hold of him and say, "I love you too, and I hope you're prepared for loving me. There could be many wars ahead."

He looks down at me with all that brown warmth that I now know is love. "I was built for loving you, baby. Not even war could keep me away."

EPILOGUE

TWO MONTHS LATER

Adeline

"The share price is up again this morning," Douglas says over the phone during our weekly chat. "And Q1 is on track to meet our predictions."

"Great news," I say, momentarily distracted by my husband who has just walked into my office unexpectedly.

"I've emailed some reports for you to look at regarding London. Everything still looks good."

"Thank you." I watch as Jameson sits on my sofa. I can't drag my eyes away. Not when he's wearing a three-piece suit with those arm sleeves rolled up exactly how I like. "I'm sorry, Douglas, I have to go."

I end the call and stand. "I wasn't expecting you today," I say to Jameson as I move to him.

He reaches for me and pulls me onto his lap. One hand comes to my neck while the other goes to my waist. His lips find mine and I feel his need for me.

Splitting our time between London and New York the last two months hasn't been easy. We've spent days and nights apart when we couldn't work our schedules any differently. I don't like being apart from him, but Jameson really doesn't like it.

"I cancelled my meetings in New York," he says after he finishes with my mouth. "I'm here for three days." Thankfully, he doesn't suffer jet lag as badly as I do, because he's the one doing most of the flying. But still, I worry about him.

I put my hand to his chest. "It's my turn next, okay? You look exhausted."

"I look exhausted because I've been dealing with Paulina Rossi."

I laugh at the look of exasperation filling his face. I find it amusing watching him deal with her. "Just remember that her strategies are working." His profits are better than before they started dropping. It helps that all the lies being published about both of us have stopped, but mostly, I think Jameson credits Paulina.

"Fuck," he grumbles. "I almost fucking wish they weren't."

"Ooh," I say as a thought occurs to me, "Does you being here now mean you'll be at the shoot tomorrow?" I forced Jameson into letting me do the endorsement campaign Paulina suggested I do for his hotels. We're filming at his London hotel tomorrow.

His grip on my neck tightens. "Yes. I need to ensure they have enough clothes on you."

I shake my head at him, but I can't help from loving him when he's like this. "You are too much, Mr. Fox."

He brings my mouth to his again, kissing me like he's thinking about fucking me. His hands are all over me like that too.

I let him have his kiss for longer than I should before putting my hands to his chest and pulling my mouth from his. "I can't fuck you," I say breathlessly.

His eyes travel down to my breasts. "Why not?"

I smack his hand away when it also comes to my breasts. "Because Shantel will be here in half an hour, and I have to chat with Lara before she arrives."

He tries to cup my breast again. "I should never have given her to you."

I smack him away again. "I appreciate you giving her to me, although giving would imply she could stay with me forever. I do recall you making it clear you expect her back working with you once she's trained my new assistant."

He gives me a pointed look. "My assumption is always that you will argue with me. I expect this situation to be no different."

When Vanessa resigned as my assistant last month so she could move closer to her mother, it left me in the lurch. February was a huge month for me with New York, London, and Milan Fashion Weeks. I didn't have time to find a new assistant. Jameson and Shantel were in London at the time, and Shantel stepped in to help. She's a fast learner and quickly picked up on what I need from an assistant.

Jameson asked her if she'd stay in London and work with me until I had time to find and train a new assistant.

We're interviewing next week for the position and then she'll work with them until they know what they're doing.

I've loved having her here. It's almost been like having Jameson here because she often shares stories about him with me.

"That reminds me," I say as I think about all this. "Shantel told me that you put Ian Swift in his place at a business lunch you and she attended in January. You didn't tell me about that."

"The less I think about that asshole, the better. He gave you enough hell to deserve far more than what I said to him at that lunch."

Shantel shared with me that Jameson told Ian in no uncertain terms that he'd ruin him if he ever spread lies about me or my family again. She told me that she has no doubt Jameson meant every word. I told her I had no doubt either. My husband is not a man to cross.

I press a kiss to his lips before going to battle with him to allow me to leave his lap. When he has me like this, he doesn't like to let go. Often, he manhandles me and forces me to stay where I am. Today, he only fights me for a few moments before letting me go.

"What are your plans for the day?" I ask as I walk back to my desk.

He stands, doing his suit jacket up. "Owen is in London at the moment. We're going to have lunch and then I've got meetings all afternoon. I thought I'd come to your red carpet tonight. What time is it again?"

I fill him in, getting distracted when his mother texts me.

Reese: Darling, Bill just mentioned that you and

Jameson will both be in New York next Tuesday. Are you able to make it for Taco Tuesday?

Adeline: No, it's the following week that we'll both be home. I wouldn't miss Taco Tuesday for the world.

Reese: Oh, I must have gotten it mixed up. I can't wait to see you. We have so much to discuss about Jameson's birthday.

Adeline: I can't wait xx

I laugh as I eye my husband. "Is your birthday always a big affair with your mother?"

"Jesus, she goes too far. What's she planning this year?"

"That is for me to know and for you to find out."

Reese hasn't told me much about her plans yet, except that it'll be a family weekend away, including Bill. He recently finished his radiation treatment and is starting to feel less tired. Reese said that he's looking forward to spending time with Jameson that weekend.

I didn't take Jameson up on his offer to come clean to Bill about our marriage. I didn't see the need. Bill wanted Jameson to find love and that's exactly what he did.

I did suggest to Jameson that he find time in his schedule to take Bill to his radiation appointments. He ended up doing that, and in the time they spent together throughout Bill's treatment, they discussed their shared vision for Bill's company and made plans for Jameson to execute once he is CEO.

Jameson comes to me, moving behind me and putting his arms around me. Resting his hands on my stomach, he brings his mouth to my ear. "You and my mother will be the death of me."

I smile as my heart sighs happily. "I thought me and Shantel would be the death of you."

"The three of you will be."

I place my hands over his. "You wouldn't have it any other way."

"That is debatable some days."

Threading my fingers through his, I think about loving him and being loved by him.

My protector.

My lover.

My soul mate.

Jameson loves me better than I have ever been loved and I never want to go a day in my life without him by my side.

He helps me take on the world every day simply by loving me, and then he wraps me in his arms at night and tends to any wounds the day brings.

I squeeze my fingers against his. "Thank God you stole my company from me."

His arms tighten around me as his lips press to my neck. "Why? So you can drive me crazy every damn day?"

"So I get to be loved by the best man I know."

Because that's what Jameson Fox is: the best man I know.

And I would let him steal anything he wanted from me if it meant he'd keep loving me.

My breath.

My heart.

My everything.

EPILOGUE

FIVE YEARS LATER

Jameson

"Daddy," Sebastian says, reaching his little arms up. "Carry me."

I lift him into my arms as we exit the elevator into our home. Looking at him, I ask, "Where do you think Mommy is?"

He smiles excitedly. "The gym!"

We play this game often when we come home from a day at my office, and he always says the gym. He's usually not wrong, and today is no different.

We find her in the gym, and I take the few moments before he announces our arrival to run my gaze over my wife's body.

She's even more beautiful now than when I married her. And thanks to her pregnancy, she's glowing. Not to mention, her curves are more pronounced, something I can't get enough of.

"Mommy!" Sebastian runs to her.

She's working out on a new piece of equipment. It's for Pilates, I think. I recall she mentioned something about it being delivered today. Whatever the fuck it is, I like it. She's lying on her back with her feet in some kind of straps. Her legs are spread wide and I'm now thinking about all the ways I want to spread those legs tonight.

"Hey, baby." She stops what she's doing, removes her feet from the straps, and sits to pull our son into her arms. Showering him with kisses, her eyes meet mine. "Did you and Daddy have a good day?"

He nods enthusiastically as I draw close. "Yes! We played with numbers."

Adeline smiles at him. "Did you? What did you play?"

Sebastian is three and splits his days between coming to work with me and going to work with Adeline. He has a nanny who comes to work with us to help look after him, but as often during the day as we can, Adeline and I spend time with him. We've both cut our hours back so we can do this. Neither of us wanted to have children we don't spend time with. It has worked so well for us that we decided to have another child. Adeline is due to give birth to our daughter in three months.

Sebastian fills her in on the numbers games he and I played today.

He's just finishing his story when my mother joins us.

"My darling boys," she says. "You're home." She holds out her arms for Sebastian who runs into them. He adores his grandmother.

Adeline comes to me. She grips my suit jacket and

pulls me in for a kiss. She doesn't take anywhere near long enough with this kiss. "Did you have a good day?"

I put my arm around her, resting my hand on her ass. I bring my other hand to her belly. "I did. How about you two?"

She looks down at her belly before glancing back up at me. "Your daughter is just like her mommy. You should prepare yourself now. She kicked all day long." She moves my hand to her side. "Can you feel her? I swear she knows when you're here. She kicks more. She wants her daddy's attention."

I feel her kick.

I feel it against my hand and against my heart.

Having Sebastian changed me, and I know having Stella will too.

I didn't think I could love anyone the way I love Adeline, and while it's a different love, it's the same in that I don't know the lengths I would go to for these three. All I know is that those lengths are immeasurable.

"Adeline," Mom says, "I'm going to give Sebastian his bath if that's okay with you."

Adeline nods. "Thank you, Reese."

Adeline loves my mother, and especially loves how Mom dotes on Sebastian. She hasn't had anything to do with her mother or her sister since that Christmas she discovered her mother had lied about her father. I know she now thinks of my mother as a mom and has formed a close bond with her.

With a smile, Mom takes our son, leaving us alone.

I pull her close and kiss her again, this time taking as long as I want.

She moans into my mouth as she presses her body against mine.

By the time I'm done with her, I'm hard as hell and she looks like she's ready to strip me and fuck me.

"I'm thinking we should convince your mother to take Sebastian home for a sleepover."

"It won't take much convincing." My mother would have him every night if she could.

Her grip on my jacket tightens. "I am so fucking horny it isn't funny. Seriously, pregnancy hormones are no joke. And then you come home wearing your suit and I can't go on. You need to find a way to get me alone and fuck me."

My lips quirk. "Perhaps I should stop wearing suits."

"Perhaps you should hurry up and do what I said."

"I hate to break it to you, but since it's your half-birthday, I planned a celebration for you. There's no time for me to fuck you."

Her eyes widen. "Oh my God, why must you be so good with these half-birthdays? And in future, can we just put sex on the calendar for mine? Like, book your mother in for a weeklong sleepover for the kids so we can celebrate with a week in bed."

I need a change in conversation. I'm too fucking hard to be discussing all the ways my wife wants me to fuck her. "This Pilates equipment you had delivered takes up a lot of space in here."

She glances around the gym. "And?"

"It's crowded in here now."

"I'm not sending it back. You can remodel."

Fuck, I love her.

I lightly smack her ass. "You need to get in the shower and get dressed for dinner."

As I follow her out of the gym, she says, "Also, your perfume arrived today."

"*My* perfume?"

"Well, it's the one you want me to wear, that I don't wear, so I can only assume you keep ordering bottles of it for yourself."

"I keep ordering bottles in the fucking hope you'll get confused and pull the wrong bottle out of your closet one day."

"Hmm, at the rate you're going, you'll need to remodel my closet again. Either that, or I'll start storing your perfume in your closet."

I boss her into hurrying the hell up and getting ready for her half-birthday party.

She bosses me into fucking her in the shower.

Along the way, we boss each other into a thousand other little things.

I wouldn't have it any other way.

I wouldn't have *her* any other way.

OWEN NORTH SNEAK PEEK

CHARLIZE

I'm going to fucking kill Poppy.

It's her fault I'm currently sitting in a hotel toilet cubicle half-naked with welts the size of I-don't-know-what under my boobs and on my back, caused by the tiniest strapless lacy bra known to womankind. I had to pull my dress down and rip that sucker off so I could have a good scratch, and now I have scratch marks all over me that make it look like I've been tackled by a grizzly bear.

It's also her fault that when I finally get up the courage to put said bra back on and fasten the tightest red dress I've ever worn back in place, I'm going to have to walk out of this restroom wearing only one shoe. The heel on the other one snapped when I skidded on the shiny tiles in the bathroom. The shoe broke as I went flying, landing on my ass. And yes, I now have a huge bruise on my ass.

Like I said, I'm going to fucking kill my cousin for making me wear a bra, dress, and shoes I would never choose to wear, to her wedding. "The society wedding of the year, Charlize" as my mother has taken every opportunity to tell me over the last six months.

Insert eye-roll.

Kill me now.

No, seriously, do it.

I love girl stuff just as much as the next woman, but honestly, when did it become mandatory to put ourselves in so much pain just to attend social functions? I can do heels, just not heels that make me look like an Amazonian woman. And dresses? I'd rather not be squeezed into one that is so tight my boobs and my lungs want to take out a restraining order on it. And that damn strapless bra with that allergy-causing stuff on it? As soon as I get home, I'm burning it.

My phone buzzes with a text, and I reach down to grab it out of my bag that I unceremoniously dumped on the floor of the cubicle. Yeah, disgusting, I know. All those germs down there, but I was desperate to get that bra off.

As I reach for the phone, the sound a woman never ever *ever* wants to hear comes from behind me.

My. Dress. Rips.

I freeze, willing it to not be true.

Holding my breath, I twist my arm around to the back of my dress to feel for a rip, and sure enough, I find it.

"Oh mother of effing God, why does this shit always have to happen to me?" I mutter as I stand. "I bloody told Poppy that I had a dress I could wear, but no, she wants me to wear this damn dress."

"It'll help you meet a man", she'd said, as if meeting a man was the highest thing on my agenda. To be clear, it isn't. No, my main priority in life at the moment is to meet someone who can print bank notes that no one would ever suspect of being counterfeit.

I kid.

Kind of.

Actually, I just need a job. That will *pay* me in bank notes. Rather than in casseroles cooked lovingly for me. See, at the moment the only "job" I can get is the one where I help my seventy-one year old neighbor, Muriel, with her art. God love her, she still paints every day. She doesn't really need my help, but after I've dedicated hours each day to finding a job, I find myself on the couch in her art room reading books and chatting about life while helping her mix colours and cleaning up once she's done. Muriel has the most amazing collection of books I've ever come across. About art, history, architecture, politics, travel and so much more. Some days I want to skip the job hunting and just curl up on her couch with a pot of tea and all those books.

My mother's voice rings loud in my head—"*you need friends your own age, Charlize, and a job. Get a damn job!*"

Ugh. *Parents!*

I grab my bra and put it back on, ignoring the itchy welts I'm covering. I then wiggle my dress up and into place. It has a zip at the back that I carefully attempt to pull up. It plays nice; however, I can feel what the problem is. When I stretched to reach for my phone, the fabric has ripped on one side of the zip, right down to my ass.

Opening the door of the cubicle, I peer out and find no one else in the bathroom. As carefully as I can, I make my way to the mirror and turn to see how bad the dress looks from behind.

Oh. God.

It's gaping open. Anyone who walks behind me will be subjected to my back, half my ass, and a flash of my red thong.

All this at the society wedding of the year.

I do the only thing worth doing right now.

I scream to let my frustration out.

It feels so good that I continue screaming until it kind of turns into a wail. No tears or anything, just a good old-fashioned release of the disappointment, resentment, and irritation filling me. This is something I should do more often. Hell, everyone should do this more often. Between screaming, wailing and having sex, I think the human race could probably resolve a lot of issues without resorting to violence.

A deep voice cuts through the air. "Jesus, are you okay?"

My mouth snaps shut as I catch sight of a man entering the bathroom. My body fills with anticipation at the same time that my knees threaten to give way.

This man is hot.

Really fucking hot.

Like, on a scale of I'd-throw-myself-off-a-cliff-to-avoid-ever-having-to-look-at-you to I'd-take-all-my-clothes-off-right-now-if-it-meant-you'd-just-talk-to-me, he has to be at the level of I'm-never-wearing-clothes-again.

He's probably the best-looking man I've ever come across. And that's saying something, because my bestie is one of the hottest dudes out there.

I'm even ignoring the way everything about him screams money. I'm not usually attracted to wealthy men in suits, but damn, this guy knows how to wear one. He also has just the right amount of scruff. And don't get me started on the way his dark brown hair falls effortlessly into place. I'd bet all the money I have in the world—a huge risk because I currently have less than five hundred dollars in my bank account—that he's had it styled, even though it looks like he simply dried it with a towel and let it do its own thing.

I grip the sink and throw out the first thing that comes to mind. "Do you always wander into women's bathrooms?" I mean, I'm all for him doing that, just not when I'm in the middle of the kind of personal crisis that is threatening to send me to the brink. My dress is gaping open, and my ass is hanging out. That's a crisis with a capital fucking C.

His brows arch as his gaze drops to my back, clearly taking in everything on display. When his eyes meet mine again, he drawls, "Only when I think a woman is in that bathroom possibly dying. You do realise you were screaming like a woman on her deathbed, right?"

I grip the sink harder. "That's because I fucking am!"

His lips twitch as if he's trying not to smile. If he smiles or laughs, I swear I'll turn around and clock him. He doesn't, though. He's smart as well as hot. "So now that we've established you're close to death, do you want a hand with that?"

My brain scrambles fast to come to a decision. I figure things could be worse. Poppy's mother and mine could have walked in on me. The Winters sisters would not be as cool about this situation as Mr I-Could-Blow-Your-Damn-Mind is being.

I nod. "Thanks. I'll just grab my bag." My emergency

kit for these kinds of crises is in there. I'm choosing to ignore the nagging feeling deep in my gut that there isn't any kit that can fix this problem.

I make my way back into the cubicle where I've left my bag on the floor, at which point I realise the flaw in this plan. If I bend to retrieve it, my dress will probably rip some more.

"Fuck me," I mutter. "Why can't anything ever be easy?"

"Problem?"

I spin to find Mr I-Could-Blow-Your-Damn-Mind standing directly behind me. Well, in front of me now. "What's your name?" It comes out like a demand. It is, really. I don't have the time to keep referring to him as Mr I-Could-Blow-Your-Damn-Mind every time I reference him in my head.

"We're dealing with your death and you want my name?"

I pull a face. "Funny." He kinda is, but this is not the time to be funny. I click my fingers to convey the urgency I feel. "Give me your name."

His lips twitch again. "Owen. And you are?"

I want to spend time drooling over his name. It's a good strong name, and I briefly imagine it falling from my lips while he gives me the kind of orgasm I bet a man like Owen can give. But I power on instead. This is no time for orgasm dreaming.

"Charlize." I step backwards, over my clutch so that it's in between us. Nodding at it, I say, "I need you to please pick that up so we can get my emergency kit out of it."

"Your emergency kit? You really think this dress can be fixed?"

My eyes widen in horror. "Don't you say that! Now is not the time to give up, Owen. If I have to walk in front of my mother again tonight, she will *not* be seeing my ass swinging in the wind."

He cocks his head to the side. "Are you Dougall's or Poppy's? I'm guessing if your mother is here, you must be family of one of them."

"Poppy's. You?"

"Dougall and I went to school together."

His words catch me off guard a little. Owen has to be early thirties, which means he's been friends with Dougall for a long time. I feel that says a lot about a person—that they look after and take the time with their friends to keep that friendship going. I probably read too much into it—God knows I often do—but I've been burned by old friends one too many times to not think there's something sacred about old friendships.

He passes me my bag. *Finally*. However, my run of shitastic luck continues, and I fumble as his hand brushes mine, resulting in me dropping the bag. Tampons, condoms, and cash scatter across the floor. None of those things catch Owen's attention. No, it's my Motley Crue vibe and my small notebook that draw his gaze.

His lips pull up in a smile as he turns to face me again. "Motley Crue, huh?" He bends to retrieve the notebook. "This looks interesting."

I snatch it from him as he straightens. Really, the only thing worse that could happen right now would be my mother walking in and finding me with this notebook full of drawings of dicks and sex acts. That I'm standing next to the hottest man on earth, in a restroom cubicle, holding said book, is mortifying. It's the kind of book a teenager would own, not a twenty-seven-year-old woman. And why the hell are we still smooshed together in this cubicle?

"My bestie gave it to me. And for your information, the Motley Crue vibe was a joke between Poppy and me." I hold the bullet up. "And also for your information, you'd be surprised what I can do to a man with this."

Poppy is deader than dead after this fiasco. And Dylan, my bestie, is, too. They will now have to spend the rest of their lives listening to me complain about the night I met the man who could have become the father of my children, only to watch him walk away laughing because he thinks my vagina has a thing for Motley Crue. And that I carry around a book of smut.

His eyes twinkle. "I bet I would."

OWEN NORTH WILL RELEASE JULY 29, 2022

This is a standalone boss, billionaire romance.

ALSO BY NINA LEVINE

Storm MC Series

Storm (Storm MC #1)

Fierce (Storm MC #2)

Blaze (Storm MC #3)

Revive (Storm MC #4)

Slay (Storm MC #5)

Sassy Christmas (Storm MC #5.5)

Illusive (Storm MC #6)

Command (Storm MC #7)

Havoc (Storm MC #8)

Gunnar (Storm MC #9)

Wilder (Storm MC #10)

Colt (Storm MC #11)

Sydney Storm MC Series

Relent (#1)

Nitro's Torment (#2)

Devil's Vengeance (#3)

Hyde's Absolution (#4)

King's Wrath (#5)

King's Reign (#6)

King: The Epilogue (#7)

Storm MC Reloaded Series

Hurricane Hearts (#1)

War of Hearts (#2)

Christmas Hearts (#3)

Battle Hearts (#4)

Stone Ops Series

COMING 2023

Easton

Zane

Liam

Bronze

Axe

Billionaire Romance

Ashton Scott

Jack Kingsley

Beckett Pearce

Jameson Fox

Owen North (coming 2022)

The Hardy Family Series

Steal My Breath (single dad romance)

Crave Series

Be The One (rockstar romance)

www.ninalevinebooks.com

ABOUT THE AUTHOR

Nina Levine

Dreamer.

Coffee Lover.

Gypsy at heart.

USA Today Bestselling author who writes about alpha men & the women they love.

When I'm not creating with words you will find me planning my next getaway, visiting somewhere new in the world, having a long conversation over coffee and cake with a friend, creating with paper or curled up with a good book and chocolate.

I've been writing since I was twelve. Weaving words together has always been a form of therapy for me especially during my harder times. These days I'm proud that my words help others just as much as they help me.

www.ninalevinebooks.com

ACKNOWLEDGMENTS

Jodie, thank you for all your work on Jameson & Adeline. You gave me strength when I needed it, and belief too, when I needed that. And God, did I need that in the final hours. I couldn't write books without you. Let's hope there's no pacing on Owen.

Rose, thank you, thank you, thank you for always working with my hectic schedule. I'm sorry I'm a last-minute girl. But man, you always come through for me and I am so appreciative.

To my author friends who kept me going on this one: Kim, Leesa, and Fiona. I love you girls. Thank you.

To my beautiful readers: thank you for still being here. Many of you have been with me for 8 years. Some of you have just found me. I am so grateful for every one of you. I hope you loved Jameson & Adeline as much as I do.

To my amazing reviewers and bloggers: thank you!!! I am so very grateful for everything you do to help me get the word out about my books.

To my friends and family who I haven't seen for weeks: I love you and adore you for supporting me and knowing I need these weeks each book to disappear and write.

PLAYLIST

"Games" by Luke Bryan
"Alive" by Daughtry
"Wicked Game" by Theory of a Deadman
"Trouble Me" by Gabriel Mann
"What She Wants Tonight" by Luke Bryan
"Man of Steel" by Brantley Gilbert
"As You Are" by Daughtry
"Pieces" by Rob Thomas
"Boxes" by the Goo Goo Dolls
"I'm Still Standing" by Allison Miller
"When the Lights Go Out" by Patrick Droney
"On Your Way Home" by Patrick Droney
"Where You Are" by Patrick Droney
"Right With You" by Patrick Droney
"Wrecking Ball" by Patrick Droney

(Can you tell I fucking love Patrick Droney?!!)

"Love Bites" by Def Leppard

"Have A Little Faith In Me" by John Hiatt
"Secret Garden" by Bruce Springsteen
"Sledgehammer" by Peter Gabriel
"Cold Heart" by Elton John
"Sledgehammer" by Fifth Harmony

Made in the USA
Monee, IL
20 October 2026

66035289R00225